INFLAME

HERITAGE OF FIRE: BOOK TWO

EMMA L. ADAMS

Want to find out how Cori and her friends met? You can get a free prequel, *Adrift,* if you sign up to my author newsletter.

"A cat," I said, "is stuck on the London Eye. *That's our mission?*"

At my feet, my friend Becks meowed pointedly. Either she meant to say, *we already said yes*, or *hey, I'm a cat shifter, and I don't appreciate being mocked.* A prod to my shin suggested the latter.

The call had said, *Urgent rescue mission, wings required.* I'd assumed we'd be tossing some faerie monsters out of a tower block or flying someone to safety through gargoyle territory. Giving a feline a lift didn't promise the huge pay bonus we needed.

Just another day in the life of a dragon shifter.

"You never know," said Zeph, my fellow dragon shifter, who walked on my right-hand side. "Some cat shifters are scared of heights, aren't they? If it's a shifter with important status, we might get a tip."

Becks gave an indignant mew, as if to say, *hey, we're not all scared of heights.* Becks herself had a bizarre wariness around rodents, but loved napping and climbing fences even when she was playing human. Her tabby form was streaked in varying shades of brown which matched her hair when she shifted to human, while she'd pocketed her glasses in case we ran into a fight.

"If it *is* a shifter, Darcy'll have to give us a raise," I acknowledged. "But if it isn't, we lose our dignity and time when they could have just called the fire brigade or a guy with a ladder or something. Why not hire a gargoyle to rescue the cat if it's someone's pet? There's way more of them around than dragon shifters."

Forcing us to rescue house pets from tourist attractions had Darcy's bullshit written all over it. It was hard not to take it personally, but our killing the two biggest mobsters in London's supernatural underworld and witnessing the criminal dragon shifter Lorne flee the city with a dangerous artefact stolen from the Mage Lords had put a bigger price on our heads than all our annual salaries combined. I didn't blame Darcy for wanting to be rid of us.

Zeph gave a shrug. "Might be a laugh."

Zeph himself wasn't even on the mercenaries' payroll, but he came with us on missions on his days off from working at the bar, claiming boredom. Like me, Zeph had auburn hair, but his was cut short while mine bounced to my shoulders in hard-to-tame curls. I was petite and 'cute', while his body was visibly toned and muscular even in a loose grey hoody and faded jeans. My plain coat and jeans hid my bright socks, T-shirt and scarf, but just the two of us standing next to one another would draw unwanted attention.

Especially from shifters, who could detect a predator a mile off.

Please say the gargoyles aren't there. I'll never live it down.

The sky was clear, cloudless, and the fresh breeze off the Thames stirred my hair and filled my lungs with the taste of rot. I held my breath in an attempt to tame my sharp shifter senses. It was no wonder the only living things we saw in the water these days were carnivorous fae beasts and the occasional hydra. Zombies, dead faeries and other junk filled the murky river, but the wheel of the London Eye stood out like a snapshot from the world before the invasion. The mages had restored it using magic a dozen or more times at the request of the human government, supposedly to improve public morale. The glass pods weren't currently in use, and I didn't see any traces of a feline presence near ground level. There didn't appear to be any spectators around, either. *Good.*

"Ready?" I nodded to Becks. "Go and see what we have."

Becks gave a despondent meow which probably meant, *don't tell anyone I did this.* Then she leapt onto the lowest level of the wheel's framework, lithely climbing higher. As the lightest among our group, Becks would have a much easier job scaling the giant wheel than the rest of us.

"The cat is probably at the top," I said to Zeph. "Hope Becks can coax it down, otherwise we might end up being the first dragon firefighters of London."

A grin dimpled his cheek. "Keeps life interesting."

"You're actually enjoying this?" As a fellow dragon shifter, Zeph shared my hot-tempered tendencies as well as the need for constant stimulation. Watching a cat climb a national monument was entertaining enough, but after two weeks of bed rest followed by another two weeks of low-risk missions, I was crying out for a real challenge. Not that I *wanted* to come face to face with my mortal enemy again, but if I handed him over to the mages, it'd be a ticket out of our financial hole. And a ticket to finding the person who was breeding dragonlings illegally. "I thought you wanted to find who's hiding the you-know-whats."

The merest hint of a flame stirred in the depths of his eyes. Zeph's true quest in London was to track down the people responsible for continuing the experiments which had led to the creation of dragonlings—artificial dragon-like beings who, unlike us, couldn't shift into human form. But since Lorne had disappeared and his allies had expired, no evidence remained behind.

A faint yowling came from above my head. "I think Becks found the cat."

I tilted my head back to watch. Becks's tail hung over the edge of the glass pod, then the rest of her followed, releasing a yowl of alarm.

I reached out my hands just in time to catch a shaking bundle of fur. Becks shifted back into a human—a wiry woman with pale brown skin, dark eyes, and hair the colour of her tabby fur. She stumbled backwards, and only Zeph catching her arm stopped her from tripping into the river.

"There's not a cat up there," she gasped out. "There's a dead body."

"A human one?"

She gagged and spat into the river. "He *looked* human, but... I don't know. Something was wrong. Magically wrong."

Zeph and I exchanged perplexed glances. The city had

been neck-deep in corpses since the faerie invasion, and the body must be in a bad way for Becks to be so freaked out. She'd lived on the streets for most of her life since she'd come to London as a baby. *Who'd put a dead body in the middle of a tourist attraction under mage protection?*

"I'll take a look," I said.

Zeph's brows rose. "You're gonna shift?"

"Nah, I can climb." I flexed my hands and shifted them to ruby red claws. With a bound, I reached for the nearest hand-hold, and stilled when the wheel dipped under my weight. I wasn't worried about falling for safety reasons—more my dignity. I waited a few seconds then resumed my climb, moving swiftly without pausing for breath.

As I neared the area Becks had fallen from, the wind blew towards me, carrying the rotten scent of the river tainted with another foul smell I couldn't quite discern.

There's our dead body. The man had been tossed onto the wheel at a careless angle. It looked like he hadn't been dead more than a few hours at most. A gargoyle kill, maybe, but they usually took their prey to pieces and dumped them in the river.

Climbing across the wheel to reach him was awkward, especially with the foul-smelling wind stinging my eyes. I used my claws for leverage, getting close enough to the body to give him a shove into the river.

The instant my hand reached out, he grabbed my wrist in a lightning-fast movement that damn near unbalanced me. I held my body still, using my free hand to steady myself, then wrenched my hand out of his tight grip, jumping out of range.

The undead did a freakish monkey-like jump to land beside me. His eyes didn't glow, which was odd. There was generally a faint blue shine around the eyes of a zombie—or so I'd noticed since I'd developed the spirit sight, anyway. *Whoa, he's fast.* Undead's movements were slow, fed by the spiritual force of the necromancer controlling them. They didn't lunge out faster than a shifter.

The undead creaked upright, its legs trembling, body intact aside from the bloodstain blossoming over the dead man's chest. At its full height, I'd guess the guy had been a gargoyle shifter. His ragged clothes exposed his collarbone, and a tattoo gleamed from just under his neck, a swirling symbol, like a witch rune, but with an odd shimmering effect.

The undead did another monkey-like leap over my head, and I ducked, my feet slipping over the edge. I caught myself by the fingertips, my heart jackhammering. "What the bloody hell are you?"

Unlike ghosts, undead had no awareness or memory of who they'd been in life. No intelligence looked back at me from his eyes. Despite his speed, he was still a walking corpse.

"Cori, you okay up there?" Zeph called.

"Just hanging around enjoying the view," I called back. "Hey—Zeph, Becks, can you see if there's a necromancer around? I think someone left their undead unattended."

Swinging by my fingers, I leapt onto my feet. My claws sliced the zombie's head off, sending it bouncing down towards the river. Bye bye, creepy.

There came a distinct meowing noise from somewhere close by. *Oh, come on.* There *was* a cat up there. Right above me.

Sure enough, when I climbed higher, I came to a small

huddle of fur clutching the wheel's framework with a death grip. "Hey." I crouched down, hands outstretched. "I've come to get you down. Also, please say you're human."

The small tabby climbed into my arms. *Okay, show's over, folks.*

I carefully climbed down, while the cat dug its claws into my arm, clinging on for dear life. "Not far now," I muttered. "Easy…"

A winged shadow fell overhead. Crap. Gargoyles.

The cat's claws pierced my sleeve, and I jumped down to the zombie's level again. His head was gone, but the rest of his body remained intact, including that weird symbol. Perhaps he'd been sacrificed. Whoever would perform a ritual on top of the London Eye, though? It wasn't exactly an inconspicuous location.

Another winged shadow joined the first. I cursed under my breath. This area was wide open, exposed. Nowhere near gargoyle territory either, but the gargoyles had reason to have a bone to pick with me after the incident with the Faulkner brothers.

You'd think ridding London of two of its most notorious criminals would count as doing people a favour, but the mess the Faulkners had left behind in the supernatural underworld had caused people to point fingers at the next available targets… us.

The wheel dipped alarmingly as the gargoyle *landed* in front of me.

"Get off," I told the shifter. "You'll make us both fall." Not that I didn't have wings myself, but gargoyles rarely travelled alone. "I'm just rescuing a cat, you numbskull. I'm not here to start a fight."

The gargoyle shifted back to human form, turning into a stocky bald man with a pierced ear. "Then get out. And leave that dead man where you found him."

"You know he was probably sacrificed, right? That's a necromancer guild matter. I'm supposed to report it to my boss, at least."

"It is no business of the guild's," he snarled. "That undead is an abomination. Get away, or you will be infected, too."

I blinked in confusion. Since when did gargoyles care what the necromancers did with their dead? "I'm not all that keen on touching him, to tell you the truth. I'll leave your friend up here."

"He's no friend," said the gargoyle. "That dead is cursed."

A rattling noise came from nearby, and the wheel dipped beneath me. I looked at the zombie, and my blood chilled. The undead stood upright, headless, hands reaching for me. He still had life left in him—relatively speaking—after all.

The gargoyle shifted into his winged form, and the rocking motion knocked both of us off balance. Moving the cat onto my back and hoping it knew to hang on tight, I bared my teeth at the gargoyle and the dead man.

Scales spread up my arms and across my back, while wings sprouted from my shoulders. My clawed hands swiped at the undead, causing him to fly back into the river. Taking flight, I unleashed a roar that sent the two gargoyles fleeing.

Damn, that felt good.

Landing at the river's side, I bunched my legs, and my

tail swung around and hit the front of the nearest building. Oops. I shifted back into human form, taking a bow.

"Damaging national monuments and causing a public menace," I said, setting the cat down on the pavement. "There you go. You can turn back into a human now."

The cat licked a paw.

Becks, who seemed to have recovered from her shock, sighed. "Real cat, then. Not a shifter."

"Ah, well." I scooped the little tabby kitten up again. "We'll still get a bit of cash."

"Not for the zombie," said Zeph. "What was that gargoyle's problem?"

"Hell if I know. He thought it was 'cursed'. It's swimming with the hydra now, besides."

Still, I made a mental note to check into the necromancer guild at the next opportunity. That zombie should not have been able to move so fast of its own accord. Not that I was an expert. Thanks to my return from death at Lorne and the Orion League's hands, I'd developed the ability to see and interact with ghosts, but nobody would ever believe a dragon shifter could talk to dead people. Or rather, that they could talk to me. Let's just say they weren't the most interesting conversationalists. No wonder the necromancers were so antisocial.

The dead man, though… I'd never seen one marked with those symbols before. Necromancers could raise the dead with a snap of their fingers. There was no need for mysterious runes or other trickery.

I glanced at Becks. "He moved wicked fast for an undead. Is that what freaked you out, Becks?"

"I just got a bad feeling." She shuddered. "He felt…

odd. Cold. And you're right, he shouldn't have been able to move like that."

"Maybe someone left a witch spell on him," I suggested. "I'd have checked, but I didn't want to turn into gargoyle bait."

"You nearly did anyway," she said. "They've been on edge since you destroyed the arena."

"Anyone would think I'd wrecked everything instead of killing the two dickheads who were forcing them to fight to the death." I heaved a sigh. "I know, I know. The gargoyles who made a living betting on arena matches are desperate for someone to blame, and they never liked us much anyway."

"That's because they didn't know or care about the shifters trapped in cages," Becks said, her fists tightening. "And they don't remember being hypnotised. Only the aftermath."

"Maybe I should show up on their doorsteps with cupcakes." I rolled my eyes. "Whether they blame us or not, they seemed as freaked out as you were about the body, Becks. Why would the gargoyles say the undead was cursed? There are zombies everywhere in the city."

"Who even knows why the gargoyles do anything?" Zeph shook his head. "Best forget it. Get the bonus and then find our next job."

"Shifts at the bar aren't exciting enough for you?" I asked. "Or don't you get enough in tips?"

"It's okay," he said. "I prefer more hands-on work, and the company here is better."

There was the merest hint of a growl in his words that made heat climb up my neck to my cheeks. One of the downsides to being a dragon shifter... blushing like a furnace. I ducked my head on the pretext of adjusting my grip on the kitten, but not before I spotted the sly grin creeping onto Zeph's face. I suspected he enjoyed winding me up more than the actual flirting, but he hadn't made an open pass at me. Given our housing situation, it was probably for the best. He was also the first dragon shifter I'd made friends with who wasn't my sister, and he'd told me he hadn't met another of his kind since his village had been destroyed eight years ago. Maybe he just wanted companionship. He got on with everyone except Astor, and otherwise, my life was way too tenuous to consider ruining our friendship by hooking up with him. Besides, with my overprotective big sister around, chance would be a fine thing.

Becks strode ahead of us through the automatic doors of Darcy's place, the local branch of the Official Order of Mercenaries. Not that 'official' meant much, considering most of the funding had been spent on the shiny chrome building rather than actually paying the employees. Darcy sat behind the desk, polishing a knife he'd probably never used. The broad-shouldered gargoyle shifter arched a brow as I deposited the wriggling feline on the desk.

"What's that?"

"It's a kitten," I told him. "You know—four paws, sharp claws, says 'meow'? We rescued it from the London Eye on *your* orders."

Darcy scowled. "The job description said a black and white kitten, not a tabby."

"He was the only cat on the London Eye that I saw."

"It also said Big Ben, not the London Eye."

"That is *not* what the client said on the phone. We did the job to the letter." I gave him a challenging stare. "I didn't climb halfway up the London Eye and nearly get attacked by a zombie and a bunch of gargoyles for you to refuse payment."

"Zombie? What zombie?"

"You know, a dead person," I said. "Slightly vacant expression, lack of any living brain cells, tendency to stare blankly at you?"

"Don't play the smart-arse, Cori," he said. "There are some downright weird reports coming in from the necromancer guild. Supposedly, there's a rogue stealing corpses again and setting them loose on the public."

"Wait, so there are more of them?"

He grunted. "Not our business. We deal with the living, not the dead."

Uh, yeah, about that. Some of us dealt with both and not by choice. "The cash?"

He handed me a twenty-pound note. "Take it or leave it."

Twenty freaking pounds? Is that all? Even with the shelter temporarily closed, there were still seven people to feed, and three of us had wasted the morning on that joke of a mission when one would have been enough. I bloody well hoped Will and Kit had sold a shit-ton of spells today. It also said something about the state of the job market at the moment that Darcy was the fairest employer I'd had in my adult life.

"Any other missions for us?" Becks asked. "Preferably more high-profile than a human-style firefighter mission."

"Return the Moonbeam to the mages."

The grimy twenty-pound note slipped from my

fingers, and Becks's hand shot out and caught it before it fluttered away.

"You what?" I took the note from Becks, lowering my hand.

"The Mage Lords have put out a warrant for the return of the Moonbeam, and Lorne along with it. Dead or alive."

"Is he even still in the city?" I stuck the money in my pocket. I'd like nothing more than to bury my claws in Lorne's spine, but I was under the impression he'd fled London to hide with the Moonbeam he'd stolen from the mages.

The Moonbeam that by rights belonged to the dragon shifters.

"Just what I heard," he said. "Other than that, we're drier than a troll's rear. No work here."

"Thanks for that mental image." Turning on my heel, I left the lobby, my feet clacking on the polished floor.

The automatic doors slid shut behind Zeph. "Maybe you should move to another guild."

"This is the only one in the area," Becks put in. "It'd be fine if we had transport, but we don't."

"Hello?" I flapped my arms in an imitation of wings beating.

Zeph grinned. "I doubt you want to fly to work every day, considering the effort involved."

He wasn't wrong. It had taken me two solid weeks to build the stamina to maintain a full shift without spending the rest of the day unconscious. But I got stronger every time I shifted. This time, I felt positively energised. "No, but I'd fly to catch Lorne if I knew where he was. Then…"

"Ker-ching," said Becks, snapping her fingers, and metaphorical dollar signs appeared in her eyes.

Zeph shook his head. "I doubt he'll be easy to track even by air. I've been circling the city in my free time and… nothing. He must be travelling on foot or not in the city at all."

"Maybe the necromancers would have paid us for the zombie." I doubted it, but it'd be just our luck. Lately, our money leaked away no matter how well we rationed it. It wasn't like we were unaccustomed to making do with next to nothing, but still.

"The cat's following us," Becks remarked.

I turned back. Sure enough, the little tabby padded along behind me.

"Hey, you can't come with us," I said. "Trust me, it's not a good idea."

"We already have a baby dragonling," said Becks.

"He's not so little anymore," Zeph added.

He wasn't wrong. The dragonling had remained the same size, more or less, for the first few weeks. Then he'd hit a massive growth spurt and was now the size of a small tiger. In another few weeks, he'd be the height of a person or bigger. And Kit was still hand-feeding him and calling him Cuddles when Will wasn't listening.

That poor kitten. I wasn't letting him within a mile of the dragonling, that was for sure.

I picked him up, and the kitten curled into my arm. "We'll give him to Keira, then. She won't mind another stray."

We turned into Magic Avenue, which rested between two ordinary streets and looked equally normal despite its magical nature. Two reasons: tradition, and safety. The road had been hidden before the faerie invasion, and while its wards no longer concealed it from view, most people living here retained the secrecy of the pre-invasion world. The gargoyle-shaped dent in the road and the roof tiles missing from our shop were proof of the targets on our backs. We'd probably devalued the cost of every property in the neighbourhood just by living here, but this was our home.

I left the kitten with Keira, ducking her attempts to reel us into conversation. She'd taken a real shine to Zeph, which came as no surprise. Everyone liked him. The day he'd shown up here, he'd wandered into a local bar and immediately got a job without even trying. Perks of being a dragon shifter—he could work in dangerous areas with minimal risk. He'd settled surprisingly well into our family despite the ongoing tension of having too many shifters crammed into an enclosed space, but he earned his keep, being the only one of us aside from Will who could cook without starting an argument or starting a fire. Or both.

Will sat behind the counter in the shop, drumming his fingers on the wooden surface. His boyfriend Kit was feeding strips of dried chicken to the dragonling, who we'd mutually agreed to name Thorn. Being a Summer half-faerie gave Kit a natural affinity with nature, and the dragonling had become attached to him the instant he hatched.

"Hey," I said, handing Will the twenty-pound note. "Sorry, the job was a bust. House cat, not a shifter. Unless you'd like to volunteer to fight a bunch of gargoyles over the zombie we found halfway up the London Eye?"

"I'll pass." He stuck the note in the cash register. "I hope your sister and Astor are having better luck."

"Sure hope so." The two of them had gone out on an earlier mission. "Darcy said the only mission left on the schedule was for the mages. They want Lorne and the Moonbeam back."

Will blinked. "You know where Lorne is?"

"Nope." *I wish.* The Moonbeam's magic might have saved my life, but I remained none the wiser about where he'd taken it. "Ah well. May as well take a nap if I have the rest of the morning free."

Getting the same idea, Becks made for the back door into our main room. I followed, preparing to sprawl on the sofa. Except someone else already sat there.

Another dragon shifter.

2

I tensed, looking at the newcomer as he rose to his feet. Typical of a dragon shifter, he had red hair, albeit streaked with grey. I'd guess he was in his late forties or early fifties, and while he could only be from the village on the other side of the two-way mirror in our basement, the mere instance of finding a stranger in our home sent alarm bells ringing in my skull.

The dragonling bounded over and bared his teeth at the newcomer, who tensed, his grey eyes flickering.

"I mean you no harm," he said. "I had no way to send a warning before I came here."

"I understand," I said. Since the village's entrance was in our basement, it might be surprising that we didn't have strangers wandering into our house more often. But the people from the village rarely came to visit us on this side.

"You're Cori, right?" said the dragon shifter. "I'm sorry for not warning you before coming into your home, but we need your help. Azalea sent me."

"She did?" I glanced at Zeph, wishing my sister was here. Ember was closer to the villagers than I was, since she knew them better. I'd never met this guy before.

"I'm Neil," he said. "And… it'll be easier if she shows you in person."

Okay… I trusted the dragons implicitly, but while my sister and I had spent our early years living in the village, the situation was a little complicated. When I was five and Ember was twelve, a war had ripped through Scotland's dragon clans. Our parents had sent us to London for our own safety, and by the time we'd re-established contact with the dragons, the survivors had changed beyond recognition after years of suffering under Lorne's rule. While the dragons had lived in peace for the last five years, they bore deep scars from Lorne's reign of terror.

"Ember's out on a mission," I told him. "I don't know when she'll be back."

I'd kind of hoped she'd be busy all day, because at least it meant she'd been sent on a job with a decent payment. But I'd never been to the village without my sister by my side. I pulled my phone out of my pocket and fired off a quick text to Ember.

A reply came—*On my way back. Job was a bust.*

Dammit. Apparently, it was one of those days.

By the time Ember returned, I needed a nap for real. Neil and I waited in an awkward silence, while the dragonling paced the room, tail brushing the carpet. At his current size, he was longer than my five feet of height when stretched out, and his pink-tinted scales had lightened to an opalescent white which shimmered when they caught the light. Nubs of horns had begun to grow on either side of his head, and his greyish eyes brimmed with intelligence.

Neil didn't seem interested in hearing the story of how we'd come to adopt him, and considering it involved stolen dragon shifter DNA and the Orion League, it was probably for the best that Thorn had yet to be introduced to the other dragon shifters.

We still hadn't introduced Zeph to any of the others either, aside from to Azalea, and Neil kept a wary eye on him as we waited for my sister to come back. His wariness of strangers was understandable, given the dragon shifters' history.

I stood, relieved, when the door opened and Ember walked in. Like me, Ember had long curly auburn hair, ashy grey eyes and a wiry frame. She wore jeans and a jacket covered in old stains, and her eyes widened at the sight of the newcomer.

"You're… Neil?" she guessed.

"Ember," he said. "I'm sorry to intrude on your hospitality, but we're in need of your help."

"Lead the way," said Ember.

The dragonling gave one final hiss and butted my hand with his scaled forehead, demanding a stroke. He tried to gnaw on my fingers, and I gave him a warning tap on the nose before following the others.

In the basement, the mirror stood beside the back door which led into the secret tunnels we'd once used to travel around the city. The mirror's surface gleamed silver-white and rippled when Ember touched it.

The four of us stepped through the mirror into

Azalea's basement. Water dripped from a leak in the ceiling, and a general air of neglect permeated the place. The village's houses were sturdy and more than capable of standing up to extreme weather—or dragon shifter skirmishes—but everything in the village showed distinct signs of wear.

The narrow stairs creaked as we climbed into the hallway. Zeph brought up the rear, his expression wary. "Maybe I should have stayed behind."

"Relax," I said. "You're one of us, you know that, right? The others will warm to you eventually. I mean, we're pretty warm in general."

Not my best joke, but Zeph grinned. The customers loved him, especially the straight female shifters. He had the sort of striking features that drew the eye, and an easy, friendly manner. On the other hand, the villagers hadn't exactly given Ember and me a warm welcome the first time we'd come here. Lorne and two of his mates had tried to strangle me, in fact, but I decided against mentioning that.

A peculiar, unpleasant smell drifted through the hall, making my eyes sting. I grimaced, and saw my own expression mirrored on Ember's face.

"Azalea," Neil called through a door off the hallway. "Ember's here."

The leader of the dragon shifters' new council strode into the hall. As usual, Azalea's auburn hair was streaked with grey and her face lined with stress. Dark circles underscored her eyes, making her look even rougher than usual. "Oh—Ember, Cori, you brought your… friend."

"Hey," said Zeph. "I'm Zeph. I hope this isn't a bad time."

Azalea's tired eyes scanned him from head to toe. "I would like very much to speak with you later, Zeph, but there's… there's a sickness in the village. I wondered if you could help us, Ember."

"What kind of sickness?" my sister asked.

Is that the source of the odd smell? It wouldn't be the first time a serious wave of illness had struck the dragon shifters, since the village lacked a lot of the magical resources the big cities had. Necromancers to handle the dead, witches to supply healing spells and other charms to stop the sickness from worsening, mages to fund proper protective wards and stop everyone from panicking. From the look of it, Azalea was shouldering most of the burden on her own.

"We've never encountered this particular sickness before," she said. "That's why I asked you to come. Six villagers are affected… including my son."

"Oh," I said. "I'm sorry."

That explained why she'd been desperate enough to come to us. Azalea had two children, both around twelve years old. Her fierce devotion to both of them was typical of a dragon shifter mother, but the villagers were used to making do alone, and pride refused to let them ask for help unless the situation was truly dire.

"He's… upstairs." Azalea beckoned us up the narrow staircase. "If you don't mind having a look at him, I'd be grateful."

The wooden stairs creaked with each step, and the unpleasant smell grew more persistent the closer we drew. Ember halted beside Azalea to peer through the open door to the boy's bedroom.

Azalea's young son lay on the bed, pale and thin. A

rash spread across his neck and his face, and his eyes were closed.

"It has the appearance of an allergic reaction," she said. "But he's also having trouble breathing. Nothing seems to help."

The boy didn't move as Ember drew closer. None of us were trained healers. We used Will's handmade healing spells whenever we had an injury that wouldn't heal naturally, and that was about it. I walked in behind her, doing my best not to breathe in the scent of sickness.

"What do the affected people have in common?" I asked Azalea. "I mean, it must have come from somewhere, right? Have you had contact with anyone from outside the village lately?"

"None," she said. "Not since we picked up the latest batch of supplies, and Agnes left those herself."

Agnes. I'd forgotten about the old woman who lived in the neighbouring village, whose sister had died to help defend the other dragon shifters from Lorne. She was part witch and part mage and might have been able to help, but I'd bet the villagers' pride had held them back from asking her, too.

I didn't know the community well enough to make an educated guess on where the sickness might have come from. The village was isolated, but wild fae roamed through the countryside, and they might be carrying all kinds of magical illnesses. Hell, it might even be a faerie curse. Dragon shifters were resilient and immune to a lot of human diseases, but that didn't make us invulnerable.

"It looks like a magical allergy," Ember said. "Not one I have any experience with. Have you used healing spells?"

She shook her head. "Our supplies are limited, and healing spells are reserved for serious physical injuries."

"I have one," she said, digging in her pocket and pulling out a band-shaped spell. "If it doesn't work, our friend is a witch. He might recognise the symptoms if I describe them to him."

She dipped her head. "That would be most welcome. Thank you."

Light flashed, engulfing the bed as Ember activated the healing spell. The boy, however, didn't stir, and when the light faded, the rash on his neck was still there.

"Worth a try," said Ember, brushing spell-dust from her coat. "Sorry."

"Who was the first victim?" I asked Azalea.

"Gregor, who lives down the road," she said. "He's barely able to walk… his young son is taking care of him now. He's had the sickness for over a week."

"Can we talk to him?" Ember asked. "It'd be easier to judge if we can compare more than one victim."

"Of course. He lives three doors down."

Relieved to retreat from the sickness-filled room, I backed out into the hallway. Zeph waited downstairs, giving me a questioning look.

"We're off to see the first person who caught it," I muttered to him, walking to the door. "Hopefully he'll have some idea how the sickness ended up in the village."

Call me suspicious, but dragons didn't catch colds or flu, or a lot of other human ailments. If this affected dragons alone, then it was no natural occurrence.

"Are you sure?" Zeph glanced upstairs, a frown wrinkling his brow. "What if you catch it, too?"

Jesus, I hope not. "First we need to figure out how it got here in the first place." I waited for Ember to catch up before opening the door into the cold, foggy street. "If it's magical, then it might be the result of a curse or a spell."

"What, you think someone cursed them on purpose?" Zeph walked out behind us, leaving the door partly open.

I raised an eyebrow. "Who'd have reason to unleash a curse on the dragon shifters?"

"Not that I've spoken to Lorne myself, but this doesn't seem like his style."

Ember gave Zeph a warning look. "Word of advice—don't mention that name aloud here. People get twitchy. With good reason."

"He's right, though," I said. "But the villagers don't have any other enemies to speak of. This place has no warring supernatural communities like London."

"Hmm." Ember halted outside the stone house three doors from Azalea's place, walking up the short footpath to the front door.

"Maybe this isn't a good idea," Zeph said. "If it's like a virus, and we take it back to London with us…"

"I know," I said. "But *you* know we're resilient to most illnesses, right? It must be a strong one. And it hasn't affected everyone yet."

Ember rapped on the door. A young man answered, maybe fourteen or so. "Hey," he said. "You're… Ember?"

"I am," said Ember. "This is Cori, my sister, and Zeph, a friend. We're here to help you figure out where this sickness came from."

"My dad's in a pretty bad way," the boy said quietly. "He can hardly breathe."

The same sickness-tainted smell drifted out of the hall

as he stepped aside to let us in. His eyes widened in surprise at the sight of Zeph. "You're not from here…"

"No, I'm from London," he replied. "I'm Zeph."

The sound of coughing drew us through an open door. A man lay on the sofa under a threadbare blanket. From what I could see of his face and neck, they were covered with the same rash as Azalea's son, and his breathing was harsh, like a death rattle.

"He hasn't said a word in days," the boy mumbled, his eyes on his feet.

"When did this happen?" I asked. "Did he go anywhere in particular? Or leave the village?"

His brow wrinkled. "He used to walk in the hills. But we know the risks. We're immune to most diseases, and the faeries know to stay far away from us."

Hmm. A faerie-spread disease was a possibility. Fae could take on dragons, and certain types could even kill a dragon shifter if they took us by surprise. Otherwise, either it was a new form of magical sickness—or a spell.

"I'm afraid we don't know what it is," Ember said. "But our friend is a witch, and we have a lot of other friends who specialise in magical spells and potions. We'll talk to them and see if we can figure out a cure, okay?"

"Sure," said the boy. "Thanks for coming over. Some of the others… they won't come near. They say we're cursed."

Cursed. An uneasy flutter went through me, a reminder of the gargoyle's fierce words when I'd found that zombie.

"Ignore them," I told the boy. "Thanks for your time."

We left the house, and I sucked in a breath of cool air with relief. I hoped none of us had caught the sickness during our visit. The last thing we needed with our dire financial situation was for any of us to be incapacitated.

"Up in the hills?" Ember pointed through the street to the rolling hills in the distance. "Maybe he ran into a toxic faerie plant up there or even a wild fae carrying an unknown sickness."

"Do you fancy wandering around the hills in this weather?" A drop of rain splashed onto my face, while so much fog smothered the landscape that it would be easy to wander into a faerie's lair and not know it. This area was rife with legends of people who'd taken a wrong turning and got lost among the hills, then returned home to find a decade had passed while they'd been gone. Faeries could be capricious and nasty on a good day, but I'd assumed most fae-centred sicknesses targeted humans, not shifters. And especially not dragons.

"We should ask Will to make a selection of cures, the same way he did when you were poisoned, Ember," Zeph said. "He got it right eventually, didn't he?"

Yeah, but only because we found the witch who concocted the poison. The perpetrator was dead, so if it *was* Lorne, he must have new witch allies.

"Yeah," I said. "He did. I guess if it *is* You Know Who and we manage to catch him at it, we'll get a decent pay day as well as the cure."

Ember made a sceptical noise, but didn't push the conversation about Lorne while the others might be listening in. Will would know the major cures, and if he didn't, there were a dozen other witches in Magic Avenue who might.

"Did you find anything?" Azalea asked as we walked back into the hallway of her house.

I shook my head. "No, but we have a few more ideas about its cause."

"We'll talk to our friends," Ember said. "Azalea, have you ever considered allowing a few witches to live here?"

"We never forbade them," she said. "But nobody wants to live in such an isolated place with no access to basic needs. We don't even have schools or hospitals. Agnes brings everything we need."

"She does?" I said. "Has she come here recently in person, aside from leaving the supplies outside?"

She shook her head. "Not for a long time. It's a long way for her, and she's not as young as she used to be."

"You should tell her about the sickness," I said. "She might have encountered it before."

Her gaze dropped. "We should be able to handle this ourselves."

"Asking for help is nothing to be ashamed of," Zeph said.

I suspected there was more than dragon shifter pride at work here. What they really needed was the protection a mage council could give them, but there was no way the mages would volunteer any of their people to live here in the middle of nowhere. Besides, they'd had their fill of being ruled by a tyrant. I wouldn't do that to them.

"We'll be back soon," Ember said, when Azalea didn't respond. "Take care."

She watched us in silence as we walked to the basement. My gut tightened. I wished I could offer her words of encouragement, but dragons were made to fight and defend one another against physical foes, not unknown sicknesses. I wouldn't even know where to start.

"Are you sure they're telling us everything?" Zeph asked in an undertone.

I trod down the stairs to the basement behind him. "Why would they lie? Some of their people might be dying."

Ember blanched. "Maybe, but you heard what she said about healing spells. Not only are their resources limited, they're short on basic needs and they're vulnerable to diseases that the rest of us would easily be able to fight off. Besides, there's only one place I've heard of a disease that specifically affects dragon shifters before."

"The poison the Faulkner brothers used?" Zeph said. "No. It didn't smell the same. I had one of those arrows sticking out of my arm, so I should know."

"Might have the same source, though." But Lorne was still in London, or close, and didn't have access to the mirror. And the Moonbeam wasn't working for him.

I hope.

The image of its glowing light filled my mind. Since I'd laid my hands on it and shifted for the first time, the Moonbeam was never far from my thoughts. Lorne had wanted its power badly enough to make an alliance with the Orion League, and had even worked with monsters who enslaved shifters and forced them to fight to the death in arena matches. Yet for all that, *I* was the one the Moonbeam had helped.

Ember, Zeph and I walked through the mirror's light into the basement of our house and climbed the stairs into the hall.

"Who wants to volunteer to watch the shop while Will's working on the cure?" asked Ember.

I pushed open the living room door. "You don't think we should be seeking alternative employment?"

"What—quit working at Darcy's?" she asked. "I don't think that would do us any favours. We have little enough cash as it is."

"Precisely." I glanced at Zeph. "I think he's deliberately denying us the high-paying missions. There can't be nothing available at all."

"You never did determine if he was in the Faulkners' pockets or not," Zeph put in.

I pulled a face. "I don't think so. Not the arenas, anyway. And Darcy's place is funded by the mages. I didn't mean we should stop working there altogether, but we have enough free hours to try something else."

"What, like pizza delivery?" Ember said. "They don't offer hazard pay."

"Nor does Darcy," I pointed out. "Zeph is the only one of us with a remotely stable form of employment."

"I wouldn't call a zero-hours contract stable," he said. "Is the shop doing that badly?"

"Not well enough to keep the shelter open." Ember lowered her voice as we entered the living room. Becks lay curled up cat-napping on the sofa, while the others must be in the shop.

Sure enough, we walked into the shop and found Will sitting behind the counter. Kit, at his side, was tussling with the dragonling over a tattered toy that might have once been a teddy bear.

"Hey, Will," I called. "We need your help."

He grunted. "Little busy."

"With customers?" I asked.

Will turned and scowled. A range of cuts marked his

face. "No, because Thorn decided to attack our only paying customer. Took a few chunks out of me, too."

"I offered to heal you," said Kit, gently tugging the toy from Thorn's mouth. "He's very sorry."

"Sorry doesn't pay rent." Will threw a rubber ball at the wall, where it bounced off, and caught it one-handed. "What do you want my help with, anyway?"

"The dragon shifters are sick with a magical virus of some kind," I explained. "I wondered if you'd heard of it before."

"Huh." He listened as Ember and I ran through the symptoms. "Sounds like an allergic reaction."

"The village isn't warded," I explained. "They get their supplies from the neighbouring village, which is a four-hour hike away."

Will arched a brow. "And I thought you guys were masochists for working for that Darcy."

"You said yourself, we need the money," I said. "A regular healing spell didn't work, but I'm guessing it'd need something more specialist."

"Yeah, that sounds like a magical contaminant," said Will. "I can brew up a few salves. Guess I've got nothing better to do." He gave the dragonling a disgruntled look.

"Why not sell more healing spells?" I queried.

"Because there are a dozen other witches on the street doing the same thing," he said. "And ingredient supplies are limited. The only way to get any business is to offer deep discounts, and most humans won't come to a place like this if they have any sense. Besides, the shelter... I don't think we're gonna be able to reopen it anytime soon."

A sober atmosphere descended, and the mages' bonus

came to mind. If we found and returned the Moonbeam to them, then we'd have more than enough cash to restore the shelter. But not only was the Moonbeam gone, I'd never felt comfortable with the idea of handing it over to people who had no idea of its true value to the dragon shifters.

Becks padded into the room. From the look on her face, she'd heard him, too. "I'm starting to think we should have hauled in that zombie."

"What zombie?" asked Will.

"When we were rescuing the cat, we found a dead person the gargoyles didn't want us to touch," I said. "He had… markings on him. Weird ones. Anyway, a gargoyle said he was cursed and almost threw me off the London Eye. I tossed the dead guy into the river, but who knows, maybe the necromancers would have paid us for him."

"I doubt it," said Ember. "Nobody needs to pay for dead bodies when they can get five for free just by walking down the high street."

"Don't say that," Kit said. "Talking about death upsets him."

The dragonling whined and chewed on Kit's sleeve, or what was left of it. While the faerie had the ability to magically heal any injury, the dragonling's teeth had done a number on most of our clothes. And the furniture.

"Maybe we should sell plushie dragonlings, then," I said. "The non-biting variety."

Nobody laughed. It was worth a try.

"I'm going to my shift at the pub," said Zeph. "I can ask if they're hiring any more staff, but I doubt they are. I'll see if I can pick up more hours."

"You don't have to," I said.

"I don't mind." He walked out of the shop, with an easy wave. "I'll see if I can earn some tips tonight."

"Breathe fire at the karaoke night, that'll stir things up," Becks said. "How in hell did we end up this destitute?"

"Because Darcy's a tight-arsed wanker," I said. "Is there a monster on the loose that needs catching, do you know?"

"Seven mercenaries killed a kraken this morning," said Ember. "I heard them talking at Darcy's. Four of them died."

I swore. "I knew Darcy was deliberately withholding the best missions. Those humans didn't need to risk their necks. I could kill a kraken in my sleep."

"The shifting's going that well?" Ember raised an eyebrow at me. "Not that I don't have faith in you, but I damn near drowned the one time I fought a kraken."

"I can shift without crashing into things now," I said. "Mostly, anyway."

"Glad Zeph's of some use, with all the private lessons he's giving you." Becks winked, and I swatted at her with a hand.

Will rubbed his eyes with the back of his hands. "Yeah, he more than earns his keep. It just feels like the rest of it is falling to pieces."

"You're telling me," said Ember. "I didn't know the other dragons were getting sick."

"Nor did I," I said. "Azalea's been keeping it quiet. Unless she didn't want to worry us."

We'd always gone through the mirror to a sea of smiling faces, but I'd assumed the only pain they were covering up was the loss that Lorne and the Orion League had inflicted upon them. Not that a new kind of trouble had come to their doorstep.

The shop door rattled. All eyes turned towards it, in hope of a customer. Instead, a dead man shuffled into the shop.

Just what our day needed—a zombie.

3

The dead man stood in the doorway, leaning on the frame. The foul smell of rot mingled with the fouler stench of the Thames, his head wobbled on his neck, and the smudged marks on his collarbone made me stiffen in disbelief. *It can't be him.*

"Want to buy a healing spell?" Will added. "You look like you need one."

"Will, this isn't funny," said Kit.

Becks, who'd shifted into a cat the instant the door opened, backed up to Kit's side, while the dragonling whined and hid behind the counter.

"You're supposed to be a vicious attack dog!" Ember said. "Is everyone going to keep staring at the dead guy instead of taking him down?"

"Uh, Ember," I said. "He's the undead I threw into the river this morning."

I'd also decapitated him. As he shuffled into the shop, his head rocked to the side, balanced on his stump of a neck. From the state of him, he'd walked all the way from the Thames. His legs were half decayed, and his head wobbled with every step. A chill crept down my neck, the chill of the grave. *Creepy. Really creepy.*

Swallowing bile, I readied my claws. The undead made straight for me, moving with the same freakish speed as before.

Not fast enough. My claws ripped through the zombie's bloated flesh, sending it crumbling into a heap. Kit gagged, and even Ember winced as the head rolled off and landed at her feet. Sightless bloodshot eyes stared at the ceiling. I didn't know whether to throw up, laugh, or take a bath. Or all three.

Astor walked into the shop through the half-open door, startling us all into alertness. He was about five-six, lean and compact with a narrow face and chestnut hair cut short. The ex-assassin barely glanced at the zombie before walking over to Ember. "I take it the mission didn't go as planned?"

"Nope," I said. "Aren't you going to ask how a zombie got in?"

"I'm assuming one of you invited it."

Shit, that was a good point. The wards on the doors were supposed to keep out threats, undead included.

"Apparently he dug himself out of the river for the sole purpose of coming here," I said. "Glad there weren't any customers after all."

"I'll get a cleansing spell," said Will, with a disgruntled look at the dragonling. "Honestly. Some guard dog you turned out to be."

The dragonling whined.

"Hey, I don't like dead people either." Kit gave the dragonling a reassuring pat on the head.

"Why not?" I queried. "He's a dragon. His fire could have melted that undead to ashes in a heartbeat. Anyway, since when did we make enemies of a necromancer?"

"You tell me," said Astor, his tone clipped.

"We didn't." Ember walked to the undead's side and tossed a handful of salt over his half-decayed head. The salt ate away at his skin and bone, leaving nothing but foul-smelling ashes.

"But we have seen him before," I added. "That guy attacked us this morning. The gargoyles told us not to remove his body, so I threw him in the river. How did he figure out where we lived?"

Maybe it was the necromancers I needed to consult, after all.

———

In my dreams that night, I hovered above a hill shrouded in mist. A ghost floated in front of me. While she was as transparent and colourless as any spirit, the hint of a flame darted in her eyes, which were otherwise as pale as the fog.

"The fire is in you," she whispered. "Coriander."

"I'm a dragon," I said. "Fire is par for the course. How do you know my name?"

"I know because I've seen your inner thoughts. Your wants, your desires."

In dream logic, I supposed that made sense.

I tilted my head. "What do I desire, then?"

Her eyes simmered. "Vengeance, like me. The Moonbeam will grant that to you."

I frowned. "How do you know about the Moonbeam?"

The ghost turned into white flames, mingling with the fog. I turned on the spot, realising my feet weren't touching the ground.

I was a ghost, too.

———

Zeph stood, legs spread apart, and watched me from across the roof.

After a rough night's sleep punctuated by nightmares, I'd woken in the early hours and found Zeph just as restless as me. Ever since Lorne's escape, ghosts had plagued my dreams. Sometimes alone, sometimes accompanied by the Moonbeam. Every time I tried to touch it, my hands passed right through it like a spirit. Then I'd wake up drenched in sweat and aching in a way I couldn't explain.

As Becks had observed, Zeph had started giving me private lessons whenever we both had a spare moment. Since the faeries had claimed every "green space" as their own territory due to their allergies to iron and their magic's habit of taking over everywhere it touched, few human-friendly open spaces were left in the city. Especially for dragons. I mean, we were kind of a public safety hazard, too. Eventually, we'd found an abandoned office block that wasn't on gargoyle territory and cleared the debris off the roof to create an area big enough to shift in. Since it was such a cloudy day, the building's upper levels were cloaked in fog which masked us from view. If any humans looked up and saw us, they'd think two angry sky gods were doing battle, which wasn't too far from the truth.

"Go on," I said to Zeph. "Do your worst."

"You might regret saying that." He grinned, his eyes simmering with heat.

Then he shifted into a dragon.

Zeph was impressive in shifted form, that was for damn sure. His scales were bright blue-white, while his seven-foot-long form—not counting the tail or wings— filled the roof space. I felt like a runt by comparison, but then again, I was a touch over five feet tall as a human, while he easily cleared six feet. Horns curled on either side of his face, but the ashy-coloured eyes carried the same hint of humour I knew well.

Go time.

Scales extended up my arms as the shift took hold, and my tail lashed out at him. Zeph jumped out of the way, his claws gripping the roof's edge. I'd broken at least a dozen windows by misjudging the shift in the last couple of weeks, but I was beginning to get the hang of fighting with an extra appendage. Not to mention the wings. Thick and leathery, they made my shadow fearsome and bat-like.

Zeph let out a growl, meaning, *stop admiring your shadow and get on with the fight.*

Then he jumped at me, claws swiping. I rolled over, letting my tough scales take the hit so the claws didn't touch my vulnerable areas. I'd learned to fight with knives and my fists from childhood, but moving a huge scaled body with wings and a tail took a little adjustment even with natural fighting instincts. I might be much more resilient in this form, but there was more of me to hit, and Zeph had had years to hone his skills.

He also had no intention of taking it easy on me.

Considering the frustrating day I'd had, I relished the challenge.

I caught his claw in mine, wrenching to the side to pull him off balance. It'd have worked on a smaller dragon, but Zeph was bigger and stronger than me in dragon form as well as human. Twisting out of my grip, he lunged, pinning me to the roof. His claws pressed against the pale scales of my neck, light but firm enough to hold me in place. I let him, pretending to give in.

Then I shifted to human form.

His claws slipped, unprepared for a wriggly human rather than a dragon. Ducking under his clawed arm, I jumped onto his back, positioning myself behind his neck. He growled, trying to shake me off, and I shifted to dragon form again. The sudden impact pushed him face-first onto the roof in a heap, pinned beneath my claws.

With a faint growl, Zeph shifted back into human form once more. Expecting it, I turned human to match him, keeping a firm grip on his arms.

"That wouldn't hurt a full-grown dragon," he said, his words indistinct and muffled against the roof.

"You *are* a full-grown dragon." I threw my full weight on him, pinning him down. "Best make the most of all the advantages I have, right?"

He tilted his head. "I should dock points from you for that. Most dragons wouldn't shift back mid-fight unless they were severely injured or knocked unconscious."

"Hey, it's a legitimate tactic." I released him and sprang to my feet. "We'll call it a draw."

"Not until you beat me in dragon form." He climbed upright and dusted himself off. His black T-shirt clung to every inch of his carved chest and biceps, and I let my human eye appreciate the view. "No trickery."

"Spoilsport." Our playful banter was a world away from the stresses of running the shelter and wondering where our next payment would be coming from. And it was certainly a welcome change from pursuing Lorne through endless nightmares, trying to snag the Moonbeam from his grasp. "Come on, you have years of experience on me. How'd you learn all this before you left home?"

"I pulled off my first shift at sixteen," he answered, some of the humour vanishing from his expression. "Not long before the League came. After, I had an incentive to learn fast, but that's why it took so long for me to reach London. I kept passing out in fields. I'm lucky I didn't get eaten."

"I did wonder." I settled back to watch the sunrise piercing the fog. "I mean, it's always just been my sister and me. I don't remember learning anything about being a dragon back in the village, since I left when I was five and nobody taught me to shift at that age."

Probably because they were fighting a war. Against Lorne.

"I think you're learning fast, considering." He sat down beside me, his long legs hanging over the edge of the roof. Our shoulders were inches apart, and that small distance hummed with tension. I wanted to run my fingertips over the curve of his arm, to lean closer and inhale his scent.

Control yourself, Cori. Did I really want to get into this with another dragon shifter? With someone who lived in the same house as us? Then again, my sister had held a five-year relationship with an ex-Orion League hunter. Anything was possible.

I turned his way, and another face stared at me from the fog. I jerked backwards, my heart kick-starting. For an instant, I thought it was the same ghost I'd seen in my dream, but I saw no fire simmering in her eyes before she disappeared into the dawn-touched fog.

"Cori?" Zeph gave me a questioning look. "Another ghost?"

I turned away. "It's best if I don't engage with them. She just freaked me out a little, since I was dreaming about one of them last night."

"Dreaming of a ghost you already met?" he queried.

"I don't know." Maybe that was why she'd seemed familiar to me. "She told me to find the Moonbeam and claimed she knew my inner thoughts, or something like that."

Maybe I had seen her before and forgotten, and she'd followed me into my subconscious the same way Lorne had. The Moonbeam was no secret, and it wouldn't surprise me if even the dead knew the mages wanted it back.

"You do want the Moonbeam back," he said. "Don't you? You always said you preferred it out of the mages' hands."

"I did," I admitted. "It was made by the dragon shifters. Lorne claimed that's why he stole it, but he doesn't have our interests in mind. Not to mention it doesn't actually work for him."

"But it does for you."

His words lingered, laced with a different kind of tension. The Moonbeam had ignited a fire within me, and

I saw its glowing form every time I closed my eyes. Lorne had tried to use it against me, but it had turned on him instead. Powerful though the Moonbeam might be, it wasn't sentient. The only explanation I could think of was that the Moonbeam recognised me as the person it had brought back to life and had spared me for that reason.

"It does, right?" Zeph went on. "You have the blessing of the dragon shifters' creation. I guess I don't blame you for wanting to keep it."

"Who said I did?" I frowned.

"Becks said she often hears you talking about it in your sleep."

I rubbed the back of my neck. "They're just dreams. And you know, the mages' bonus would solve all our problems in one. It's a little hard to forget that."

"I know," he said. "I know how much that shelter means to you and your friends."

I drew my knees up to my chest. "The Moonbeam *does* belong to the dragon shifters. But it's also way too powerful to be allowed outside of a secure environment. Every time it's got loose, someone's stolen it and used it for evil purposes."

No matter how often I dreamt of holding it in my hands and feeling its power humming through my veins, like living fire, I wasn't the only person who coveted the Moonbeam.

Even though I suspected I *was* the only person its magic had brought back to life.

"Want to spar again?" Zeph rose to his feet. "See if you can beat me as a dragon this time."

"Challenge accepted."

I flexed my claws, bounded to my feet, and shifted once more.

————

"You have got to be shitting me," I said to Darcy. "We did our jobs."

"Not well enough." He coughed. "Sorry, Cori, but there just isn't enough work coming in that's suitable for you."

"Suitable?" I echoed. "In what way?"

'We prefer people who can more easily pass as human."

"What part of me, exactly, doesn't look human?" I'd got my claws out in front of him on one occasion and that was when a wayward undead had wandered into the building. It wasn't like I'd even used them on Jake, my ex-co-worker. Mostly because he was missing, presumed dead.

Darcy glared back, his eyes red-rimmed. He looked sick. Work getting to him, maybe. "Don't like it, find another guild. You're done here."

Becks's body tensed, and I grabbed the back of her coat before she leapt at him. If he changed his mind later, we didn't need to be blacklisted by every mercenary outlet in north London.

Becks pulled herself free when we got through the automatic doors. "What an utter bell-end."

"We'll try the next mercenary office," I said. "Someone must want our services."

Or they did, before the city's most notorious mobsters met a fiery end.

I was tempted to blow the whole thing off and fly around in search of Lorne's hiding place, but finding someone who didn't want to be found was near-impossible in the supernatural world. The best method was to lure him out, and while he wanted me dead and surely knew where I lived, he'd made no open attempts on my life since his escape.

Walking everywhere was a pain, but most people in London hadn't owned cars even before the invasion. The Underground was still infested with dead, the buses and taxis cost the earth because of the impracticalities of avoiding the various obstacles in the way, and air travel was restricted to the few who could afford a private plane or helicopter. Most of us were grounded, unless we happened to have wings, and Becks refused point-blank to ride on my shoulders.

An hour of walking in the cold brought us to the next-nearest mercenary office. A squat red-brick building with murky, cracked windows, it was a lot more run-down than Darcy's place, and a sign stuck to the crooked blue-painted door said, NO SHIFTERS NEEDED. HUMANS ENQUIRE WITHIN.

I turned to Becks. "Are they seriously excluding shifters?"

"Looks that way." Becks spat at the wall underneath the sign. "Prejudiced fuckwits."

"They could get a bollocking from the mage council for that." Unlikely, though. The mages rarely ventured outside their preferred haunts to enforce the rules, but I would have thought a mercenary outlet would *want* shifters to work for them. Some missions were too dangerous for humans, and shifters were the best supernaturals at combat and had more endurance than regular humans. Okay, most shifters also went berserk during the full moon, but dragon shifters weren't affected by that particular quirk. A lot of places excluded faeries and half-faeries from applying despite the mages' rules, but this was a first.

I peered through the glass. "Do I look human enough to pass as a non-supernatural?"

"No," said Becks. "You also smell like a bonfire."

I gave her an eye-roll. "Want to call Astor and ask him to sign up? He's human. What does he even do for a living, anyway?"

"Ask Ember, not me. Maybe he's still assassinating people for cash."

You never know. He must contribute towards the shelter's funds or Will wouldn't let him live in our house, but the ex-assassin was uncommunicative at the best of times.

Through the grimy window, the place looked deserted. "Is anyone in?"

"I'll check." Becks shifted into cat form and nudged the door open, slipping inside with her brown-striped tail wagging behind her.

I took a step back from the window and spotted a ghost floating in the mouth of the alley between the guild and the shut-down building society next to it. He stared ahead, his transparent hair floating in a breeze that didn't exist on the other side of the veil.

Ghosts were often tied to the place they'd last been before death. Did that mean he'd died here?

"Hello!" said the ghost, spotting me looking at him. "You can see me. But you're not a necromancer. I assume you're not, anyway. You're not wearing one of their cloaks."

"It's at the dry-cleaners," I said sarcastically, regretting looking in his direction. I wasn't in the mood for chit-chat with the dead.

"Really?" The ghost approached me. "I considered signing up to their guild. The necromancers are known for being able to coax talent out of most people with the spirit sight, though their pay rate leaves much to be desired. Almost as much as the mercenaries, but with fewer risks, I imagine. Unless the work involves zombies. Ghosts I don't mind, but zombies... not so much."

Why did I always run into the talkative ghosts? Okay, if nobody else could hear a word I said, I'd feel pretty desperate for human contact, too.

"How did you die?" I asked.

"I got sick," he said, his brow crinkling at the sight of the mercenary office. "I was walking home, and that's the last thing I remember. Are you here to escort me to the afterlife?"

"Not quite," I said. "Sick with what, flu?"

"Something like it," he said. "It came on fast. Started with a rash and dizziness and then went downhill from there. I survived the faeries and the riots, but I died from the flu? It's insulting. And now I'm stuck here, and I don't know how to move on."

"Did you say... a rash?"

No way. London was a world away from a village up in the Highlands. The only connection was our mirror, and the disease couldn't have spread that fast even if one of us had picked it up yesterday.

"All up here." He indicated his neck. "I was struggling to breathe, but I have a family to feed, so I kept coming into the office. I assumed a monster would finish me off, but…" He gave a helpless shrug. "I have a four-year-old. Can you tell her—tell her I'm sorry?"

My throat went tight. "Uh, I'm not a necromancer, but I can try."

Making promises to ghosts didn't carry quite the same risk as making one to a faerie, but we were neck-deep in debt already. My gaze went to the poster on the door. "Why is there a sign banning shifters from applying to work at the mercenary's guild?"

"They know the shifters were the first to catch the sickness," he said. "I'm half shifter, so it took longer to affect me."

"The sickness?" My heart sank. "Where did it start? Who got it first?"

The door slammed closed behind Becks, and the ghost startled, disappearing. Becks's fur stood on end and her eyes were wide.

Damn. What now?

"Becks, speak to me." I crouched beside her, but she bit my fingers when I tried to stroke her. It was her way of saying, *hey, I'm not a house cat.* Standing, I pushed the door open, and Becks gave a plaintive meow.

I stepped into the dusty lobby and swore. A dead man faced me, sitting at his desk with his eyes staring blankly ahead. A purplish rash covered his face and neck, and his eyes were bloodshot.

Who was I even supposed to report him to? Destroying his body would also remove the evidence, and there was something quietly sinister about the way he just sat there, unnoticed by anyone. I checked his name badge. Eric Galwood, owner of this branch of mercenaries. *Another possible employer bites the dust.*

I backed out, finding Becks shivering on a low wall. Her eyes were round, and her fur stood on end. Becks had the paranoia and sense of danger born of living on the streets, but her reaction seemed out of character. I tentatively stroked her, and she bared her teeth at me.

"Good, you're still in there," I said. "I was beginning to worry."

Becks gave me a swipe with her claws, dragonling-style.

"Watch it," I said. "I'm the one who looks like a complete tit talking to a cat on a wall. We can't leave that guy in there, though..."

An idea sparked, kindled by the sight of the spirit hovering beside the building.

Becks turned human again. "Cori, what are you scheming? I know that look."

"I'm going to summon his ghost," I said.

4

"Cori, I really don't think this is wise," said Becks. "Have you ever summoned a specific ghost before?"

"Well… no." I opened the bag containing the set of necromancer candles Ember had bought me as a present a few years ago. Tipping them onto the carpet between the chairs in the living room, I flipped each one over. They resembled plastic models of regular candles, lit by internal magical lights rather than by striking a match.

"And don't you need to be near where they died?" Becks sat opposite me, legs crossed. "Not trying to piss all over your idea, just imagining what Will would say if you set a ghost loose in the house."

"It won't be loose, thanks to these." I tapped one candle with a fingernail. "It'll work anywhere in the city as long as we have the guy's name."

"You should ask the necromancer guild instead," she said.

"They're like the mages." I laid the candles out in a circle of twelve. "They charge a fortune for summonings, and we have no spare cash. Besides, we're perfectly capable of doing the summoning right here." Okay, I hadn't even read a basic guidebook, and I had no necromancer friends whose expertise I could call upon. All I could do was follow what I remembered from my education before the faerie invasion.

"All right," she said. "Get this over with before Will kicks up a fuss about us conducting necromancy in the back room."

"It's hardly worse than his witchcraft experiments." I set the last candle down. "I'd rather do it before my sister gets back. Ember will give me an hour's safety lecture and the ghost will be long gone by the time she's done."

According to Will, Ember had taken a collection of healing potions and charms through the mirror to the dragon shifters. If they cured the sickness, I'd have no real need to worry, but still… what if the same sickness *had* wound up here in London?

I surveyed the candle circle. I didn't think all twelve had to be evenly spaced, but aside from my ability to see and talk to ghosts, I didn't know how to do other necromancy tricks. Like reanimating bodies, for instance. Not that I knew *why* rogue necromancers liked doing that so much. Keeping rotting bodies in the basement seemed way too high-maintenance.

One at a time, I hit the switch on the back of each candle. Blue lights flare, connecting to one another to form a wobbly circle. When all twelve were lit, grey smoke bloomed within the circle's boundaries. *That's a good sign, right?*

The candles' magic combined to open the spirit realm.

Now all I had to do was speak the name of the ghost I wanted to summon.

Becks backed away from the circle. "That smoke looks like the arena did when we were trapped in there. Is that —the spirit realm?"

"Yeah, it looks that way all the time to people with the spirit sight," I said. "Normal people can't see it unless the spirit lines are screwed up, they're on a key point, or they're buddies with a necromancer. It's just Death."

"Just Death, open in our back room." Becks shuddered. "Get it done, Cori, before it goes horribly wrong."

I leaned forward, unsure how close to the circle I was supposed to sit, and said, "I summon Eric Galwood."

The grey swirled. My heart kick-started, and I fell back into a sitting position as a transparent figure appeared in the middle of the candles. He was the spitting image of the man we'd found dead in his office.

"Are you Eric Galwood?" I asked.

"I… yes, I am. Who are you?"

I flashed Becks a triumphant look, then turned back to my captive spirit. As long as the candles remained lit, he wouldn't be able to get out.

"Hey," I said to the ghost. "Uh, sorry for dragging you across the city like this. I wanted to make sure I summoned you before you moved on to the afterlife."

"The what?" he mumbled. "Who are you people?"

"My name's Cori." Since he was dead, it wasn't like he could tell the whole world I'd summoned him. "I found you dead in your office at the mercenaries' place."

He squinted at me. "I dozed off again, didn't I? Is this one of those lucid dreams?"

"Nope," I said. "Was there some sort of sickness going around your office?"

"Yes," he said. "Every shifter got sick, and then the humans. Nobody's coming into work. It's a bloody nightmare, and of course the mages won't do anything. I need to wake up now, though. It's nice meeting you, Cori."

Damn. He doesn't believe he's dead. This was going to be rough.

"Where'd the sickness come from?" I asked carefully. "Please—it's important. Some friends of ours have it, too."

"I don't know where it came from, but there's no cure," he said, his tone despondent. "I left four messages for the mages, but they didn't pick up the phone. It's getting worse by the day…"

And he faded, mid-sentence, drawn back into the grey.

Dammit. I stepped up to the circle, and said clearly, "I summon Eric Galwood."

This time, the grey smoke remained as obscure as ever, swirling between the candles.

"I think he's gone," Becks observed. "Turn the candles off before the angel of death swoops into the house."

"There's no such thing as the angel of death." But she was right. Eric had moved on. Beyond Death's gates, or so the necromancers called them. I hadn't stayed in Death long enough to see what actually waited on the other side of the veil.

The candles' chill pierced through my naturally warm body temperature. Crouching, I hit the switch on one of them. At once the twelve lights died, taking the swirling smoke with them.

After checking the spirit realm was thoroughly gone, I set about collecting the candles. Each one contained a finite amount of spiritual energy, or so it said on the box. From what I'd heard, spiritual energy didn't appear in many places, so for all I knew, it might have come from humans. Or the spirit lines, which were active currents of energy. No sane necromancers dared to use their power on a spirit line, for fear of stirring up every spiritual force in the area. For lunatics like Lorne and rogue necromancers, on the other hand, that instability was exactly what they wanted. To suck out souls, cause a second invasion… or raise the dead.

Becks eyed the candles as I put them back into the bag. "I don't think you should make a habit of using those."

"Since when were you so superstitious?"

"Since the arena." She heaved a shudder. "And Lorne's attack on the spirit line. You know how bloody terrifying it was for me to just… lose control of my senses? It wasn't like the full moon. When the moon's full, my shifter side is in control, but at least that's a part of me. The Faulkners' spell… Lorne's spell… it took away my free will. I wanted to fight, and I had this endless *rage* that wouldn't go away."

"I wouldn't know how to do that even if I wanted to, which I don't," I said, closing the bag and shaking it so that the candles rattled against one another. "I think necromancers have an unfairly bad reputation, to be honest."

"Uh, yeah, because too many of them decide it's funny to crash people's parties with zombies. Are you planning to take up amateur necromancy as a side income?"

"At this rate, it would be our *only* income." I tossed the bag of candles onto the sofa. "I guess we might get work just for the novelty value. *Hire the first dragon shifter turned exorcist in the city of London!*"

"Pretty sure you need a permit from the guild to set up an independent business. Like the witches do."

I pulled a face. "You sound like my sister, Becks. I was just kidding."

We didn't need to make enemies of the local necromancers on top of the gargoyles. Not to mention the mages, who were the ones who'd set up the *you need a licence* rule in the first place. Will had easily acquired a licence to sell potions and spells to the public in the post-invasion days, but I'd have to go through years of necromancy training to qualify as an independent, and the other ghost had implied that expelling poltergeists from people's houses didn't pay much better than mercenary work.

Speaking of ghosts… "Eric said he left four messages for the mages and they didn't pick up the phone. Do they even know about the sickness?"

"Maybe," Becks said. "They know most things, but then again, if it started with the shifters, maybe not. Never thought I'd say this, Cori, but I think we should report it."

I was inclined to agree. "All right," I said, resigned. "But if they find out the dragon shifters have it, too they might blame it on us."

Not that they'd have reason to, considering the sickness must have hit London before we'd even known the other dragon shifters were affected.

But if that was the case, where had it started?

———

Since Will and Kit were running the shop and Ember was still with the dragon shifters, Becks and I headed to the mages' place alone.

Mage territory covered the city's more affluent areas, and the central headquarters of London's Mage Lords were located in Kensington. Becks and I looked positively drab compared to the pristine houses and warded gates, but at least we could freely walk around without the threat of being dive-bombed by a gargoyle.

If the sickness spread, the first thing the mages would do was quarantine their territory. They'd done so at least twice following the invasion, and preventable illnesses were prevalent among humans and less fortunate supernaturals already thanks to the shortages of vital medicines. The mages oversaw shipments of goods from mainland Europe alongside the human governments, but one in two ships disappeared en route, swallowed by the monster-infested waters of the English Channel. As a result, rationing was still tight, people lacked vital medications, and it wasn't a surprise that this new sickness had spread so quickly. As to how it'd wound up in the middle of the Highlands as well, though, I could only guess.

Since the mages had installed a new security system, we had to stand outside the iron gates to their headquarters. I fired off a text to Ember while we waited. She'd be ticked off that we'd left without telling her first, but a man was sitting dead in his office and the mages hadn't even picked up the phone to hear his pleas for help. Lord Smyth and the other Mage Lords had some serious explaining to do.

The gates slid open, inviting us up the neat path to the

doors of the mages' headquarters. The large chrome and glass construction gave the air of a modern office block rather than an ancient organisation dating back to the dawn of the supernatural community.

The woman waiting at the door wasn't the mages' leader, but the second in command. Blond, tall and stern, Lady Clare had never been my biggest fan. I'd helped Ember save her from a murderous necromancer a few years ago, but if anything, that seemed to make her resent me more. That I'd predicted Lorne's escape was just fuel on the fire.

"Yes?" she asked. "What is it?"

Undeterred by her terse tone, I launched in a quick explanation of what I'd found at the mercenaries' office.

"Humans, were they?" she asked.

"Not all of them," I said. "Shifters, too. The guy who owned the place was sitting dead at his desk, and he left a message for you on the phone. For the mages. Nobody picked up."

No need to let on where I'd acquired that information.

"We get a lot of calls," she said, as impassive as ever. "He was likely put on hold by one of our assistants."

"There was more than one message," I went on. "It sounded like he was desperate. I wondered about calling the local necromancers to remove the bodies, but their families deserve to know, so I came here first. Since they already tried to contact you."

Trying to stir up some sympathy was lost on Lady Clare, who'd probably never set foot in a shifter neighbourhood in her life. "How did you end up in that office? It's out of your area."

"We were looking for work." I hated admitting that we

were struggling for money in front of her unsympathetic stare, but lying to a mind-reader would be pointless.

"If nobody was alive, how did you find out how they died?" She arched a perfectly plucked eyebrow.

"The mercenary mentioned it in the message he left on your phone." If the mages found out about my conversation with the ghost, they'd throw me on the mercy of the local necromancers and we'd never find out if the mercs had died of the same sickness as the dragon shifters.

Becks nudged my leg, but I didn't know what she wanted me to say.

"We didn't know who else to report it to," I added. "Since even the owner of the place was dead. Where's Lord Smyth?"

"He's meeting with the leaders of the local shifters," said Lady Clare.

"About the sickness?" I asked. "I think he should hear about this."

"I'll leave a note on his desk," she said. "And please don't waste Lord Smyth's time. He's a busy man."

That's friendly. I expected nothing less from the woman who'd locked my sister in jail when she'd committed no crimes. She probably blamed me for Lorne's escape, too.

"I heard about the reward you're offering," I added. "For Lorne and the Moonbeam."

"And do you have information to share?" Her stare was cutting, like she could see into my mind. Which she could, to some degree. I bloody well hoped she hadn't picked up anything incriminating. Not that I had much to give away as far as Lorne and the Moonbeam were concerned. If he was behind the sickness, he'd left no visible traces to follow.

"Only that the Moonbeam doesn't work for Lorne," I said. "That I know of, anyway. He might have sold it for all I know, since it's not much use to him."

"You claimed it belonged to the dragon shifters," she said. "Who was the original owner?"

Well... actually, I have no idea.

The first I'd heard of the Moonbeam was when I'd woken up from the coma the Orion League had put me in when I'd been their captive. The League had intended to use it to turn shifters into killing machines, but Astor's friend Giselle had taken it from their grip and sold it to someone in London's supernatural underworld. Needless to say, it hadn't lasted long there before it'd wound up in the League's—and Lorne's—hands again.

As for who'd created it in the first place? Even the villagers didn't know.

"If you return it, you'll receive a generous reward, Cori," she said. "We keep our word. If you want the bonus, please tell us if you have any information to share about Lorne's whereabouts."

Damn her. I never should have hinted at our financial woes. "I will if I find out."

Becks shifted to human form again as soon as we'd left the grounds. "Why not tell her you think Lorne did this?"

"Because they might stop us from using the mirror to visit the dragon shifters," I said. "We're already being blamed for what the Faulkners did. I notice the mages aren't falling over themselves to defend us."

"Have they ever?" Becks snorted. "We're shifters. Bottom of the heap, even below the necromancers."

"Speaking of whom, I should have told her about that undead, too, in case it's linked." I rubbed my eyes. "The sickness… it *is* the mages' business. If the virus doesn't stop with humans, it'll reach the mages, too."

"Do you honestly think they'll let it?"

I growled under my breath. "Nope, they'll throw another shield around their territory until we're all dead. But if we don't know where it started, I guess there's someone else we can ask for help."

Namely, the local necromancers.

5

I'd never visited the local guild of necromancy. Mostly because I'd wanted to avoid the inevitable conversation about where I'd acquired my spirit sight.

The necromancers made their home in an old funeral parlour, appropriately enough. The dull grey bricks were worn with age, while the windows were curtained in black. The necromancers, I'd long since come to assume, revelled in their reputation as sinister figures who haunted crypts and cemeteries at night. If necromancy was truly my calling, I should have felt more of a pull towards the place, but I didn't know whether to laugh or back slowly away.

Becks hung back by the fence, her fur standing on end, so I made my way to the black-painted door alone. There wasn't a doorbell, but a tall thin man stood on the doorstep, wearing such a vacant expression that I mistook him for a statue at first. Until he blinked, his gaze sliding back into focus. "Can I help you?"

"Can I speak to your leader?" I asked.

"I'm afraid this isn't the best time," he said. "He passed away this morning."

"Oh." What was with our luck today? "Is there anyone else I can speak to?"

"He'll be back in soon," he said. "But there's normally a period of adjustment for new Guardians."

"Sorry, I have no idea what you're talking about," I said. "Who's guarding what?"

"Guardians?" he said. "You know, those who guard the gates of Death."

"Oh, of course." Did they assume everyone else had taken advanced necromancy classes? "Are you implying your boss is coming back from the dead?"

"Of course not," he said. "He's taking an induction to Death's gates, then he'll be returning to resume his position as guild leader as he stated in his will."

That sounded like coming back from the dead to me. Bloody necromancers. Half of them spent so long in the spirit realm that they had no idea how to exist in this one, let alone talk to normal people. A lot of the most competent necromancers had perished in the invasion, while the survivors couldn't be doing well, if their leader had just kicked the bucket. Talk about bad timing.

"I'm sorry, was there something you wanted to ask me?" he asked.

"I wanted to report an unusual undead," I said. "We were attacked in our home and I think a rogue necromancer might be after us."

He blinked. "I'll mention it to the boss when he comes back, and you can file a report then."

That sounded familiar. I doubted Lady Clare would

actually bother to leave a note on her fellow Mage Lord's desk. "Uh-huh. Sure."

"Take one of these." He handed me a business card with the guild's details on it. On the back was a form where I could write my number. "I'll ask him to call you."

"Oh, sure." I scrawled my number on the card and handed it back to him. At least he'd been a little more helpful than Lady Clare had. "Okay, thanks. Um, who do I report dead bodies to? We found the body of a dead mercenary who died from some form of sickness, but I'm not sure it's in your area."

"We leave it to the families first," he said. "Otherwise they won't appreciate it if we take the bodies away without permission."

Ah. I ran into so many zombies that I'd forgotten it was supposed to be against the law to reanimate them without permission from the necromancer guild.

"Also…" I hesitated. If I told him I was seeing ghosts, then he might call me a liar and refuse to have anything more to do with me. "Can ghosts communicate through dreams?"

"Dreams?" He blinked his owl-like eyes again. "No. People often dream of loved ones they've lost or think they see their shades. Is it like that?"

"Not exactly." The spirit I'd seen in last night's vivid dream wasn't real, then. It wasn't worth expending energy worrying about it.

I found Becks around the corner, sitting on the kerb in cat form. She didn't turn human again until we'd left the necromancers' place behind. Then she shifted, shaking out her hair.

"God, that place is freezing," she muttered. "Is the spirit realm like that all the time?"

"Pretty much," I said. "I didn't see any ghosts, but I guess they have the spirit realm under control in their own headquarters."

She wrapped her arms around herself. "Did you tell them about your little… talent?"

"Chickened out," I admitted. "If I told him I came back from the dead, he might have interrogated me on how it happened, and I didn't want Ember dragged into it."

"Right… because Ember brought you back," she said. "That's all I remember. Ember holding the Moonbeam and glowing. She asked it for…"

"A miracle." I hunched my shoulders. "I'm not… ungrateful for that. Ever. But ever since then, the mages have claimed they deserve to keep the Moonbeam for themselves. I mean, they thought it legally belonged to them anyway, but you heard what Lady Clare said. I know nothing about it."

Not even where it had originally come from.

"Neither do they," Becks said. "So the necromancers didn't offer you a job?"

"I didn't ask for one. And the mercs are a bust. Unless we get a bonus for handing their bodies over to their loved ones. Might as well, since the day can't possibly get any more depressing."

I angled my footsteps in the direction of the abandoned mercenary headquarters once more. If the mages wouldn't help, then I could at least move the dead where they wouldn't rot—or worse, fall victim to a rogue necromancer.

Becks ran alongside me. "Are you sure?"

"We can't leave that dead guy sitting there in the office," I said. "At the very least, we should contact his family. I don't expect the mages to put it at the top of their priority list, and besides, if anyone else stumbles across the body, they might catch the sickness, too."

"Uh, like us?" she said.

Good point. Dragon shifters weren't immune—a first. "Then I'll ask permission to destroy the bodies, like they do when other sicknesses hit the shifter communities. The head of the guild isn't a gargoyle, it's not like he has a clan at his back ready to swear bloody revenge on us."

Having spoken to the poor guy's ghost, I was even less inclined than before to let him rot. He seemed decent enough. Not to mention the other guy from the alley, who'd begged me to speak to his daughter. It'd be a dick move to just leave him there.

Becks tensed. "We're being followed."

I spun around, but the curly red hair of our pursuer could only belong to one person. Smiling, I waited for her by a low-rise wall.

"Hey!" Ember caught us up, the wind stirring her auburn curls. "Cori, where're you marching off to?"

"Did any of the cures work on the villagers?" I asked her.

Ember's eyes darkened. "No. Will's brewing some others."

"It's bad news." I drew in a breath. "The sickness is killing people here, too. Shifters *and* humans. We're going to check out one of the bodies now. Wanna come?"

Her mouth tightened. "Here? Are you sure?"

"Looks that way," I said. "We reported it to the mages, but Lord Smyth's off on a mission and the necromancers can't haul in the body until his family have been informed. It wouldn't hurt to have a poke around and see if there are any more dead people who'll talk."

"Did you say any *more* dead people?"

Ah. Well, I had to tell her eventually.

I told Ember about the morning's unexpected events while we walked—including my conversations with the dead. Ember's expression grew sterner and sterner with each word, but she only got one line into her lecture before a shrill noise interrupted.

"Oh, Thorn," she said over her shoulder. "I told you not to follow me."

The little dragonling flew over and landed at my side. Relieved of the distraction, I gave him a stroke on the forehead.

"We might as well bring him along," I said to the others. "It's not like there's anyone alive in that place who might report us."

"And if the mages change their minds?" Ember enquired.

I shrugged. "They're distracted. Besides, I doubt they haven't heard about him by now. He's bitten enough customers."

We reached the mercenary outlet, and Ember halted at the sign in the window.

"No shifters?" she echoed. "Why?"

"They were the first to pick up the virus," I said. "But it did end up affecting humans, too."

Ember walked to the doors, pushing them open. Becks

seemed content to stay outside with the dragonling, so I left the two of them out there and walked into the lobby.

"Is there supposed to be a dead guy in here?" she asked.

Ah, hell. The desk was empty, save for a few scattered papers. No sign of Eric's body, but I couldn't tell whether he'd been moved by the authorities, the necromancers… or someone had stolen his body.

The image of the dead man who'd appeared in our shop flashed through my mind, bringing a chill to my skin. What was the matter with me? I'd summoned a ghost in our house. I had no reason to fear the dead.

"If the authorities took him, they'd have locked the place up," Ember said. "To prevent it being—" She broke off, staring through a half-open door.

"Ransacked?" I finished. Sure enough, the room she stared into had clearly been a weapons room until recently. Given how expensive good weapons were, it wasn't a surprise that everything save for a few broken knives had been taken, leaving the shelves bare and dusty.

I checked the other rooms on the ground floor, finding them similarly ransacked. Thieves moved fast, and most mercenaries were humans, starving and desperate to keep their families alive. Of course they'd have taken what they could and run if a disease had killed all their supervisors.

But Eric had gone beyond the veil. I couldn't summon his body back without a soul.

I re-entered the reception area and moved behind the desk, opening the drawers.

"What're you doing, Cori?" asked Ember.

"Aha." I produced an address book from the desk drawer. "This will have all the guild employees' details. What're the odds that some of them stopped coming into work when the sickness kicked off? We only saw one supervisor in the office this morning. If we call everyone, we might be able to find where it started."

"Good thinking." Ember nodded. "There's not much else worth taking in here."

I gave the office another scan. "Thieves took anything valuable, but mercs wouldn't have reason to remove the record books."

"Like this?" Ember leaned under the desk and lifted a thick spiral-bound notebook. "Looks official."

A warning trill drew me to the door. The dragonling. Tensing, I stuck the address book in my pocket and walked outside.

Eric Galwood stood on the doorstep. Or rather, his reanimated body did.

"Nice to see you again," I said, falling into a fighting stance. "Don't let me keep you from your work."

His hand shot out, faster than any undead had the right to move. My claw snapped up, catching his hand before it closed around my throat.

The dead man wrenched at my claw, and alarm flickered through me. No mere human should be strong enough to move a dragon shifter's claw. I tugged back, and Ember smacked him over the head with the logbook. He swayed, his grip breaking, and swung a fist at her. Ember darted out of the way. Damn, he was fast. His strength and speed were supernatural—literally.

A burst of fire ignited over the dead man's head, and the dragonling landed on him, biting and tearing. He went limp, and the dragonling spat out a mouthful of undead flesh with a shudder of revulsion. Despite his destroyed body, symbols were visible on his collarbone.

I pointed. "Look at that."

"What, a tattoo?" she queried. "What's so odd about it?"

"It's the exact same as the tattoo on the undead who attacked us at the London Eye." The one the gargoyles had proclaimed *cursed.* "Got a bag to carry him in?"

Thorn spat a mouthful of fire at the undead. His singed clothes ignited, his body evaporating, tattoo and all. *Damn.*

I turned around to see if there were any witnesses, but this entire neighbourhood was a ghost town. My spirit sight didn't turn on automatically, but in a place as touched by death as this one was, the pale grey of the veil wasn't far away. Greyness smothered the already dilapidated houses, and a chill swept the air. But no ghosts. Not close, anyway.

Sighing, I turned off my spirit sight to find my sister watching me, her head tilted on one side. "Cori… is it still happening?"

"Only when I let it." When I summoned dead mercenaries into our living room, for instance. "I was seeing if there was anyone else still around to give their testimony. I guess we could try summoning the other mercs, but they've probably moved on."

Ember's mouth thinned. "Messing with the forces of life and death never ends well, Cori."

Becks nodded in agreement.

"I'm a walking exception to that rule," I said. "So's Thorn."

The dragonling jumped into my arms, and I staggered under his weight. He really was getting too heavy to carry.

"See, he agrees with me," I said. "Okay, I guess we're

calling Eric Galwood's relatives to tell them about his fate."

I gave the pile of ashes one last look. The image of the tattoo flashed through my mind again. I'd seen it somewhere before… on the Orion League's elite soldiers.

Or more specifically, on Astor.

6

When we got back to Magic Avenue, we found the shop closed and Will up to his neck in spells in the lab, preventing me from trying any more illicit necromancy. Instead, I took out the address book and set about tracking down the former employees of Eric Galwood's mercenary outlet.

After the first failed to answer, I dialled the second number in the address book.

"Hello?" I said. "Is this Norman Jones?"

"No," said a quiet feminine voice. "It's his wife. Who is this?"

"The inspectors," I improvised. "We're wondering why he failed to show up to work this week."

"You're too late," she whispered. "He's dead."

My throat went tight. "I'm sorry to hear that. May I ask if this was related to his mercenary work?"

"Possibly," she said, her voice choked. "He died of a sickness, and I think he picked it up on the job."

"That's what I've been asked to look into," I improvised. "It's not the first story I've heard, so we're looking for signs of possible magically-spread sickness. Did you see anything else?"

"I don't know," she said. "He was fine, then he came home from work and claimed he had a headache and was going to bed early. A few days later..." she cut off in a sob. "He developed this awful rash and could hardly breathe. Nothing we bought over the counter did anything for his symptoms."

"Did he mention having had contact with anyone else who had the same symptoms?" I asked. "We have reason to believe this sickness has a magical origin, and if we find its cause, then maybe we can prevent it from affecting anyone else."

So the disease had been here in London for at least a week. But then, how could it be the same as the sickness affecting the dragon shifters? The only people with a connection between both places were us—and Lorne, if he'd reactivated the Moonbeam's portal.

My chest tightened. Poison wasn't Lorne's style, but then, what did I know? He'd used a spell to turn all London's shifters against one another. He certainly wanted all of us dead, or at least not to get in his way. On the other hand, you'd think he'd have targeted my sister and me directly. He'd made no secret of the fact that we were top of his hit list.

"I'm sorry," said the woman. "I'm afraid I don't know."

Undeterred, I apologised for her loss and dialled the next number on the list. Nobody answered this time. The third call turned out to be the relatives of the ghost I'd met in the alley, which was about as painful as I'd expected. I opted not to admit that a dragonling had burned the bodies. Afterwards, I passed on the message to the second ghost's four-year-old, which was even worse, if possible.

"Maybe this is why the necromancers can't get any business," I said to Becks. "It's depressing as hell, and everyone either burns their dead or loses them to unscrupulous rogues. And their ghosts aren't talking."

As for the mages? An entire mercenary outlet had gone up in smoke and nobody even seemed to care. Sure, it wasn't a revolutionary concept that the upper echelons of society—supernatural and otherwise—lived a literal world apart from the rest of us. With so much destruction and ruin in the city already, what was one more closed-down building, a few dozen people without jobs, and a few people without loved ones? There was no sense in even blaming the mages. There were a few hundred of them, and more than a million people in London. They couldn't look out for all of us.

A full afternoon of phone calls yielded no leads. By the time I'd reached the end of the list, I had nothing but a headache and a well-rehearsed spiel of condolences.

"Maybe Lord Smyth's back from his mission now," I muttered to Becks, who'd been cat-napping on the rug while I paced the living room speaking to ex-mercenaries and their bereaved family members. "He's got to take an interest in it if someone's pilfering these corpses and reanimating them, but I don't know which branch of necromancers is supposed to be in charge of that area."

The necromancers were more numerous than the mages, but consisted of cobbled-together collectives made from the survivors of the invasion. When the invasion had screwed up the spirit lines, those people who'd already been close to the spirit realm had been dragged into Death en masse. Unfortunately, the more powerful a necromancer was, the closer they were to the realm of Death. The result? Amateurs abounded, at least half of whom didn't belong to a guild at all. Which explained why someone had swiped those dead bodies so damn fast.

The question was, who'd sent the dead man from the London Eye after us? Was it the same necromancer who'd raised the others at the office, and if so, how did they know where we lived?

The gargoyle's words came back. *Cursed,* he'd said. Astor hadn't shown his face yet and Ember had marched out to 'get some air' an hour or so back, which left me with nobody to tell my theories to except for a sleepy Becks—and Will, who'd spent the entire afternoon in the lab.

Becks yawned and didn't respond, so I walked over to the lab, coughing on the smell of burning herbs. Will's blond hair stuck up in all directions and his eyes were red-rimmed.

"No luck?" he asked. "I can feel your frustration from over here. It's messing with my concentration."

"Are you sure it's not your own frustration about the lack of customers?" I asked. "Anyone would think *we* had the plague."

"Maybe they do," he said. "It doesn't take much to start a rumour, and you saw that sign on the guild saying *no shifters.*"

"Oh come on, nobody can possibly know we've inter-acted with the other dragon shifters," I said. "That's a little paranoid."

He turned around, his eyes bloodshot. "Ember has

tried every popular cure, and nothing has worked. I'd almost call it a custom-made poisoning, except no antidote seems to work on it either."

"Seriously?" I said. "Have you tried asking a witch who specialises in poisons? Not that you aren't good at magic, but healing isn't your area of expertise and neither is poisoning."

Unfortunately, the only person I could think of was the witch who'd worked for the Faulkners, who Astor had administered an unfortunate end to.

"I asked around," he said. "Nobody knows. Did the mages have anything useful to say? You did tell them, right?"

"Yes, but Lady Clare was the only mage around and she doesn't give two shits if we all die," I said. "Maybe it was for the best that she wouldn't listen. They'll probably put us in quarantine if the sickness reaches us here."

The mages might owe my sister and me for saving the city, but that didn't mean they'd hesitate to throw us under the bus if they thought we were responsible for the sickness. If they found out we'd seen evidence of it elsewhere, it'd be easier to blame us than anyone else.

Will tossed a heap of leaves into the cauldron bubbling on the kitchen stove. "If it's not a poison, it's perhaps an engineered virus, created using a rare and banned substance. Or it could be a spell, I guess, but that'd be tricky to administer. Or a rare animal got loose and started biting people, but again, it doesn't match up with any that I know."

"So a witch definitely did this?" I asked. "Even if it *was* Lorne, I didn't think he had any witchy friends."

"Whoever said it was Lorne?" He scowled at the mess

of ingredients on the counter. "I don't see him being this subtle."

"Look at his plan to get out of jail," I said. "He can do subtle when it suits him. I just find it suspect that the virus hit London and the village at the same time. Who else has access to both places?"

"What, you think he reactivated the Moonbeam?" he asked. "Have you checked on the mirror?"

"Well… no. I'll do that now."

"Good," he said. "Go and mess with the mirror for a bit and please take your pacing somewhere else. You're distracting me."

My mind buzzed with thoughts. Poison, Lorne… the Moonbeam. The image of its glowing white form filled my mind and guilt assailed me for coveting it even though Lorne might be using it to spread the sickness. The Moonbeam might have saved my life, but that didn't give me a claim on it. For all I knew, trying to track it through the mirror would transport me instantly to Lorne's side. Ember would pitch a fit if I confronted him without her beside me, but the mystery nagged at me like an unreachable itch.

The mirror stood in its usual place, glowing with silver-white light. My palms touched the surface and I thought, *take me to the Moonbeam.*

The mirror's surface remained opaque.

I tried again. And again. Since the Moonbeam could only be activated by a dragon shifter, then… then Lorne couldn't be using it after all.

I gave one last try, and my feet caught on the mirror's edge. My head popped through, and the sound of sobbing reached my ears. Tossing caution aside, I stepped into the basement of the dragon shifters' village. The sobbing grew louder. It sounded like… Azalea.

My chest constricted, and I ran to the stairs and up into the hallway. Azalea's office lay half-open. She sat slumped in a chair, her knees drawn to her chin in a manner that made her look startlingly vulnerable.

"Azalea," I said, breathless.

"Cori." She startled upright. "The cure. Do you have it?"

I shook my head, the despair on her face cutting through to my very core. "I'm sorry. The sickness… it's in London, too, and it seems to have come out of nowhere. Is your son okay?"

"He's worse," she mumbled. "Half the council has it, too. The first victim died this morning."

"I'm sorry," I said, my stomach lurching. One person had died. How much more time did the others have? And if I couldn't track Lorne via the mirror, then maybe it wasn't him who'd done this. "We're doing our best to work on potential cures. Is there anything else new?"

She just shook her head. It was too dark outside to go wandering around, so I headed back to the basement.

I stepped through the mirror, hearing the door open above me. *Astor's back.* I climbed the stairs into the hall. "Hey, Astor."

He jerked his head by way of a greeting. "Cori."

You'd think he hadn't been dating my sister for the last five years. I figured their relationship was built on really hot sex and both verbal and literal sparring, but I was reasonably confident he wouldn't rip my head off for asking a harmless question.

"I have a question for you," I said. "Astor, when did the Orion League tattoo you?"

His eyes narrowed a fraction. "Why?"

"Curiosity." I knew he'd covered most of the marks with a tattoo of a dragon as a tribute to Ember, but it'd been a while since I'd seen them up close. Ember would know, since the two of them spent most of their time alone together rolling around naked. I hid a grimace at the mental image. "I remember you had these, uh, marks. She said they made you an Elite, faster than normal humans. I just wondered how that worked. Are they like witch marks?"

"No," he said flatly, and turned his back, heading into the living room.

That went well. Maybe I was overthinking it, but that zombie had been no normal undead, and now I'd seen the exact same symbol on two of them. If those symbols *were* magical… then that brought a whole new dilemma to our rapidly growing heap of problems.

"I'm off to meet Zeph at work," I called through the living room door, for Ember's benefit. She didn't like me walking around at night alone, but my claws could decapitate a faerie beast as easily as a mugger.

The cool night air soothed my nerves, cooling the frustration boiling in my chest. Give a dragon an unsolvable puzzle and they'll just breathe fire on it. Wandering around questioning spirits and making phone calls to dead mercenaries' relatives wasn't our style. The necromancers never had called back either, so I gave up on the notion of anyone coming to help us.

The pub where Zeph worked was one of few with the lights still on, though no customers sat at the bar or played pool in the corner. Zeph paced behind the counter, polishing a glass, and his eyes brightened when I walked in. "Come to save me from boredom?"

I sat on a bar stool. "I'll get whatever the beer of the day is."

Zeph put down the glass. "I shouldn't give you one on the house considering how crap business is, but I will."

"Good. Ember will flip a lid if she finds me wasting our finances on booze."

"Hey, you deserve to blow off steam. My shift ends in ten minutes, anyway."

He poured a glass of beer and passed it to me over the bar.

"Cheers." I took a sip, while he filled another glass. "This place is deserted."

"I know, right?" He moved around the bar. "I've polished everything to a sheen, I've swept the floors, cleaned the windows…"

"I saw the iron wards around the pub," I observed. "From the mages?"

"Nah, the owner knows a local witch." He settled on the stool beside me and sipped the foam from his glass. "The mages wouldn't be seen dead in a place like this."

"All the more beer for us." I took a swig from the glass. "From the way you talked about your job, I expected to see trolls brawling in the corner and wolf shifters fighting with the pool cues."

"Nah, that's our Tuesday night special," he said lightly. "There are a few troublesome locals, but they backed off the first time they saw my claws."

"I bet." I took another drink. The stuff tasted foul, but I hoped for a decent buzz to distract myself from the failures of the day. A drink with a hot dragon shifter, like in another life, where we could go on a normal date.

"Does Ember know you're here?"

I pulled a face. "She's not my mother. She's just seven years older than me and still thinks I'm twelve."

He shrugged. "It's good to have someone who cares about you like that."

I choked on my beer. "Sorry. I know that was kinda insensitive—"

He waved a hand. "Don't worry. Just making an observation. She's looking out for you, like you all look out for each other."

"You're one of us, too." I put down my glass. "Things might be strained at the moment, but you are."

"I know." He inched his stool closer to mine. "Is it bad to say I prefer some of you more than others?"

I tilted my head. "Depends who."

The glasses rattled as the door creaked open. Zeph swore under his breath. "We're closed."

"I don't think he cares," I remarked.

A zombie stood in the doorway, so quiet that I wouldn't have noticed him if I hadn't heard the creak of the door. Sliding off my bar stool, I got out my claws in time to catch the zombie in a forward lunge.

The undead flew back, striking the salt barrier on the inside of the door. He was on his feet a moment later, but Zeph struck first, sending his head flying. As his body crumpled over the threshold, the salt dissolved his rotting flesh.

I heaved a shudder. "How the bloody hell did he get in? Did he step *over* the salt?"

"Not this time." Zeph strode over to the dead man's

twitching form. "Most undead aren't smart enough to avoid the barriers. Someone gave him orders." Since undead were quite literally lacking in a functioning brain.

The undead's limp hand reached up and I snagged it in my claw, ripping it clean off. Then I lifted his twitching torso, and sure enough, I found a set of familiar symbols carved on his collarbone. "Enough of this bullshit. I'm taking him to the necromancers."

"Seriously?" Zeph raised an eyebrow. "Are the necromancers even open now?"

"They're open until midnight, at least." I kicked the dead man's still-twitching arm. "It's the best hour for speaking to the dead, or something. The necromancer guild can find the summoner."

For a fee. But maybe the necromancers had seen those symbols before. The Orion League's soldiers might be long dead, but the necromancers had disposed of enough of their corpses. Okay, I was grasping at straws, and carrying a squirming bag of dismembered zombie parts was not how I'd hoped our brief attempt at a date would end. The bag was really starting to stink by the time we reached the darkened street leading to the necromancers' place, as though the body was older than it'd looked. Holding my breath, I tugged the sack of zombie parts over my shoulder and spotted the same necromancer as before standing on the door. Perfect.

"Hey there," I said, depositing the dead man at his feet. "This guy just attacked me. I wondered if you could find the summoner?"

The necromancer peered down at the bag then jerked back when the zombie's dismembered hand jumped out and began a crab-like crawl over the pavement. "Who is that individual? We need to inform the family—"

I caught the zombie's hand and dumped it back in the bag. "Please, can you do that later? I think someone is sending undead to attack me and my friends. This is the third zombie to attack us in the last few days. He showed up at Zeph's workplace and walked over a salt barrier like he was living."

The necromancer blinked at me. "He walked over it?"

"As in, stepped over it." I mimed it. Zeph cracked up in silent laughter, and I shot him a warning look.

"I see," said the necromancer. "I will ask Lord Glover if he is willing to see you."

And he disappeared in a sweep of his cloak.

The bag of undead pieces twitched again. "I have to say, this isn't how I hoped tonight would end," Zeph said in a tone which would have had a very different effect if there wasn't a dismembered hand trying to jump out of a sack next to my feet.

"You're telling me." I trod on the bag to keep it from squirming off the pavement. "This isn't our day, is it?"

The necromancer poked his head out of the door. "Lord Glover is ready to see you now."

We entered the gloomy hallway, which was about what I'd expected. Bare floorboards, cobwebs, lamps placed at strategic angles to make the shadows look longer and more menacing. And no ghosts. At least until we came to the main office, where a transparent figure floated above the desk. I hesitated, not sure whether I was supposed to be able to see him or not. If I gave away my spirit sight, I'd get dragged off on an unnecessary tangent and might never get to the bloody point.

"Well?" said the ghost. "What have you come here to bring to me? Do you have any idea how infuriating it is to be surrounded by paperwork and not be able to touch any of it?"

"Um... don't you prepare for it?" I asked. "I mean, death is kind of... all around you, isn't it? Ah, never mind. I brought a zombie. I think a rogue necromancer is sending these weirdos after me. They also seem to be faster than regular undead."

The zombie's hand shot out of the bag and clawed at my face. I swatted it away, and it shot across the room. Ack.

"Owen, catch that runaway hand!" bellowed Lord Glover, and his second-in-command moved in.

"There's something you don't hear every day." I crossed the room and picked up the wriggling hand from the bookshelf. "It has a mind of its own, as you can see. We wondered if you could track the person responsible."

"What kind of question is that?" said Lord Glover. "Owen, take them to the summoning room, and get that zombie out of my office."

Owen approached us with an apologetic look on his face, and I reluctantly grabbed the wriggling bag of zombie bits again. "He's having trouble adjusting to his incorporeal state."

"I noticed," I said. I guess being dead took some adjustment even for a professional summoner of ghosts. He was also the most lucid ghost I'd ever met—not that that was saying much.

Owen led us to another small, cold room, in which twelve candles were laid out in a circle on the floor. "Put the zombie in there—the hand will do. It shouldn't be able to escape."

"I'll take your word for it." I let Zeph do the honours, removing the zombie hand and tossing it into the candle circle.

The necromancer leaned over the circle. Blue light shone from his hands, moving to the zombie's twitching hand.

"I'm not getting a reading," he said. "That's… odd. It's not attached to a practitioner. It must have risen of its own accord."

"It can't have," I said. "Undead aren't sentient, and it showed up at Zeph's workplace as though someone sent it there."

Owen stepped back from the circle. "It's reanimated using residual spirit energy alone. Nobody raised it."

That's impossible. The dead guy had stepped over the salt barrier as though he'd known it was there. Even now, the bag twitched and moved by itself. Yet within the circle, no blue traces of necromancy surrounded the reanimated hand.

"I'm sorry," he said, "but that body was not revived using necromancy. It must have been a side effect of another spell, or an accident on the spirit line. These things happen."

He was right—the dead did often rise of their own accord. What they *didn't* do was target a specific person, unless they'd been ordered to.

Maybe it's to do with the sickness. "Owen, have you had reports of any deaths from a certain sickness lately?" I asked. "A rare magical illness?"

"Generally, we're called to help victims of homicide,

not sickness," he said. "I won't charge you for this visit, Cori, don't worry."

Well, that's good news.

But if the reanimator had left no traces on the body, how had they raised it from death?

———

Ember paced in front of the house when Zeph and I arrived back at Magic Avenue.

"*There* you are," she said. "Cori, where have you been?"

"She came to see me at work and an undead attacked us," Zeph explained.

Ember scowled. "*Another* one?"

"We took it to the necromancers." I walked after her into the shop. "To see who summoned it. Here's a tip for carrying a bag of squirming body parts: don't."

I was in dire need of a long, hot shower to wash the smell of the dead off my skin. The stench seemed to linger around the shop, too, perhaps from the first undead.

"Luckily," said Zeph, "since there was no summoner, they didn't charge us."

"First bit of good news we've had all day." I walked into the living room to find Will and Kit on the sofa with the dragonling curled up between them, taking up as much space as a full-grown man.

"The wanderer returns," Becks said from the armchair. "Did I hear something about squirming body parts?"

"I don't think I want to know, thanks," Will said.

I rolled my eyes. "You probably don't want to know how it feels to carry a dismembered zombie from the high street to the necromancer guild, either."

"How can there be no summoner?" Ember took a seat in the other armchair.

"According to them, it rose from the grave, walked over to the pub and stepped over a salt barrier to attack us of its own accord," I said. "This coming from the experts. I don't get it either."

"Maybe the summoner's magic wore off when it was destroyed," said Will. "That's normal, right?"

"It was still *moving*, though," I said. "I hacked it to pieces but left it intact enough that they'd be able to see if there was anything screwy. The hand jumped out and tried to strangle—"

"Enough!" Kit squeaked. The dragonling ducked his head behind the half-faerie, making quiet whimpering noises.

"Sorry," I said. "But it's true. The undead had no pilot."

"Which is bullshit," Zeph said. "It stepped over a salt barrier. If it was walking around at random, then it'd never have bothered."

"Was it their leader who tried to find the summoner?" asked Ember. "If not, perhaps another necromancer would be able to get a result."

"I think that Owen guy is pretty high up in the guild," I said. "Also, I'm not sure if their leader could have helped, since he's a ghost."

"The boss is a ghost?" Will blinked, nonplussed. "How does a ghost get paid?"

"Why would that be the first thing I thought of?" I asked.

"Probably because we're broke," Kit put in. "Zeph, did you get any good tips?"

"Nope," he said. "The place was deserted all night. Guess word of the sickness has spread."

An uneasy silence passed through our group.

"If everyone's talking about it now, doesn't that mean we're more likely to find out where it started?" Ember finally said.

"Of course not," said Becks. "Now the rumour mill has got hold of it, there'll be a hundred separate theories by the week's end."

"Wonderful," said Will. "Did you at least check the mirror, Cori?"

Ember gave me a questioning look. "You went through the mirror?"

"I wanted to make sure Lorne isn't using the Moonbeam to hop around," I said, as everyone looked at me. "And I don't think he is. But… I heard Azalea crying. The first victim died last night."

Ember's face crumpled. "Oh, no."

I looked at the floor. "Her son's in a bad way as well. I checked the mirror at least a dozen times and it won't connect to the Moonbeam, so Lorne can't be using it to travel around."

"Maybe it's not him," Will said. "We've already tried the most common antidotes. I'm inclined to think it's a new thing."

The dragonling made a quiet whining noise and tried to chew on Will's sleeve.

"The necromancers haven't even heard about it," I said. "Guess they get their gossip from the veil, not the real world. And we're still out of a job. What the hell are we supposed to do now, go to every mercenary outlet in north London until we find one who'll take us in and isn't filled with corpses? Besides, I'm not sure the mercs are long for this world at this rate."

The image of Darcy's coughing behind the desk came to mind, and an uneasy skitter went down my spine. Sure, I didn't like the guy much, but if the sickness had spread this close to home, then it was only a matter of time before it landed on our doorstep.

7

____

The Moonbeam lay in my hands, cradled between my palms. Its white glow spread from my hands to my wrists, and its surface seemed to pulse in time with my own heartbeat.

"The fire runs in your veins, Cori."

I looked up. The same ghost as last time faced me through the fog, her hair wild and curly, her eyes sharp and grey and brimming with intelligence. She appeared young, and yet her voice sounded old, much older than I was.

"You again," I said. "Who are you?"

The Moonbeam vanished from my hands. Nothing but air and fog remained, and the ghost, staring at me with eyes which kindled with the hint of a flame.

"I am fire, Coriander," said the spirit. "I am the fire that runs in your veins, the longing you feel to fly, to hunt, to kill." She hovered before me, the light in her eyes burning brighter. "Find the Moonbeam. Feel its rage and set me free."

"Aren't you just a figment of my subconscious?"

"I gave you your fire, Coriander. Now it's time for you to return the favour."

My eyes opened. I jerked upright, at first convinced I saw the ghost watching me, but it was only the light streaming in from the landing. My hands were freezing, and I shivered violently as I sat up. Becks wasn't in the other bed, as usual, because she liked roaming at night.

I checked the time. Six in the morning. My teeth chattered, and I bloody well hoped it wasn't the first sign of the sickness. Grabbing my clothes—including my favourite dragon-patterned socks Ember had got me—I walked to the bathroom and took a long, hot shower. I was probably wasting half our water supply considering I'd had to spend half an hour washing every trace of the zombie off me last night, but I didn't typically wake up freezing cold. Dragons had a higher natural body temperature than humans did.

And what the bloody hell was the deal with the Moonbeam? I had no business craving something that didn't belong to me any more than it belonged to Lorne. Besides, the Moonbeam wasn't a friend. As Lady Clare had all too recently reminded me, I didn't even know where it had originated from. *Please say weird dreams aren't a symptom, too.*

I dried myself off, then dressed and went downstairs. Zeph lay asleep in the living room on a fold-out bed, wearing nothing but a pair of boxers and a thin T-shirt that did little to hide the definition in his arms and chest. We'd offered to lend him one of the rooms at the shelter, but he'd refused in case we needed to use them. I halted beside him, wondering if he'd mind me waking him to ask if I could curl up next to him until his body heat banished the chill from my limbs.

"Cori," hissed a voice from the dark kitchen, and I jumped. Ember sat at the table in the dark, surrounded by Will's spell ingredients and a pile of official-looking documents. "Can't sleep?"

"Nightmares," I said, hoping it'd been too dark for her to see me ogling Zeph. Ember and I shared almost everything with one another, but still.

"Anything you want to talk about?"

I walked to the table and read the topmost page over her shoulder. "He's selling the shelter." My shoulders slumped. "Guess I can't say I didn't see this coming."

"It's that or shut down the shop," Ember said. "Sorry, Cori. We always knew the funding was limited. We weren't all supposed to stop bringing in any money at the same time."

"It's nobody's fault." I went to the cupboard and poured cereal into a bowl. If I was going to spend the day job hunting, I might as well get started early. "Maybe I should sign up to the necromancer guild."

"Hey, it might work," she said. "People are always looking for someone to summon their dead spouses and solve murders."

I rolled my eyes. "I guess that's why the necromancers were so confused when I asked if they'd heard of anyone with the illness. The ghosts they summon are ones who didn't die of natural causes."

The sickness seemed suspicious to me, but I doubted any of those cash-strapped mercenaries could afford to hire a necromancer. Good thing Lord Glover hadn't charged us yesterday.

I pulled out a chair and sat down. "Ember, what do Astor's tattoos mean? I tried asking him, but it went about as well as you'd expect."

"Ah." She took a sip from her mug. Hot chocolate, judging by the smell. "He covered them up, but... now you mention it, I'm not sure. He got them at the Elite ceremony when he was promoted, I think. Why?"

"The undead who attacked us all had the same tattoos." I stirred my cereal with a spoon. "And they were much faster and stronger than regular undead. I wondered if it might be the same kind of magic that marked Astor."

"What, you think the zombie was a League member?" Ember's brow furrowed. "That's not possible. They all died or fled, and a corpse can't stay in one piece for five years. Also, Astor said the marks weren't magical."

"He would say that." I shovelled cereal into my mouth. "Doesn't make it true. Astor's human, yet he moves as fast as a shifter. So did that undead. I figured he'd be more likely to talk to you than to me."

"You're not wrong there." She stood, putting her mug in the sink. "I'll ask him, but I don't think those mercenaries were involved with the League."

"I'm not sure it *is* the League." I took another bite, but my appetite was gone. "Maybe someone else found out how to use their magic. If it's not necromancy, then what else could it be?"

Cursed, the gargoyles had called the undead. Cursed... and yet not reanimated in any common manner.

If the League's anti-dragon technology had stayed in development even after they'd died out, then perhaps more of their creations had, too.

I stirred my cereal, feeling bad for wasting food when

resources were so low. I went to give it to the dragonling instead, who was asleep on the sofa. He lifted his head and snapped it up in three quick bites.

"I know who to blame our low supplies on," Ember whispered in my ear. "That dragon ate an entire chicken yesterday. Raw."

I picked up the bowl. "Maybe we can send him to hunt his own food."

"Uh… maybe not," she said. "We don't need another mob showing up on the doorstep if he eats someone."

"They're whispering about us? And him?"

She shook her head. "I heard the neighbours talking about how the shifters are saying we're harbouring an illegal animal, but it was probably nothing. Half of them have illegal pets, besides."

Right...

I dumped my empty cereal bowl in the sink and poured a glass of water. "I guess I'm off job hunting, then. Maybe I'll run deliveries like Zeph used to. I can easily fly supplies from one end of the city to another, assuming it pays better than raising the dead."

"Bit degrading, though," Ember commented.

"Better than starving to death." I sipped water from the glass.

Things weren't quite that dire yet, but with seven of us, supplies went down fast. And that was with us all living in the same house, too. It'd end up being even more expensive if anyone took off alone. Now we were too dependent on Zeph, and I felt bad considering he was the last to join our group and didn't have to go down with our sinking ship.

I glanced at him. He looked like he was still asleep, but

for all I knew, he might be listening to our conversation. We hadn't exactly been keeping our voices down.

"You're going out now?" Ember asked.

"I have to start somewhere." I rinsed out the glass. "Besides, I wanted to check in at Darcy's place. He looked sick yesterday, and considering the way our luck's going at the moment…"

Ember grimaced. "I'll go with you, then. If he's dead, the body snatchers might come for him."

"Hope you're wrong." Since Zeph was still sleeping, I didn't object to Ember coming with me. Becks hadn't come back from where she'd been wandering last night, and I could use the company.

The cool morning air revived me, though most humans without a dragon's high body temperature would find it too cold to walk without a jacket. Now the iciness of my dream had gone, I felt a bit better, though my mood dimmed when I reached Darcy's place. While the man himself worked 9-5, the place stayed open 24/7 for the sake of the mercenaries running late-night missions.

For a heartbeat, I expected to find him sitting dead behind the desk like Eric Galwood, but a stranger sat in his place.

"Hey," I said to the guy on the desk. "Is Darcy coming in?"

The mercenary, a tall Asian half-shifter I didn't know, said, "He called in sick. Didn't he fire you?"

"Not in so many words," said Ember. "What's wrong with him, do you know?"

"Sounds like flu. Why?"

"We heard there's a weird sickness going around," I

said carefully. "Another mercenary outlet shut down, do you know? Eric Galwood's."

The merc shrugged. "I dunno, I don't talk to the guy. Ask Darcy when he's back in. What do you want?"

"Work," I said bluntly. "Darcy claimed he wanted to let us go because we don't pass as human. Firstly, that isn't true. Secondly, if anything that'd be an advantage, not a weakness. Most monsters would hesitate before taking a bite out of a shifter."

He drummed his fingers on the desk. "I'm not in charge of the rota. Take it up with Darcy, not me."

"I'll do that." *Right now, in fact.*

Ember and I turned heel and left through the automatic doors. A chill breeze swept the street, blowing litter and debris in our direction.

"Do you even know where Darcy lives?" Ember asked.

"Ten minutes from here," I said. "I know two angry dragons are the last thing he wants to see if he's on his sickbed, but if it *is* the same sickness, maybe he'll know who he caught it from."

———

Darcy's flat was nicer than I'd expected, a low-rise townhouse with a proper security system. Not quite efficient enough to stand up to an unlocking charm, however. Ember and I slipped into the building and climbed to the first floor.

Darcy answered the door after the third knock. He looked even worse than yesterday, his eyes bloodshot and a nasty rash on his neck. From outside appearances, it *was* the same sickness. Oh, hell.

He coughed, his breathing strained. "What the bloody hell are you two doing here?"

"Sorry to bother you outside of work hours, but we heard you were sick," I said. "There's a rare disease spreading around, and we're looking into its possible cause."

"For the mages," Ember added, catching onto my plan. "They asked us to look into it because it seems to affect shifters in particular."

He coughed again. "What do you want to know?"

Huh. He believes us? "When did the symptoms start showing up? And did you see or interact with anything unusual on that day?"

"Yesterday," he said. "And what do you mean by unusual?"

"We suspect magical contamination," I said. "That is, a magically created, or engineered virus. But we're not sure how it's spreading. Did you interact with anyone else who had the symptoms, or handle any new substance?"

"No," he said. "If anything, the last few days have been quiet. Just saw the usual suspects. No mystery monsters, a few false alarms... and Jake came in the other day with some bullshit excuse for disappearing."

"I thought Jake faked his death and then ran away." Suspicion flared. Jake had been known for working with the Faulkners, delivering packages to mobsters... and ingredients to poisoners.

He gave another cough. "Just what I heard. Can I go back to sleep now?"

"Of course. Thank you for your time." I turned to Ember as the door closed. "That was illuminating. I know where Jake's apartment is."

"You think he's involved?"

"He worked with the witch who made the poison they used on you." He hadn't actually known that was what he was delivering, being a low-grade messenger, but I didn't believe in coincidence. "He's known to be a gullible fool who doesn't ask questions."

Her eyes flickered with the hint of a flame. "All right. We'll pay him a visit."

"Good. Also, watch out for low-flying gargoyle porn."

———

Halfway to Jake's apartment, my pocket began vibrating.

"Cori, your phone's ringing."

"Huh. So it is." I pulled it out of my pocket. "Unknown number. Maybe I won the lottery. Hey, I can dream."

Clicking on the screen, I said, "Who is this?"

"Hello," said Owen of the necromancer guild.

"Oh, it's you," I said, without much enthusiasm. "Did you find anything out about those zombies?"

"I have the Mage Lord here," he said. "He wishes to speak with you."

"Me? Are you sure?"

"Yes." And he hung up, leaving me staring at the phone in confusion.

"Who was it?" asked Ember.

"Head of the necromancers," I said. "Lord Smyth is at the necromancers' guild and wants to speak to us. Or me, anyway."

Ember frowned. "Why not invite us to his own head-quarters?"

"Maybe they found a lead." Not that the zombies

concerned me nearly as much as the illness did, especially as we had no more leads on a cure. On the other hand, if anyone could give me permission to storm into Jake's apartment, it was the head of the Mage Lords.

"Who is the necromancers' leader, anyway?" Ember asked. "I've never met him."

"He's dead," I said. "But he's okay. They keep their members employed past their sell-by dates. Don't ask me why."

She raised an eyebrow. "A dead man used the phone?"

"Nah, that was his assistant," I said. "He's not great at remembering to explain things. I don't think he spends much time around living people."

As for the mages? If the necromancers had told tales on me, it was either because Lord Smyth was taking the zombie issue seriously—or they knew I had the spirit sight.

———

Lord Smyth waited in the office, with the necromancers' deceased leader standing behind the desk. Or more *in* the desk, really. Lord Smyth was a tall black man who looked much more alive than the spindly assistant in front of me.

"Lord Smyth," I said, following Owen into the room. "You wanted to speak to us?"

"Yes, I did," he said. "I understand that you brought an undead here yesterday that was afflicted with some unusual magic."

"It attacked us," I explained. "But when Owen used his magic to figure out who raised it, there was no result."

"And this was not your first encounter with an undead in that condition?"

I weighed the odds, then said, "We found an entire mercenary outlet had dropped dead of a sickness. Eric Galwood's. His body was reanimated and attacked us. I reported it at the mages' guild, but you weren't in. Lady Clare said she'd tell you."

"She did?" He frowned. "Must have slipped her mind. In any case... am I correct in assuming you know something of the cause of death?"

"The sickness?" I asked. "Our old boss, Darcy—he caught it, too. We have reason to think it may be the work of... someone linked to the Faulkners."

"The mobsters?" His eyes sharpened. "Their helicopter mysteriously burst into flames during their escape from the city, reports tell me."

"Odd, that." Oops. I doubted the mages planned to punish me for ridding the city of those two shitheads. Nobody would miss them, and while they'd never been convicted of a crime, the mages must have been aware of the underground fighting rings.

"It's not the Faulkners," Ember said. "But they hired witches to make a poison targeting dragon shifters, and I don't doubt they came up with other concoctions."

"That sounds like mere speculation," he said. "We took in everything known to have belonged to the Faulkner brothers and found no evidence of this... virus. If it is engineered, as you implied."

"And the undead?" I asked. "From the way they attacked us, the person who's raising them set them upon us deliberately. I assume they're either someone who resents us for taking down the Faulkners, or they're linked to Lorne. I heard you put out a bounty for his capture?"

"Yes," he said. "Lady Clare's idea. I disagreed with her approach, particularly with regard to the Moonbeam. I don't believe that exposing its powers is wise, considering how coveted it is."

The mages had had a disagreement? Huh. "I don't think so either," I admitted. "I think announcing there's a rare and powerful item missing is a great way to make sure everyone tries to sell it to the highest bidder rather than turning it in."

"That's not quite it," he said. "The bounty is, of course, worth much more than the artefact itself."

"How much?" Apparently, the avaricious dragon from my dreams had taken over my waking thoughts. I didn't need to sit on a hoard of gold coins. Real dragons cared for family far more than riches. Even if the money *would* stop our shelter going under.

He tilted his head. "I thought you wanted to keep it for yourself."

For a baffling moment, I wondered if he'd seen my dreams. Then I remembered the incident five years ago when I'd requested that he hand the Moonbeam over to us after the battle. He'd refused, of course.

"Unless," he went on, "you have any more clues as to Lorne's whereabouts? The mirror, perhaps?"

"No," I said. "I checked. The Moonbeam is cut off from the mirrors. I guess it broke during the battle."

Unlike Lady Clare, he wasn't a mind-reader. And he knew I'd protect the other dragon shifters to my death. But if he suspected Lorne might be using the Moonbeam to skip between his hideout and the dragon shifters' village, the first thing he'd do was confiscate the mirror so the mages could use it to track the Moonbeam down. Then we'd never be able to reach the other dragon shifters and help them.

"Then how do you suspect Lorne might be involved?" he enquired.

"We're assuming he never left London," said Ember. "And he wants us dead. Sending undead after us isn't really his thing, but who else can it be?"

"Don't forget those symbols," put in Owen.

Ah, hell. Lord Smyth turned to me. "What symbols?"

"The dead were all marked with odd symbols," I said, resigned. "The one we brought here and the two who attacked us this week all bore the same marks. They looked similar to the marks used by the Orion League on their elite soldiers to make them superior to humans. Since I spent time in their labs... I got to see things the others didn't."

Not strictly true, but I knew Ember would appreciate me not giving the mages reason to go after Astor, considering he'd nearly been jailed once already.

Lord Smyth frowned, but he couldn't fault my reasoning. He and the mages knew I'd been a prisoner. No need to let on that I'd spent most of my captivity unconscious.

"I see," he said. "We'll look into these symbols. In the meantime, if you do find the Moonbeam again, then you will be given the full payment when you hand it over to us. And Lorne himself, dead or alive."

"And... the sickness?" Ember asked.

"This is out of our area," admitted Lord Smyth. "We are contacting every witch available, but in the meantime, we would be most grateful if you would use your resources to find information. If you succeed in finding the source of the sickness, you will also be handsomely rewarded."

And there it was. The mages had offered me a job more than once in the past. Since Ember had helped save the city, they'd made no secret of the fact that they wanted the reputation of hiring the city's only dragon shifters. I'd be one step up from a lab rat, which was hardly better than giving up my future to the Orion League.

Until now, we'd managed to make do. But to save my friends and the other dragon shifters, I had to set my pride aside.

I nodded to Lord Smyth. "All right. We'll do it."

8

"How much did the mages offer you?" Will asked.

We gathered in the living room while Ember updated the others on Lord Smyth's unexpected offer. Will hadn't opened the shop yet, claiming nobody went out this early in the morning. He and Kit sat with the dragonling on the sofa, while Becks had returned from her night-time wanderings and was napping on the carpet.

"Enough to save the shelter," I said. "All we have to do is find the source of the sickness. And if we find the Moonbeam and Lorne as well, we'll be set for life."

"If you say so." Will dragged a hand through his hair, looking weary. "But the only lead you have is your old boss, who might drop dead by the week's end."

"Gotta stay optimistic," I said. "Darcy didn't see anything out of the ordinary… except Jake came back."

"Who's Jake?" asked Kit.

"Cori's mortal enemy," Will said. "Right?"

"More like minor annoyance," I said. "He faked his own death once already. And he worked for the Faulkners. I doubt he knew Lorne personally, but—"

Zeph interrupted by walking into the back room from the hall. From his wet hair, he'd been showering. "Did you say the mages think Lorne is responsible?"

"They don't know what to think," I said. "Never thought they'd admit to being clueless, but there you have it. We need to address all the leads we have. I'd say it's worth seeing who's got Jake ensnared this time. He delivered poisons to a witch once before, and Darcy said he came back into the office right before he got sick."

A shadow fell over Zeph's face. "You think this is a witch's doing?"

I thought of the symbols and a chill raced across my skin. "A witch playing mad scientist, maybe. Zeph, you said the League was developing anti-dragon shifter defences while you were their prisoner... do you know if this sort of thing was in development, too?"

"Yes," Astor said. "It was."

Kit jumped and the dragonling bounded off the sofa, baring his teeth at Astor, who stood silently by the door in a manner that suggested he'd been standing there the whole time we'd been talking.

"I don't suppose you're gonna tell us where you've been all night?" Will asked.

"No." Astor stepped into the room. "To answer your question, there were plans in development for years. One of the methods discussed was the use of a plague to remove supernaturals from the world without the need to deploy teams of soldiers. Since supernaturals outnumbered League members, it was deemed more effective than an army. But they couldn't come up with anything that didn't affect humans, too."

"The sickness *is* affecting humans, though," I said.

Astor shrugged. "Perhaps the person using these methods isn't concerned about that side effect."

Zeph's entire body tensed. "And were *you* involved in these schemes?"

"I'm no scientist, so no," he said. "None of them ever came to anything. And if that's what it is, then it certainly isn't the League using them. I'd be surprised Lorne chose that method rather than confronting us in person, but then again, he cares little for innocent lives."

Zeph let out a low growl. "Yes, and he's not the only one. You're saying Lorne stole the virus from the League? And you decided not to tell us until now?"

Astor retained an expression of absolute calm. "No, I'm not suggesting anything. But if we assume that it *is* a League creation, then Lorne knows the location of at least some of the League's strongholds. I assumed most of them were destroyed, but perhaps not. I can't say I know the specifics. If I knew, I would have told you."

"Would you?" Zeph said.

"Of course he would," Ember said. "We aren't immune to the sickness either, you know. Dragons included. And humans, too."

Including League soldiers? Those symbols… if London's entire shifter population perished in a plague, unscrupulous rogue necromancers would rake in a fortune. Maybe they already were.

"Astor, are there any strongholds near London which might have been the source?" I asked.

Zeph and I had yet to find the place where they were

breeding the dragonlings, but no more eggs had shown up on the black market since the Faulkners' deaths. If we found the source of the sickness, then maybe the dragonlings would be there, too.

Astor shook his head. "The Stronghold near Windsor was never used for that, and Ember completely destroyed it. There were no other major strongholds near London or inside the city and all the minor ones were abandoned. I checked."

"Then it's either not in London or they made a new base," I surmised. "All right, we'll go to Jake's place and use our newfound authority as permission to search his property. If that doesn't work, then…" I gave a shrug. "Summon another ghost? Stalk the mercenaries?"

"Deliver the latest batch of potential cures to the dragon shifters?" asked Will. "Come on, there aren't many ways it could have reached them. You're more likely to be able to track the source up there in the middle of nowhere than you are here."

"Fair point," I said. "I just don't see how Lorne can be hopping between the two places if the mirror doesn't link to the Moonbeam. It didn't work for me, anyway."

"Maybe it's a countrywide thing," Ember said, her lips pursed. "It's not like we get a ton of news from outside London. The mages ought to be responsible for tracking the spread of new magical diseases."

"They admitted they're clueless, though," I said. "Ember, if you have another look around the village, I'm going to storm Jake's door down and then I'll come and join you if you're not back. Deal?"

Her gaze slid to Zeph. "All right, but don't go alone.

That Jake might be a wimp, but for him to have stayed alive this long, he must have powerful allies."

I was more inclined to think he'd been hiding underground, but I wouldn't object to taking Zeph with me. I still felt bad that he'd been left to pick up the slack because the rest of us were woefully underemployed.

"All right," Zeph said. "Coming, Becks?"

"You bet." She shifted to human form and yawned in a catlike manner. "Let's go see what that slimy dude's hiding."

"Rat shifter porn, probably." I waved goodbye to Kit and Will—who were engaged in a tussling match with the dragonling over a shoe—and walked with Zeph into the shop.

Despite my reservations about working for the mages again, I couldn't deny that their cluelessness was worrying and reassuring in equal measure. Ember had a point that it seemed unlikely that the illness was only present in London and the village, which made it the mages' responsibility. The mages knew most of what went on in the supernatural world, but only intervened when it threatened their own interests. Not all that different from the shifters, when it came down to it. Except they had the resources to survive. Not just survive, but rule.

With the Moonbeam.

I shook off the thought. The mages had held the Moonbeam locked up for five years and had never touched it. They didn't want to rule over shifters any more than they wanted Lorne to have his way. Those weird dreams were getting to me again.

When the three of us reached the brick building where

Jake lived, I eased an unlocking spell off my wrist, tilting my head to see through the window.

"Becks, can you see if he's in?" I asked. "He upped the security, but I doubt it's cat-proof."

She nodded and shifted to cat form, scaling the drainpipe with effortless grace. A few seconds later, she dropped to land on four paws, turning human again.

"There's someone inside his flat," she said. "Gargoyle."

Great. "Either he's being robbed, he decided to shift indoors, or we're risking walking in on a live-action play of his pornography. Wanna flip a coin to check who gets to go in first?"

Zeph tensed. "Or," he said. "It's not him."

A shadow passed behind the glass door. Then it opened and a gargoyle shifter shouldered his way out. To be precise, one of the gargoyles who'd cornered us on the London Eye.

"You didn't take our advice," he growled at me.

"Who, me?" I feigned ignorance. "What are you doing at Jake's flat? I didn't know you were buddies."

"We aren't friends," he said. "I've come to strip the flesh off his bones."

"Oh… kay." I took a step backwards, my claws pushing against my fingertips. "Couldn't you just call him? You know, chat on the phone like normal civilised people rather than this *stripping the flesh off his bones* business? There's no need to be hasty."

His lip curled. "I saw him handling one of those cursed dead. Like you."

Ah. "You know, we're looking for information on those zombies," I said. "The Mage Lords—"

His words cracked like a whip. "Keep the Mage Lords out of this."

"Too late," I said. "Jake's one of our suspects. Is he involved with whoever is raising those dead? Who—"

"Do not ask me of them, dragon shifter," he growled. "If you poke your nose where it doesn't belong like those mercenaries did, you'll suffer the same fate."

He made to storm past, but Zeph blocked his path. His grey eyes danced with the beginnings of a flame. "What did the mercenaries do? Is it to do with that sickness?"

"It's her fault." His sharp gaze pierced me. "In killing the Faulkners, you unleashed a curse."

"Uh… what?" I blinked. "You're blaming *me* for it? You know the Faulkners were plain old humans, right?"

Gargoyles had a reputation for being superstitious, but that was absurd. Nobody in their right mind would believe *I'd* cursed everyone, right?

"Everyone knows," he said. "The curse began to strike our community immediately after the Faulkners passed. And death is not the end. When they die, they rise as those… things."

"Tell that to the necromancers, not me," I said. "You're seriously telling me you're scared of a few zombies?"

"Those dead aren't natural," he said. "They are cursed, and whoever touches them will be next."

Oh… kay. Maybe he believed that, but it didn't make it true. I mean, the gargoyles had frequented the arena, where hapless shifters fell for scams every day.

"You're right," Zeph said. "They're not natural. Someone in the city released that sickness, and they have a necromancer working for them who is raising the dead in an effort to sow discord. We're not the enemy, and we're trying our best to stop whoever is responsible."

It wasn't like Zeph to avoid a fight, but the gargoyle's words worried me. All the gargoyles in the city couldn't believe *I'd* caused the sickness, right?

"We're not behind this," I said, "but we think Jake was involved. Did you see him?"

"No," he said. "We live in the skies for a reason. And we will not interact with the dead any longer."

He shifted to gargoyle form, taking flight in a single bound. I tensed, prepared to get out my claws, but he flew over the rooftops without looking back.

"He's lost it," said Zeph, shaking his head. "And it sounds like Jake did a runner."

"Doesn't mean we can't raid his flat and get Will to make a tracking spell," I said.

Becks turned human again, her hair standing on end in place of her fur. "That won't do much good if he's dead, which he will be when those gargoyles catch up to him. Also, I'm not collecting his toenail clippings or hairs."

"Tracking spells work better with something belonging to the person you're looking for," I explained to Zeph. "I draw the line at using his nail clippings, but anything of his will work. I bet that gargoyle left his door wide open. And if he *is* dead, I can always summon his ghost."

"Hey, I thought you weren't making a habit of doing that," Becks said. "And you wonder why rumours are spreading that we're cursed?"

Cursed with bad luck, was more like it. Scowling, I activated an unlocking spell on the door and marched upstairs to Jake's flat.

There was nobody in there, and there hadn't been for a while. Dust covered every surface, while the furniture had been overturned. It smelled stale but not of dead people, and when I looked below the surface into the spirit realm, nobody stared back.

Zeph waved a hand in front of my face. "What're you doing, checking for ghosts?"

"Yeah. Nothing here. Guess he really did run off." I gave the room another scan. "Find anything?"

"Nope," he said. "No packages. He hasn't lived here since he faked his death, I'd guess."

I kicked at the carpet, stirring a cloud of dust. "Then what the bloody hell was he doing at Darcy's place?"

"Who knows," said Zeph. "Are you going to ask Will to make the tracking spell?"

"Yeah," I said. "Are you working today?"

He shook his head. "Nope. Wouldn't surprise me if my boss closed up the place until the hysteria dies down. If the gargoyles are flitting around wailing about curses, it's no wonder none of them are coming over for Happy Hour."

"Ugh." I coughed on the smell of dust. "Ember's still in the village, looking for clues. Not that there are any experts up there, aside from… wait, Agnes. We haven't asked her yet."

"Come again?" Zeph said.

"Agnes," I said. "Friend of the dragon shifters. She's a witch. Or a mage. Not sure, but she's the person responsible for delivering supplies to the village. She's also the person who cast a spell on Ember and me to erase the time we spent in the village from our memories."

"She did what?" His eyes widened.

"Our parents didn't want our enemies to find us, so they took us to Agnes," I explained as we left Jake's apartment block. "Ember and I woke up on a train to London with no memory of how we got there. Just a note and a bunch of instructions leading us to a shelter for rogue shifters. I was five at the time. Ember was twelve. We didn't get our memories back until we found the village and this woman... Madison, she explained what our parents did. She was Agnes's sister, but she died."

"So the dragon shifters used to live with other supernaturals, then?" he asked.

"They did, once," I said. "Not many, though. I'm not sure why Madison was the exception. But Lorne murdered her along with anyone who opposed him when he joined up with the Orion League in London."

He'd wanted the dragon shifters to have nobody to help them. A familiar anger stirred inside my bones, and I ducked my head.

"Sorry," Zeph said. "I guess you were close..."

"Yes, and no," I said. "I mean, I was a kid when I left the village. The earliest memory I have of Agnes is from five years ago, where she undid the spell blocking my memories. I'm not sure if she'll be able to help us with the sickness, but it's worth a try." Since her sister had died to protect the other dragon shifters, maybe she knew more about Lorne and his plan to wipe us all out.

Maybe she also knew about the Moonbeam.

9

This time when we walked through the mirror, nobody was crying. Hoping that was a good sign, I climbed the stairs into the hallway of Azalea's house and found her pacing from one end to the other. From the stairs to the doors, and back again.

"Oh, hey, Azalea," I said. "Is Ember around?"

"She's outside." Her expression was distant, and she looked exhausted. "My son has taken a turn for the worse."

"I'm sorry." My heart sank. "We're going to talk to Agnes, if that's okay. Has she been around?"

"No," she murmured. "Nobody has. Except for you. I'm glad you two have each other... Cori."

I felt Zeph's eyes on me but didn't look his way. I could see her mind ticking over the image of seeing the two of us together. There were so few younger people in the village that I knew the next generation was a worry to her. The population was dwindling, and the number of people who could pull off a full shift into a dragon was on the verge of dying out. Half-shifters had a decent chance of being able to shift or at least partially shift, but the age of the dragon shifters had been coming to an end long before Lorne had decimated the dragon clans.

Maybe there really was no place for us to survive in the modern world, but the sickness was no natural thing. I wouldn't let it be the end of us.

I gave her a kind smile and walked to the door with Zeph. "I assume Ember's wandering around looking for clues, like she said she would."

"Hmm," he said. "I don't see her."

"We can walk from one end of the village to the other in ten minutes, it's fine."

Sure enough, we found Ember wandering near the hills by the far end of the village. She looked up as we approached. "No luck?"

"Nope," I said. "Found anything?"

"I circled the whole village," she said. "Nothing. Except a nest of dead piskies, and a few redcaps I had to scare off. Was Jake no help?"

"He did a runner," I said. "We have Will concocting a tracking spell so we can find where he's hiding. In the meantime, I thought we might to talk to Agnes."

"Agnes?" She frowned. "Why?"

"She's the most knowledgeable witch I know," I said. "Don't tell Will I said that. But if nobody in London knows about the sickness, she might."

"Good point," she said. "I suppose it's not too far off… and I'm not being much help here, to be honest."

"The cures didn't work, then?" I asked.

She shook her head. "We need to find the root cause, and I have no idea."

"Yeah, fair warning, some of the gargoyles think *we're* spreading it," I said. "They got it into their heads we unleashed a curse by killing the Faulkner brothers."

"Just great," she muttered. "All right, let's go and see Agnes. Zeph, that means we're flying. I'll lead the way."

"Sure," he said. "Cori, is it a long flight?"

"Not too long for me to handle." This would be my first longer flight since I'd learned to shift, since Agnes lived in another isolated supernaturals-only village in the Highlands, easier to reach by air than on the ground. Anticipation hummed in my veins, almost as potent as when I'd held the Moonbeam.

Ember shifted into her dragon form. Zeph followed suit, his huge wings extending behind his powerful shoulders, his claws splayed on the grassy hillside.

"Race you there," I said to both of them. The shift took hold, scales creeping up my legs and arms. Wings sprouted from my shoulders, and I bounded into the air, joining my sister in flight.

Excitement pounded in my chest. I inhaled the fresh taste of the air, stretching out my wings. Clouds billowed around me, and the village shrank to a small gathering of houses among rolling hills. Zeph flew alongside me, his wings wide enough to touch mine. I brushed against him, teasingly, and rolled onto my back in mid-air. He flew higher and executed a loop-the-loop that set me bristling with jealousy. *Show-off.*

All the stresses of the city melted away with the sheer rush of flight. Cold air blew past, barely touching my rock-hard scales. Seconds melted into minutes, and I glanced down at the rippling hills, which ended at the jagged coastline. Too far off course. I steered my path back to join my sister, though I suspected Ember had taken a detour or three, too. In flight, we covered miles in seconds. But we'd come here for a reason.

Skimming lower, I searched for the shape of the neighbouring village. Ember dipped low over a vast loch, and towards a rippling transparent line. *That's the Ley Line.*

As we drew close to another small tangle of stone houses, Ember came into land on a muddy dirt track from the village. Sensible idea, since we didn't want the human villagers to think they were being invaded by dragons. Reluctantly, I touched down and shifted back to human, shivering in the cold air and wishing I could carry my scales with me back into my human form.

Ember turned human again. "Are you okay, Cori?"

"Of course," I said. "That was *amazing*."

Zeph landed beside me and shifted into a human, too. "You did great for your first major flight. Much easier than flying in London. Where's Agnes's place?"

"Somewhere in the village." My cheeks heated from his praise. "Ember, do you have her address?"

"Uh, no," Ember said. "She was waiting for us last time we came here. I got the impression she's pretty well-known, though."

We walked down the muddy path, which ran alongside a graveyard next to a squat brick building with dark curtains that I'd bet belonged the local necromancers. Villages like this one tended to have a lot of witches and necromancers, a few shifters and half-faeries, and very few mages.

The first person we asked knew who Agnes was, and pointed us in the right direction. We came to a small shop with cracked windows, and, strangely enough, claw marks on the door.

"Was another dragon here?" I asked Ember.

"Haven't a clue." She pushed on the door. "It's open. I didn't know she owned a shop."

We crowded inside, marvelling at the sheer number of magical artefacts Agnes had managed to cram into such a small space. Rickety shelves filled with portable charms, glass cabinets containing leather-bound books with jewelled covers, and crooked hat stands adorned with what appeared to be costumes.

"Check this out." Zeph put on a pointed hat with bells jangling on its frilled edges. "New style?"

"No. You look like the offspring of a wizard and a cowboy, only sixty years older." He'd also sprouted a grey beard and wrinkles. "Look in the mirror."

Zeph grinned. "At least I aged well."

"Put those down," came a gravelly voice from the back, and Zeph dropped the hat. Immediately, he turned back into his normal auburn-haired self.

Ember scooped up the hat and put it back on the stand. "Is Agnes in?" she asked the man who'd spoken.

"Who is it?" he called.

We walked to the counter, careful not to knock anything over. A man sat behind the counter, his features not unlike the bearded person Zeph had turned into when he'd put on the hat.

"Hey," I said. "I'm Cori, and this is my sister Ember and our friend, Zeph. We're here to see Agnes."

"She's back there. We're watching the Lynns." He said this in a tone in which one might say, *we're just hanging onto this live bomb.* "I'll keep an eye on the kids while you talk to her."

Agnes had kids? I hadn't seen any the last time we'd been here, but I hadn't stayed for long. Hadn't known she ran a magical shop stocked with rare artefacts either. I admired an ornate mirror beside the front desk while we waited.

The door behind the counter flew open and two shrieking girls ran out of the back room into the shop. With a look of alarm, the man darted out after them. "Stop! Ilsa, put that down."

One of the girls, who was maybe seven or so, had taken a glittering amulet from the nearest display case.

"What does this do?" asked Ilsa, her eyes gleaming with interest. She gave the amulet a shake, and it lit up.

Then Ilsa turned invisible.

A little boy who was maybe a year or two older than the girls walked in, aiming a water pistol around.

"Ilsa is *gone,*" the other girl said, her eyes as round as saucers. "She disappeared."

"I'm still here," Ilsa's voice said from the spot where she'd vanished.

The boy aimed the water pistol at the invisible Ilsa. "Hey, I can still hit you."

"I'm going to kill you, Morgan!" shrieked Ilsa. "Hazel, stop *laughing* at me."

Before anyone could get murdered, Agnes appeared in the doorway to the back room. Her silver-white hair hung down her back in a long braid, and her mouth was twisted in annoyance.

"Put that amulet down," she commanded. "Do as Everett says and let the customers... oh, it's you, Ember."

"Hi," said Ember. "Is this a bad time?"

"Not at all—Everett, can you please keep an eye on the children while I speak to these three?" She stepped into the back room, and I made to follow her.

"Hello," said the little girl who was still visible. "I'm Hazel. Who are you?"

"I'm Cori," I said. "A friend of Agnes."

"Everyone's Agnes's friend," she said in self-important tones.

"But she likes our mum the best." Ilsa appeared with a popping sound. Everett held the amulet out of reach, returning it to its cabinet.

"Our mummy is in F—" Hazel cut herself off. "She's away."

"It's a *secret*," Ilsa said, pressing a finger to her lips in an exaggerated movement. "We're on our very best behaviour." She gave a solemn nod and then burst into hysterical giggles.

"Come on," said Agnes. "You three, stay in the shop and try not to break anything. And don't look in the cursed cabinet, is that clear?"

"Cursed cabinet!" yelled Morgan.

"You're cursed now!" shrieked Hazel.

"I'd watch those three." I stifled a laugh as Agnes ushered us into the back room.

Agnes closed the door behind us, scowling. "Their mother is off gallivanting in Faerie, and they're supposed to be my responsibility. Frankly, I think a curse or two will teach them not to poke their noses where they don't belong."

"Did you say their mother was in *Faerie?*" Ember asked. "They're human."

"Special circumstances," muttered Agnes. "I'm too old for this nonsense. Not that you were ever trouble, Ember."

"You knew me when I was a baby?"

"Both of you," she said. "Cori, you won't remember. Gods, one of them is bad enough. I hope Everett can handle three."

I did my best to ignore the shrieking noises from the shop and launched into an explanation of Lorne's recent escape, and the sickness affecting shifters both in London and up here in Scotland.

"It's been so long since I heard from them, I was beginning to wonder," she said. "That sickness, though… nobody mentioned it to me. I heard stories from Edinburgh along those lines, though."

My heart sank. So it *was* happening everywhere?

"The mages are clueless," I explained. "I though Lorne might have used the League's old methods to spread the sickness, like the poisons they made to target dragon shifters. But he's not using the mirror to do it."

"Lorne… and the League?" Her eyes widened. "I heard he escaped, but not that he was using the League's technology."

"It gets worse," said Zeph. "This all started when a pair of mobsters started gambling dragon eggs on the black market in London, working behind the scenes to engineer Lorne's escape from jail."

Agnes swore eloquently when we explained about the engineered wild dragonlings, created using dragon shifter DNA.

"Do you know where they might have been breeding these creatures?" she asked.

"That's why I was in London," Zeph said. "But I never

found the source. They must have a secret lab hidden somewhere close, but after the Faulkner brothers died, all our leads disappeared. It's not too much of a stretch to assume the virus came from the same place."

"Is that so?" She frowned. "I'm at a loss to explain how it got all the way to Scotland without the mirror, but perhaps the scheme has been in the works for a while. As for the sickness, though… if it's a magical creation, then you'll need to find its source to make a cure. I could maybe develop one with a blood sample from someone suffering the sickness, but honestly, anyone with experience in antidotes could do the same. Given that it's affecting people across the country, even if it had unnatural causes, it may be too late."

My heart sank. "That's not all, though. There's also some kind of rogue necromancer stealing the bodies and turning them into undead with strange powers. Their bodies have these weird… markings on them."

Agnes went still. "Markings?"

"Like tattoos," Zeph said. "They move faster than any undead have the right to, and the necromancer guild couldn't help us figure out who raised them."

"I see." Agnes paused. "That's because it wasn't a necromancer who raised them. It was a witch."

My stomach lurched. *I was right.* "But—a witch can't raise the dead, right?"

"There's one type of magic that can, given the right application," she said. "I assume you've encountered the Orion League's Elite soldiers when you fought the League?"

I shot Ember a pointed look. "Yes, we did. And I thought the marks looked the same, but I didn't think it was possible to use magic on the dead, except necromancy."

"It certainly *is* possible, but undead are devoid of consciousness and their power is limited," she said. "Using that art on a *living* person, however, was what enabled the League to give humans the ability to go head to head with shifters."

"And they got it from witches?" I surmised. "Azalea told us that the League captured witches, once. Is that why?"

She made a noise of disgust. "Yes, they did. My sister was one of the lucky ones. Most of the others didn't escape."

I swallowed. "I'm sorry."

"But none of our witch friends know that type of magic," said Ember. "They haven't even heard of it."

"That's because it died out with the League," said Agnes. "Plainly, an ally or two of theirs survived. I'd be inclined to blame Lorne, if he's using the Moonbeam to move around."

"That's it—I don't think he can." I glanced at Ember. "He couldn't use the Moonbeam on us the last time we saw him. It didn't work for him."

"Interesting." Her gaze was piercing, and I wondered if her ability to remove memories extended to mind-reading like Lady Clare. It was bad enough that the mages had an insight into my thoughts. "I suppose the Moon-beam might sense the betrayal... After all, it was Lorne who traded the Moonbeam to the Orion League in exchange for their help."

Shock punched the air out of my lungs. "He *what?*"

She folded her wrinkled hands on her lap. "I assumed

you'd guessed. The Moonbeam did not end up in the League's hands by accident."

Damn. Of course not. We already knew that Lorne had sold out his fellow dragon shifters to win the war, but not that he'd traded the Moonbeam away, too.

The only other time it'd refused to work was when we'd met a pregnant dragon shifter who'd been carrying Lorne's child. He'd gone as far as to mark her with tattoos so her son would develop powers, and we'd used the Moonbeam to undo the damage...

My heart lurched into my throat. "The Moonbeam would cure the sickness," I said. "Wouldn't it?"

Agnes's face was grave. "At a guess? Yes, it would."

Ember swore. "Is that the only way? We have to find Lorne?"

"Have you no leads on him?" she asked. "I assumed he'd *want* you to find him."

"Apparently not," I said. "If he plays human, he can hide anywhere. Even if he's flying—let's be real, he'll have left London behind."

But where would he have flown to? It was the Faulkner brothers who'd once claimed they wanted to hide out on an island until it all blew over.

An island...

"Go through a list of his favoured haunts," said Agnes. "I wish I could help you. My sister... she might have known, but I've lived away from supernatural society for too long to be up to date on recent developments. I don't make much use of my powers anymore."

"But you undid the spell erasing our memories," I said. "Right?"

"I did," she confirmed. "But in using my powers on

you, I robbed you of any memories of your childhood for most of your life. There are some kinds of magic which should be used with great care. Especially those which give you dominion over others."

Does she mean the Moonbeam?

"Thanks for your help," Ember said. "We'll go now."

I waited for the others to leave, then said, "Agnes, there was something else I wanted to ask you. I didn't know who else to go to…"

"Yes?"

"Do you know anything else about the Moonbeam?" I asked. "Uh, I don't know if you heard the full story about what went down in the battle with Lorne and the League five years ago, but Ember used the Moonbeam to save my life. And since then, things have been… weird."

Her expression turned speculative. "In what way?"

"I think I'm a necromancer."

Her eyes widened. "You can see ghosts."

"And summon and speak to them," I said. "I don't know if it's enough to train as a full necromancer, and I'm not sure I want to. But I *saw* the spirit lines when Lorne attacked the city. That's not common, is it?"

"No," she said. "If you want to know more, I'd advise you to speak to a knowledgeable necromancer. Lady Montgomery of Edinburgh's necromancer guild is probably the best person to ask, but I understand if you can't make any more detours."

She was right. We needed to cure the sickness and stop Lorne first, and when I found the Moonbeam, using it to cure the shifters was our priority. I'd worry about its past, and future, when that was done.

"It's not linked to those symbols, is it?" I asked.

She shook her head. "If the Moonbeam saved your life —I've never heard of such a thing before. How did it happen?"

"Ember used the Moonbeam to return my soul to my body," I said. "When Lorne's army and the League knocked the spirit lines out of whack, I was ripped from my body. Ember managed to use the Moonbeam to... to wake me up, somehow."

Her eyes were wide, shocked. "I've heard of several incidents where a very skilled necromancer managed to return a lost soul to its body before they were separated for good. But an *object*—I'm afraid I don't know any more than you do."

"Lorne probably does," I said. "Even though I have my memories back, I was five when I left the village. I feel like I'm stumbling around in the dark."

None of the villagers knew where the Moonbeam had originated—or they hadn't been willing to share, anyway.

"You're a good person, Cori," Agnes said. "You won't go bad like Lorne."

"No chance," I said. "He has no sense of humour and is dull as ditchwater."

She smiled. "Take care."

Feeling a little better, I walked out into the shop to find all three Lynns had climbed onto the shelves and were in the process of staging a bank robbery.

"You'll never take me alive!" shouted Morgan, and Hazel tackled him, sending both of them crashing into the shelf and knocking over half of Agnes's spell display in the process.

Ilsa yelped and hid behind me. "They're like *animals*," she said.

"Where's Everett?" I asked.

Ilsa giggled. "Not telling."

"Hazel did it," Morgan proclaimed.

"It wasn't my fault!" She grabbed a handful of his hair and pulled on it, and he yelped.

I scanned the shop and spotted Everett locked inside a glass cabinet.

"It doesn't open from the inside," he said, his voice muffled. "Please can you give me a hand?"

Poor guy. "Hang on, I'll get you out of there."

I grabbed the door handle and yanked it open. Everett stepped out to a chorus of boos from the Lynn children.

"Agnes will never let me live this down," he muttered.

Ilsa giggled again. "It wasn't my idea."

"Uh-huh," I said. "I'll let Agnes and Everett decide that. And your mother, when she's back."

"Don't tell our mother," Ilsa said, panicking. "It was my sister, not me. Sisters are annoying. Do you have one?"

"I do," I said. "Ember's my big sister. Seven years older. Pretty sure she never locked anyone in a cabinet." Probably because we'd spent most of our childhoods in hiding, avoiding the Orion League. I wouldn't know the first thing about parenting. My parents had died when I was five, and the handful of memories I retained were hazy.

"*I'm* seven," Ilsa announced. "So is Hazel. We're twins. Everyone keeps calling me Hazel. It's really annoying. Are you magical?"

"Kind of," I said, figuring that shifting my hands into claws might traumatise them. "Are you?"

"Not yet, but I will be," she said.

"Nice meeting you, then, Ilsa." I headed for the door. "Behave for Agnes and Everett, okay?"

I opened the shop door to find the others waiting outside.

"I am never having kids," I said, once the door was firmly closed.

"Just avoid twins," Ember said. "What did you ask Agnes about?"

"Ghosts," I said vaguely. "We should get back, anyway. No time to lose."

And I had an inkling I knew exactly where Lorne was hiding.

10

"The lab?" Ember said. I'd told her and Zeph my theory on the walk back through the village to Azalea's house. After our flight back, exhaustion threatened to pull me into slumber. I'd pushed too far with two long flights in the same day. "Are you sure?"

"I should have thought of it earlier," I said. "Someone was smuggling the dragonlings into the city from outside, right? The lab's off the coast, but since Lorne can fly, he'd easily be able to find it again."

It was the perfect hiding place… and the perfect place to manufacture a virus to infect London's shifters.

"I can't believe even Agnes didn't know," Ember murmured. "I suppose she's been isolated from the supernatural world at large, almost as much as the other dragon shifters are."

"She knew about the symbols, though," I said. "If Will's made the tracking spell, we might be able to track the dickheads reanimating corpses. Then at least one problem will be solved."

It might not help us find the source of the virus, but hell, maybe it would. Besides, if they used those symbols on dead people, then there was nothing stopping them from using them on the living, too.

Inside the main room, Becks and Will stood in conversation by the lab, while Kit and the dragonling were playing an involved game of catch. The dragonling came up to Kit's waist by now, and he was the tallest of our group aside from Zeph. If Thorn kept growing, he wouldn't want to stay cooped up all the time and would start wandering around outside. That, however, was a conversation to have later.

"Any luck?" asked Will.

"Sort of," I closed the door behind me. "Agnes doesn't know what might have caused the virus. But she did confirm where those marks on the undead came from. They *are* the same as the ones the League used. Which means someone—a witch—is loose in the city who served the League, and now serves Lorne."

Will grimaced. "Ugh. Who'd willingly work for him?"

"Half the gargoyle underworld," Becks reminded him. "Until recently, anyway."

"Exactly," said Zeph. "If we track Jake, he might know. Will, did you finish the spell?"

"The tracker? Knock yourself out," he said. "If you want me to poke around and see if any witches know where Lorne is, I can try, but nobody's talking."

"I think I know where he is," I said. "I think he's using the old fortress. The one on the island."

"Damn, I should have thought of that," said Becks. "Makes sense. Are we going there?"

"Not today," Zeph interrupted. "We've flown a long distance today already, and Cori is exhausted."

"Hey!" I protested. But he was right. If I knocked myself out cold, I wouldn't do us any favours. "We need a plan first. You know how well guarded the fortress was the last time around. Also, I'm betting that was where he was breeding the dragonlings, too. He smuggled them into the city somehow."

"Killer dragons and freakishly fast zombies," said Will. "Count me out. I'll stick to brewing poison cures, thanks."

"Are you going to use the tracking spell now?" asked Ember, picking it up.

"Might as well," I said. Exhausted though I might be, Jake was on the run and I'd regret it if we waited until he'd disappeared—or died. Not that he didn't deserve it, but still. I was sure he knew something.

I took the tracking spell in hand. The dragonling spotted the shiny light and padded over to watch, tail twitching with excitement.

Hands on the table, I activated the spell. Green light flared, and a familiar tunnel appeared, blurred and indistinct. Then it vanished.

"Damn," I said, lifting my hands from the table. "I didn't know he was literally underground."

"What—in our tunnels?" asked Ember.

"Looked that way," I said. "He might be behind the door in the basement for all we know."

"He won't undo the defences," Will said. "I check them every day and nobody's come through that way in years."

I mostly forgot about the door in the basement that led into the warren of tunnels that ran underneath London. I'd thought nobody used those tunnels at all, not since half of them had collapsed when Malkin had forced a rogue necromancer to conduct a ritual under there. A shudder ran through me at the memory of nearly plummeting to my death. I'd never liked the narrow, cramped spaces or the unstable ground. What had once been a safe way to travel between shelters had filled with the dead and enabled the League to corner us.

But if Jake had fled underground, he might bring his pursuers right into our house.

Ember nodded to me. "I'll lead the way."

Once more, we descended the stairs into the basement. This time, Ember made for the locked door rather than the mirror, unlocking it with Will's key and revealing a narrow earthen passageway. The passages snaked between tube stations, accessible through entrances that had once been hidden with magic before the faerie invasion. Now, no sound disturbed the silence, no rumble of an oncoming train or chatter of commuters. Nobody living would be foolish enough to try their luck against whatever might be lurking here in the dark.

Ember hissed out a breath. "Look at that."

I squinted into the gloom. Footprints darkened the ground behind the door. Damp, recent ones.

"There are seven of us in the house," Zeph said. "All of us have sensitive hearing, including the assassin. How can none of us have heard—"

A faint breath on my neck. Then a hand locked around my throat, pinning me to the wall with impossible strength.

I snarled through my teeth, shifting my hand to a claw. The others moved all at once—drawing weapons, claws or otherwise—as a half-dozen silent figures popped up out of the darkness. My claw wrenched the man's hand away, eliciting no reaction. An undead, then.

With a furious snarl, Zeph tore the man's head off. The dead man didn't hesitate even then, hands moving with blinding speed. I caught his wrist in mine and snapped it, using my claws to take his body to pieces. Once he crumpled in my hands, I glimpsed now-familiar tattoo marks on his collarbone.

Ember and Zeph made short work of the other attackers, claws flaying flesh from bone. I kicked each body aside to check their faces, but none of the attackers was Jake. I didn't think tracking spells worked on the dead, so he must have been alive when I'd used it.

Ember turned one of the undead over with her foot. "He has different marks to the last one."

"Stealth," I guessed. "Total silence, if they've been walking around here without anyone hearing them."

And they'd tried to break into our home. Anger surged, and I grabbed one of the limp corpses by the throat, tapping on my spirit sight. Grey fog rose, but no ghosts. There'd been ghosts all over here before, but the one time I actually needed to speak to a spirit, they were gone.

Cursing, I dropped him. "Let's go and find Jake."

"One of us should warn the others," Ember said.

"I will," Becks said, her hair standing on end in a fur-like manner. "Your claws are more practical for taking those bastards to pieces."

I didn't blame her for wanting to get out. The enclosed space made the dragon within me feel stifled, trapped, and worse was knowing that our privacy had been violated so recently.

"What did they want to break into the house for?" I said. "There's nothing to steal."

"Except Thorn," Ember put in.

"Do you think he'd have let anyone carry him off?" I glanced at Zeph. "He'd have screamed bloody murder."

Zeph frowned. "Wasn't Lorne ticked off that Thorn picked you over him?"

"True," I acknowledged. "Unless… unless he was trying to get through the mirror."

Ember's shoulders tensed. "You know, that door is stable, but those undead are enhanced to be invincible. If the witch used a spell which allowed them to open the basement door without being heard…"

"Then what are we supposed to do?" I asked. "Move the mirror out of the basement?"

"Maybe." Her expression was grim. "I think it's safe to say Lorne's got the best of us again."

I shook my head. "Not if I have anything to do with it."

We continued into the darkness, finding more bodies. None moved to attack us, but I destroyed them anyway. Anger burned in my blood and at the sight of yet another dead person, I snarled, hooking my claw into his chest.

It was Jake. Or most of him. His head was nowhere in sight. I detached him from my claw, swearing.

"Oh, lovely," said Ember. "I guess they caught him."

"The gargoyles?" I dropped what was left of his body. "I guess that's why the tracker cut out. Should I summon his ghost?"

"You can do that?" asked Ember.

"Probably not without candles," I acknowledged. "All right, let's get out—"

Something hard crashed into the back of my head.

Ember let out a soft gasp and I turned to see Jake's severed head bounce past. Then a pair of gargoyle claws grabbed the scruff of my neck, yanking me into an alcove.

The gargoyle barely fit into the tunnel, his leathery wings hunched against his back. There wasn't room for me to shift, but my hands turned to claws and I twisted them until I got at the right angle to stab him in the palm. The gargoyle's grip broke, and I kicked at him.

"You're cursed, too," he snarled. "You will die this time."

"I'm not cursed." Oh hell. He'd heard me talking about summoning ghosts. There was no way I could leave him alive.

The gargoyle's talon gouged at me. I ducked, and it sank into the wall instead. Before he could recover, I buried my claws in his chest.

A rattling gurgle escaped his throat. "Death will take you back, Coriander."

"Cori!" Ember ran in behind me as the gargoyle fell to the earth, shifting human again in death.

"He thought I was cursed. He's cracked." I shook droplets of blood from my claws, grimacing.

"That's ridiculous," said Ember. "They saw us with Jake and probably assumed we're working together."

"I think he was just deluded," said Zeph. "Cori, you okay?"

I cracked an unconvincing smile. "Sure. Let's go and summon Jake's ghost."

Leaving a dead gargoyle and a bunch of zombies behind risked bringing more trouble on our tails, but then again, I'd killed him in self-defence. Besides, the mages wouldn't care, nor would they even know the dead were missing.

By the time I dragged myself back into the living room, there was nothing I wanted to do *less* than summon the ghost of my former nemesis. But his death was as bewildering as his final loyalties.

While I fetched the candles, Ember and Zeph updated the others on our discoveries down in the tunnels. I scrubbed the blood from my hands in the bathroom, but it was harder to banish the gargoyle's words from my mind. *Death will take you back.* Yeah, right.

"So you're saying super-stealthy zombies tried to creep into our basement while we were sleeping?" Will was saying as I walked back into the main room carrying the bag of candles. "How did none of us hear them?"

"They used spells to mask every sound," I said. "You should have seen them sneak up on us. It was like…"

"The assassin," Will finished. "He's *still* not in. I swear, if he's done a runner…"

"He won't have," Ember said. "Oh yeah, and we killed a gargoyle, too."

"I did," I said. "He murdered Jake for reasons that made no sense, so I'm going to speak to his ghost."

"Right here?" Will's brows shot up as I laid the first candle down on the carpet.

"Relax, she already did it once," said Becks.

The dragonling whined, and Kit petted him. "He doesn't like ghosts. Neither do I."

"I don't *like* them," I said. "I just don't have much choice about dealing with them at the moment. Let's face it, the living aren't much help."

"She's not wrong," Zeph said, moving to help me with the candles.

Bolstered by his encouragement, I finished putting the candles into place and knelt before them. "I summon Jake Frey."

The smoke swirled. Then Jake's hovering form appeared. His eyes were wide, mouth stretched open, and he let out an awful scream. The dragonling hissed and hid behind the sofa.

"Hey, stop yelling!" I said.

"I'm in hell!" Jake moaned. "Make it stop."

"Shut up!" Will put his hands over his ears. "Is this what ghosts are like all the time?"

"Mostly." If Jake had been solid, I'd have slapped some sense into him. "Jake, for god's sake, you're dead. Nobody can touch you. A gargoyle killed you—why? What were you doing with the undead?"

He sobbed. "It was a mistake, it was all a mistake. I don't wanna die!"

"Too late for that, mate," I said. "But you can help us."

"Nobody can help you," he said. "He was right. The dead are cursed. And they're going to kill us all."

"*He lies,*" a voice whispered. I stiffened, staring into the whirling fog. Behind Jake appeared another ghostly form, a female figure, almost like—

The circle cut out, the smoke vanishing. Blinking in confusion, I counted the candles. Ten, eleven—"Hey!"

The dragonling took flight, one of the candles in his mouth, and crashed into the wall. Kit ran after him in pursuit, while I gave the others an exasperated look. "I was just getting somewhere."

"Sounded more like you were about to reach into the

afterlife and strangle Jake," Becks commented. She'd shifted to human when the circle had vanished.

Wait, was I the only person who'd heard that voice at the end? Weird. *I must have imagined it. It can't have been her.*

"That was a bloody waste of time," Will said, taking the dragonling's spot on the sofa. He looked exhausted, like he hadn't slept in days. "I always heard the dead were melodramatic drama queens, but really. The cursed dead are going to kill us, are they?"

"He's talking crap," I said. "Like those gargoyles."

"If anything, we'll starve to death first." Becks aside as the dragonling loped over, spitting the candle out at my feet. "I noticed our rations are down. What do we do, start wagering food on poker games?"

"Nah, we'll just have to choose who to kill and eat first," Will said, his light tone not fooling anyone. "For the record, I'm not volunteering."

"Yeah, right," I said. "As soon as the food runs out, the dragonling will probably eat us all."

"What in the world is going on in here?" Astor stood by the door, as quiet and still as one of those zombies. He scanned the candles with narrowed eyes. "Summoning spirits, were you?"

"No, we decided you're the first person we'll feed to the dragonling when our supplies run out," said Zeph. "Also, that stealth spell of yours is doing the rounds on the local undead."

"My what?" said Astor. He sounded more irritated than puzzled.

"Hey, Astor," I said. "I was right. The marks *are* the same as the ones the Orion League used on their soldiers.

It's witch magic, not necromancy. And their latest trick is to send stealth zombies around the tunnels."

"Didn't you already come to that conclusion?" he said.

"Yes, but we didn't know the specifics. Now we do," I said. "As for the virus, we think it must have been manufactured in the fortress."

"The League's sea fortress?" Astor shook his head. "I doubt it's still in use."

"What makes you say that?" Zeph strode to block his path before the former assassin could disappear. "If you're trying to sabotage us, then I suppose it means nothing to you if we all die."

"Don't be a fool." Astor's jaw locked. "As far as I'm concerned, you're welcome to do as you wish. I'd prefer it if you didn't get me killed in the process, but I have my own way out planned for Ember and me. I'd suggest you do the same."

Zeph's hand shifted, but Astor's hand closed around his wrist before he could move an inch. I'd seen him fight, and Astor moved damned fast, but not as silent as the undead did. Close, though. The marks the League had put on him were definitely the same type. I should have trusted my instincts from the start.

"Don't push me, Elite," hissed Zeph, his claw inches from Astor's neck. "Tell me what you know about those spells they used on you. Don't try to wriggle out of answering."

"They aren't spells," said Astor tersely. "A League member used a pen to ink several markings on me during the ceremony that made me an Elite. It looked like an ordinary pen to me, and I didn't think of it as magical. Of course, I considered the possibility after I quit the League, but considering the majority of my former League contacts are dead and their Stronghold destroyed, I don't know where their equipment ended up."

"Pens," said Zeph, but he dropped his claw when Astor released him. "Right."

"Hey, I did all this with chalk," Will said, indicating the pile of handmade spells on the kitchen table. "The person who did that to you wasn't a witch, Astor?"

"I assume not," he said. "But those portable spells of yours can be used by anyone who isn't a witch, even a human."

"The loophole," Will muttered. "Even dead people… damn, they're smart. Why waste that intelligence on turning zombies loose in London's tunnels to terrorise everyone?"

"Because they're not smart," answered Zeph. "They stole those methods from others. Supernaturals."

Astor scowled. "I already said I wasn't involved, so if you don't mind—"

"Zeph, we still need to clean those undead out of the tunnels." I caught his arm. "And make sure the back door is thoroughly sealed. Right?"

With a final frown at Astor, he obligingly came with me down to the basement.

"I still don't trust him," he muttered.

"I do," I said. "Because Ember does. She's not thick."

He shook his head. "I know. His attitude just gets up my nose. Sorry I keep provoking him."

"We've all tried it at one point or other." I pulled out a handful of spells and set about destroying the zombies' remains. Zeph did likewise, moving alongside me. Even in the gloom, embers gleamed in his eyes, hints of his annoyance.

"That doesn't mean I'm not keen to stick around," he said. "I like you."

"Good," I said. "Because I like you too."

More than I probably should.

His scent infiltrated my personal space, conjuring images of flickering flames and open skies, distinct from mine and yet still recognisable as belonging to a dragon shifter. A spark danced in his eyes as he lowered his head to mine and kissed me. My lips parted beneath his, and he made a faint growling noise. When I drew back, I knew my eyes were glowing with the same orange light as his.

He released my shoulders. "Sorry, I didn't want to make a complicated situation even more complicated."

"Are you kidding me? I need the distraction." His closeness had chased away the chill of the zombies, his warm scent masking the smell of grave dirt and decay. All my senses were trained on him, and while part of me knew it was simple dragon shifter biology at work, a bigger part of me was all too keen to leap into the flames along with him.

Recklessness seized me. I kissed him hard, fisting my hand in his soft auburn curls. He growled again, his heartbeat thundering alongside my own. Then a rattling sound infiltrated the silence, drawing my attention to the half-open door to the basement.

"If either of us was carrying the plague, we probably both have it now," I said, sobering a little.

He stepped back from me. "Let's get back to the house before your sister comes looking for you."

11

"Oh," I said to the ghost. "It's you again."

The female ghost looked at me, her grey eyes simmering like a dragon shifter's. "Yes, it's me, Cori."

"Was it really you I saw?" I peered into the fog, but no other ghosts appeared, only her. "Did you appear when I summoned Jake?"

"Terrifying mortals is my only source of entertainment," she said. "You're different, Cori. The fire that runs in your veins is the same as mine, as I made you."

She seemed more lucid than she had before. And, considering this was supposed to be a dream, startlingly lifelike.

"Are you real?" I asked. "Am I actually talking to you?"

She tilted her head. "Are you?"

"Okay, I'm ready to wake up now."

Her hands shot out and grabbed my wrist. The pain burned my arm, and I jerked awake in an instant. My skin chilled with cold sweat as I flung the covers off, my breaths coming in quick pants.

A singed mark covered my wrist in the shape of a handprint, stinging with heat, yet the rest of me was icy cold.

Okay, this was too much. Dragons didn't burn. I could stick my hand in an open flame and feel nothing. So why had a *dream* affected me?

If I woke Ember, there was a chance I'd wake Astor, too, and dealing with an angry assassin was too much for me right now. I padded to the bathroom and took a long shower to wash away every trace of the dream. Not that recalling my plan to infiltrate the Orion League's old base were much better. I hadn't set foot in a lab belonging to anyone from the League since I'd woken up after my sister had rescued me from the Stronghold.

I forced the memories to the back of my mind. We had a mission: find Lorne and destroy his lab. If we got to destroy the source of the virus, too, so much the better.

I came downstairs and found Will asleep at the kitchen table, head resting on his arms. He looked pale and tired, which came as no surprise considering how hard he was working on potential cures for the sickness.

Backing away, I saw Zeph's eyes were open, watching me from the sofa. Thinking about our kiss in the tunnels, maybe. Heat curled low in my belly, drawing me closer to him, to inhale his scent. To lose myself in his warm gaze.

The image of the ghost in my dream flashed before my eyes. *Go away.*

Zeph's expression turned serious as I sat down next to him. "Worried?"

"Only about the hundred things that could go wrong today. For all I know, Lorne won't even be there." Something cold and sharp touched my hand. The dragonling put his head in my lap, scales pressing into my palm. "What is it?"

"You want to come with us to the lab?" Zeph asked.

The dragonling made a chirping noise.

"It'll be dangerous," I said. "Lorne won't make this easy for us. And… you know, the lab might be where your egg was kept before it was sent to London."

Thorn made another chirping noise, and something clicked into place. Did he want to find his fellow dragonlings?

"Okay, but I think we ought to ask Kit first." I reached to stroke him.

Zeph's eyes widened as he took in the mark on my wrist. "Cori, where did that come from?"

I lowered my hand. "Uh… this is going to sound weird, but I dreamt it."

Zeph's expression grew more and more concerned as I explained the weird encounters with the spirit—including when I thought I'd seen her staring at me when I'd summoned Jake's ghost.

"You saw this spirit in real life, too?"

"You believe me?" I touched the hand-shaped mark with my other hand gingerly. "I didn't think it was possible even in the magical world for something to walk out of a dream into reality."

"No," said Zeph. "You said she mentioned the Moonbeam, though. Maybe it's linked to what it did to you."

"Maybe," I said doubtfully. "She knew the Moonbeam brought me back to life. Perhaps it's another side effect.

As well as seeing ghosts in the real world, I'm seeing them in my dreams, too. I guess I should have asked the necromancers about that one."

Not that it mattered. Finding Lorne was more important. I'd deal with the Moonbeam when I had my hands on it again.

Never mind what the weird spirit stalking my dreams might do when I held it for real.

———

"Are you sure about this, Cori?" Ember asked for the fifteenth time.

"Of course I'm sure." I pushed aside my irritation at her acting like I was five and off to school for the first time. It was only natural for her to worry. I was pretty damn jittery myself, and taking the dragonling along to the Orion League's former haunt didn't seem a wise idea. Kit wasn't happy either, but Thorn had the half-faerie wrapped around his little finger. Or rather, smallest claw.

"Just a head's up that the headquarters is on an island-fortress that's also a giant ship," Ember told Zeph. "And there are kraken and hydra in the water."

"Didn't you take a swim last time?" I'd been in a coma when Ember and the others had gone to the fortress to confront Malkin and nearly lost their lives, so I'd only heard the highlights after I woke up.

"Exactly," she said. "I'd rather you didn't take the risks I did."

"You didn't fly there last time," I pointed out. "Relax, I'm not planning on taking a bath in the ocean."

Rather, my eyes were on the sky.

For the second time in two days, I shifted into dragon form and launched myself into the air. Flying over a city wasn't the same as soaring over the wilderness, but it was just as freeing. London shrank to a tangle of buildings, winding roads and open green spaces. I grinned and waved a claw at the spot where our house lay. The little dragonling flew alongside me, his wings pumping frantically, his tongue lolling. Seeing him next to Ember reminded me how much he'd grown. Unlike us, he'd never be able to shift into a human. I hoped Kit didn't expect to keep him in the house forever.

Before long, we were soaring over the ocean. The sea air made my eyes sting, but I kept them wide open to enjoy the view. A rippling expanse of blue spread below, and my breath caught. *Beautiful.* Sea monsters or not. Dragons didn't like water as a rule, but watching it from afar was a sight I wanted to remember. Then the blocky shape of an island came into view. *There it is.*

There only seemed to be one platform to land on, a wide concrete space. No ships or boats were around, suggesting that if Lorne had been there at all, he'd flown in. Ember landed in front of a huge construction built like some kind of fortress, blocky and unappealing-looking. Rails surrounded the platform, and its shape was more oblong than square. As Ember had said, it wasn't just an island, it was a huge ship.

Ember shifted to human and said, "It's not being steered, don't worry."

I landed beside her and turned human, blinking as the sea's salt spray stung my eyes. "Are you sure?"

"Ninety per cent. I doubt Lorne knows how to steer a ship."

"Doesn't mean he's alone." Zeph landed and shifted into human form, looking up at the towering fortress. "What was inside the fortress before, do you remember?"

"We… didn't actually go in," Ember admitted. "The League soldiers tried to execute us on this platform and then I jumped into the sea to avoid them."

"So we don't know the way in," I said. "Great start."

The dragonling strode up to the door and spat a mouthful of fire at it. The fire dissolved on contact with its metal-looking surface.

"Fireproof." Ember pulled out a witch spell. "Not immune to Will's spells, though, I bet."

Sure enough, the door clicked open the instant Ember activated the unlocking spell, and lights automatically came on. A long corridor stretched ahead. The fortress had only one floor, which appeared to be made up of corridors laid out in a neat grid-like pattern. If we had a map, it would have been no problem to navigate, but not knowing what was in each room meant we had to move slower than I liked to avoid running into any traps.

By mutual assent, Thorn took the lead. His sense of smell was as good as a dragon shifter's, but he'd also be able to pick out the scent of his own kind. Our footsteps echoed, amplified by the metal floor. Dragon shifters and stealth went together about as well as cat shifters and flying, but I didn't much care if Lorne knew we were here. *Bring it. Let them all burn.*

Despite the fortress's size, there were only a small number of rooms, each one bigger than our house. The dragonling sniffed at each door and nudged one of them with his nose, emitting a faint whining noise.

I pushed open the door. The room was filled with

cages. Huge cages, big enough to fit a full-grown dragon shifter inside them—but empty. Every one of them.

"I think it's abandoned," Ember murmured.

"No kidding." I scanned the room. No dragon shifters, and while their faint scent hung around the cages, it wasn't recent.

Despite the empty room, bad memories began knocking on the doors at the back of my mind. Cold hands grabbing me, tearing me away from my sister. Choking the air from my lungs. The sharp jab of an injection in my arm—then blackness, so deep that not even Ember could pull me out of it.

Then the glow of the Moonbeam, a siren's song luring me back into the waking world.

Was it here? The Moonbeam?

A humming noise sounded in my ears, growing louder as we reached the next room. Zeph opened the door first, and I held my breath as I entered behind him. My gaze snapped to the source of the humming—a tank, hooked up to a bunch of machines. The tank was empty, traces of what appeared to be water in the bottom. Along with—

Shattered pieces of scale. Dragonling eggs.

But no dragonlings.

"They evacuated," Ember said. "They must have hatched the eggs, and—taken them."

Zeph strode into the room, moving among the shattered pieces of scale. He picked several up. "These would work in a tracking spell."

"Not if he flew them out to sea," I said. "Or packed them on a boat. Depends how many there were."

Few humans would agree to transport living dragonlings around without asking questions, surely. Unless the dragonlings had hatched earlier, but I'd thought the ones in London had started out as dragon eggs sold on the black market.

"This must be where he created them," said Zeph, his voice low, his head bent over the machinery. "Or the League did, anyway. I don't think it was Lorne's idea."

"I think the idea of an army of dragons who'd obey him without question would have been appealing." I glanced at the dragonling, who sniffed at one of the broken pieces of scale, his tail drooping. "Then again, it didn't work last time."

Lorne had used the dragonling to help him escape jail, but in the end, his loyalty to Kit and the rest of us had won out.

Zeph sucked in a breath. "What the hell is this?"

I moved to look. He'd picked up a bottle filled with some kind of liquid, which had been left behind the tank. I sniffed it, grimacing at the foul stench. "Smells awful, whatever it is."

Awful… and familiar. Suspicion spiked, and Zeph's expression told me he'd had the same thought. "Whatever was in this tank… they tested the virus on."

I tasted bile. "This is… this is the virus?"

"A distilled form of it." Zeph held up the bottle. "Wait —don't break it. Can Will engineer a cure out of this?"

"If they left it behind on purpose, probably not." Anger thrummed within me. In order to see if it worked, they'd have used dragonlings as test subjects. "I guess they couldn't kidnap enough shifters and bring them here to use as lab rats, so they decided to breed them instead."

Ember's mouth twisted. "If you bring it back with you, for god's sake don't spill a drop."

"If we show the mages, they won't be able to deny it was engineered in a lab," I said. "A few detection spells later, and…" I snapped my fingers. "That, or we load it into a water pistol and use it to shoot Lorne in the face."

Ember gave me a look. "And I the mages would let that slide?"

"Don't ruin it." My light tone didn't quite hide the rage boiling inside me. Lorne thought as little of our lives as the League did. Even if he hadn't originally created the virus, he'd used it for the same purpose—utter domination.

All because he couldn't get the Moonbeam to work for him.

Since he couldn't force all shifters to obey him, he wanted to destroy us instead.

Whatever Ember said, there was something immensely satisfying about the idea of bringing Lorne down with the same virus he'd intended to use to destroy us.

As for the dragonlings? There weren't many options for smuggling small dragons off the island. He must have taken a boat. Hell, he might have vacated the premises weeks ago. Or the Faulkners had. There was no evidence Lorne himself had ever set foot in here. The virus might have been their idea, if their plan to use the spirit device had backfired.

"The next room probably contains a trap," I said. "Bet you ten pounds it's zombies."

"Only ten?" Zeph tilted his head.

"It's all the cash I've got left," I said.

"I'll give you some of my tips."

"Oh, no." I threw up my hands. "We're not at that point yet. Though you probably shouldn't miss any more shifts."

We left the lab behind. The dragonling sat huddled in the corridor, looking dejected. I tried to give him a reassuring stroke and got a sharp nip on my wrist for my trouble. Wincing, I put my hand in my pocket and continued on to the next room.

As the door folded inward, a coppery tang teased my nostrils. Blood. Shoulders tensed, I led the way into the room.

A nightmare exploded out of the shadows, crashing headlong into me. Claws dug into my arms, only to bounce off hard scales. I half-shifted to my elbows, batting the nightmare away. A pair of pitted eyes stared at me, and below, sharp teeth dripped red-tinged drool onto the metal floor. Long talons ended in razor-like claws. What the hell was it? Not a dragon, though it had a long, scaled body striped in red and black. Fae, maybe.

The monster emitted a high-pitched scream. The sound made my ears ring, distorting my vision. Cursing, I gave another swipe. This time I managed to hook my claw under its tough scales, yanking a handful out. Red-and-black scales came free, not iridescent like a dragon shifter's but in stark, brutal shades. Its eyes were dark pits, masking the pupils, while its claws were longer than a dragon's with three per hand rather than five.

"What are you?" Ember hit out, sending the beast flying into the wall. Its wings splayed behind its back, claws dragging on the metal floor with a horrible screaming noise. "Get away from my sister."

The monster lunged again, crashing headlong into my

claws. Wrenching, I tore off more scales, piercing the vulnerable flesh beneath. Ember leapt onto its back, claws digging into the tip of its spine.

The beast gave a lurching spasm, spitting out blood. Zeph strode in, and we pounced, tearing into its neck. The beast shuddered, let out one feeble cry, and lay still.

"Ugh." I shifted my hands back and released a breath. "Is this one of their lab creations?"

"I… don't think so." Zeph indicated the back of the room.

My breath caught. Bodies lay on the floor in a careless heap, blood splattering the metal wall behind them, and underneath was a scrawled chalk circle.

"A witch's circle," Ember muttered. "A sacrificial summoning."

Sour bile filled my mouth. Those people hadn't been murdered, they'd been sacrificed to summon that clawed, scaled monster.

"Doesn't Lorne have enough of his own monsters?" I inched towards the bodies, shivering. They were dead, all right, but tossed into a pile. Forgotten.

And that meant there *had* been witches here, not just Lorne and the League. From what I'd heard, using blood in a summoning was like summoning a ghost, except replace 'ghost' with 'mystery monster'. Given that the scaly monster had been as tough as a dragon shifter, I wasn't all that keen to meet the others.

"He must have reasons for employing a witch to conduct a blood summoning." Zeph strode to my side, scanning the bodies. "They weren't tortured. A single wound killed most of them."

"Bullets," I concluded. "Can't tell if they're shifter or human, but given how fast they died, I'd say shifters."

But they'd died recently. That meant…

"The witch is still in here," Ember said.

The lights went out, plunging the lab into darkness.

"Seriously?" I said, trying to keep my voice steady. "Why is it always darkness? Why can't you use flashing disco lights or something instead?"

A cool breeze wafted through the room. Ember's eyes shone like twin candles in the blackness. My keen sense of smell ought to have picked up on anyone close, but the copper scent of blood and the dead, not to mention the lingering stench of the bottle of liquid in my pocket, dampened my senses.

Icy grey fog swept around me. Death, close enough to touch. My body locked to the spot.

It wasn't real. It couldn't be real. We were miles from any spirit lines, and the spirit sight didn't just turn on by itself.

Or did it?

The air swam with greyness, the only colour in the gloom. Lost souls whispered at me, begging me to join them.

"Help us," murmured a voice, so close that cold breath tickled my ear. My heart kick-started, hammering against my ribcage, and the urge seized me to run—to fly, as far from this nightmare as possible.

"Help us."

"It's been so long…"

Faces watched me from the fog, overlapping, a cold and endless mass begging to be freed. They were trapped in here. Like the arena, someone had turned it into a fortress that even lost souls couldn't escape from.

Chilled hands caught my arm and I jumped violently.

"Cori, is that you?" whispered Zeph.

"Yeah," I managed to croak out. "Where's Ember?"

"I don't know. God, it's foggy in here."

"You see it too?" I swallowed, my throat dry. "You know how the arena had that spell on it, blocking the dead from getting in or out? I think this place is the same."

Zeph swore softly. "I can't see a thing. Is this what Death looks like for you all the time?"

"You've got it," I said. "Generally, I can control my spirit sight, but this place is… contained."

I'd managed to break the boundaries on the arena. Might I be able to do the same here?

A dead man floated through the wall in front of me. "You're new."

"Hey there," I said. "Can you turn the lights back on?"

He floated right up to me, making me wince at the chill. "You should leave," he said. "Otherwise you'll get trapped here. Like us."

"I can set you free," I said. "Just—I need some information. We're looking for someone. Goes by the name Lorne. Big bad-tempered guy, red hair kinda like mine… seen him around?"

I'd never seen a ghost flinch, but there was a first time for everything. "You're one of his shifters."

"I'm not with Lorne. I'm trying to stop him." My breath fogged the air. "Can you tell me where he took the dragonlings? What he did with them?"

"I saw him carrying a cage," whispered the ghost. "I can't see beyond this room. Please, living shifters—run."

Carrying a cage. That implied he'd either carried the dragonlings to the mainland himself or had a boat waiting, and I couldn't picture Lorne with a cage sitting on his back, flying over the ocean. Whether they were still on the boat or it had docked in London, though—who knew.

"He was engineering a virus to use against shifters, wasn't he? What exactly—" I broke off. The room had gone very quiet, and Zeph had disappeared in the fog. Cold greyness smothered everything, as though I'd wandered right into the middle of one of my dreams.

Dead hands brushed against me. I shuddered, feeling the phantom touch of ghostly skin as they floated through me, leaching all warmth from my body. "Stop doing that."

"You're warm," whispered the ghosts. "So warm… so alive."

"Yes, and I'm sorry you're dead, but you're creeping me out."

They were trapped in here… which meant candles. To break the spell on the arena, I'd had to find and break the boundaries of the spirit circle. Maybe the candles were in the wall here, too. But they'd have to be around the building's entire perimeter to keep the ghosts caged inside.

"Ember," I called into the fog. "Zeph?"

Silence. They wouldn't leave me alone in here, right? Come to think of it, I wasn't sure I was even in the same room.

I also couldn't feel the ground beneath my feet.

Oh, bugger.

"Living shifter… you will soon be with us, among the dead," hissed one of the ghosts.

"Not a chance." I recoiled at a ghostly touch, pushing the transparent hand away with my own.

My own hand, as transparent as a ghost's.

No wonder I couldn't feel anything… somewhere back then, I'd left my body behind and floated into Death along with the other spirits. And if I wasn't careful, I'd be a permanent addition to the nest of restless dead.

12

I floated on the spot—floated, not stood, because I didn't have a bloody clue where my body even was. When Lorne had tried to use the spirit device to draw my soul out of my body, the Moonbeam's magic had stopped him. This time, I'd floated out of my body without even noticing. It shouldn't be possible, yet my hands were transparent, and the fog thickened all around me.

A ghostly woman's hands touched mine. "Join me in death."

"She won't," said another female voice.

I knew that voice.

The ghost from my dreams, her eyes flaming, hovered at my side. She *was* real. In a ghostly sense, anyway.

"What the—?" My mouth dropped open. The female ghost looked as solid as I was, her hair long and curly, her eyes ashy grey.

The first ghost's hand touched mine again. "Join me..."

"No thanks." I yanked my hand away, unable to take

my eyes off the newcomer. She'd walked out of my dreams. Or rather, walked *into* my dreams.

"I told you," said the fiery-eyed ghost. "The fire runs in your veins, Cori."

The fire runs in your veins. The same fire that had brought me back to life.

I wasn't a prisoner in a cage any longer.

Magic hummed inside me, the echo of the Moonbeam's power. I reached out and *shoved* the spirit away, and she went, floating backwards from my touch.

I turned to the fiery spirit. "My body—"

"You know the way back, Cori. Follow the Moonbeam's fire."

Fire. I imagined flames, crackling to my fingertips, triggering the shift. A breath choked my lungs and I dropped to my knees, cold—*so* cold. But solid. Pain shot up my knees, and I braced my hands on the metal floor.

Try to trap me in Death, will you?

The shift took over, and flames burst from my lungs, banishing the fog, sending the ghosts fleeing.

When the smoke cleared, Ember and Zeph stared at me across the room. "Damn, Cori, give some warning next time."

The lab… I was still in the lab. I blinked around, my wings scraping the ceiling. Ow. Right… I'd shifted. I must have been standing frozen in here while my spirit drifted away.

Taking a careful, measured breath, I turned human again. "You've been here all along?"

"Yeah, but where have you been?" Ember's eyes pinched with concern. "You went really quiet."

"We found the witch who summoned that monster,"

Zeph said. "Dead, back there. Must have been quick. Not a wound on her."

The ghosts had pulled her out of her body. Just like they'd tried to do to me.

And the fiery-eyed ghost… was real. An ally, even. It shouldn't be possible. Dragons and the dead were polar opposites, I'd thought. Then again, the dragon shifters had created the Moonbeam, and the Moonbeam embodied life and death.

So who was the woman? A dragon shifter? How had she got into my dreams?

Thorn whined, poking his head out from behind Ember's leg.

"Is he okay?" I asked.

"He's scared," said Ember. "Can you blame him?"

"Nope." *What a waste of time.* Not that the alternative was any better. We'd left the others to deal with the fallout of us abandoning the mages' request to go on a wild dragonling chase, while Lorne must have already taken his other dragonlings back to the mainland. We might have a container of the virus, but no cure.

"If they're hiding in London, then maybe Thorn can sniff them out," said Zeph. "The person with the dragonlings, I mean. It looked like at least some of the eggs hatched. If they're that hard to track, they can't be spread around, someone would have seen them. He likely has only one hideout."

"Maybe," I said. "I'm going to destroy the candles around this place, then we'll get out."

"Uh… candles?" asked Ember.

"This place is a death trap—literally," I said. "The spirits can't leave. Just like in the arena. Destroying one candle will break the circle, and considering we're surrounded by water, I'm guessing they're inside the fortress, not outside."

Navigating the corridors was easier without the fog. The others insisted on checking each room, but I knew we'd already found everything Lorne wanted us to. He'd seen us coming weeks back and left no tangible clues behind except for a bottle which had 'trap' written all over it.

Turning on my spirit sight was the last thing I wanted to do after my literal brush with death, but I calmed my breathing before tapping into the greyness on the other side. Ghosts murmured, drawn to me, but none was the fiery-eyed ghost from last time.

"Cori, what're you doing?" Ember's voice drifted from a brighter glow just behind me. *Living spirits glow, too? I didn't know that.*

"One second." To the right, a glowing line indicated the boundaries of the circle. *Gotcha.*

I walked, spotting an alcove in the ceiling and a candle hidden within it. Taking a swift jump, I hooked my claw in and swung myself up. The alcove wasn't wide enough to stand in, but the gleaming candle had no shield over it.

One swipe, and the candle wobbled. Two more grabs and it came free, still glowing, into the palm of my hand.

"How do you put it out?" Ember asked as I dropped to land beside her.

"There should be a switch…" I found it, clicking the light off.

The fog returned, and the whispers of the dead rose, becoming louder, more joyous. My hands pressed to my ears as the noise rose to a crescendo. The others stared open-mouthed, watching the ghosts leaving the fortress in a pale tide of relief and joy.

"Damn," Zeph said quietly. "I've never seen anything like that."

"Too weird for you?" I quipped. "Is this a bad time to say I saw the weird ghost from my dreams earlier, and she stopped me from being dragged out of my body?"

His jaw dropped. "What?"

"I'll tell you on the way out."

———

One long flight later, I landed in front of our house. I shifted to human again before the neighbours got too alarmed, joining Ember and Zeph.

Becks paced outside the shop's door in cat form, hissing when we approached. The door opened and Will strode out, wielding a hat stand.

"Whoa, it's me," I said. "More zombies?"

"Five," said Kit's voice from behind the door. "Oh —Thorn!"

The dragonling bounded through the door and the two fell into a half embrace, half wrestling match. The rest of us followed, closing the door behind us.

Will's mouth pressed together. "The mages asked after you."

"Oh, hell," I said. "What did they want?"

"They heard about the dragonling and wanted to search the premises," he said. "Lady Clare came alone, for some weird reason. Obviously, she found nothing. But she's a mind mage. I think her power's based on eye contact, and I *tried* to avoid thinking about what you were doing, but I don't know if she saw through me or not. It's a good job Kit glamoured himself and hid."

"And the mirror?" asked Ember.

"She had a long hard look at it. I didn't let her touch it, but she knows what it can do. I know the mages are seriously ticked off about how the Moonbeam slipped out of their grasp."

"Shouldn't they be more concerned with the sickness and the zombies?" asked Zeph.

Will shrugged. "I think someone might have tipped her off that we were involved."

One mage had betrayed them already. A chill raced down my back. Our safety was in such a precarious position, it wouldn't take much more than a rumour to erase it altogether.

"Sorry," I said. "It's not great news from us either. Lorne already evacuated. Put everything that was left in the lab on a boat, I'm guessing. Not sure if it went to London or otherwise. The lab was swarming with ghosts and not much else."

"Except a blood summoning," said Ember. "We found a pile of bodies a witch had sacrificed to summon... something."

Will pulled a face. "Ugh. Why would he want that?"

"It's a mystery." I extracted the bottle from my pocket. "So is why he left this behind. I'm pretty sure this contains the essence of the virus."

Will jumped back into the shop counter. "Are you out of your mind?"

"Don't you need it to make the cure?"

"Yes." He sank into a sitting position on the desk. "I do,

but the bloody mages just came through here. If they find that, we're doomed."

The dragonling hopped over onto the counter and butted Will's shoulder with his head. Will gave him a half-hearted stroke.

"We'll destroy it afterwards," said Zeph. "If there's any chance of getting a cure out of that thing, we have to give it a shot."

Will took the bottle from me. "I'll do my best, but I'll make no promises."

"We appreciate it," I said. "You keep us sane."

"You all drive me *insane*," he muttered, rubbing his eyes.

"It really didn't feel like that place was the main base," Zeph commented. "Are you sure there wasn't anywhere else in Scotland?"

"What makes you say that?" asked Ember.

He shrugged. "London wasn't originally Lorne's base. I assumed it was the dragon shifters he wanted to conquer, and the rest of the humans and shifters were more of an afterthought."

Maybe he was right. The Orion League had originated somewhere in Scotland. They'd captured local witches, Azalea had told us, and Agnes had confirmed the same. We'd seen no traces of the zombies in the fortress, but those symbols had come from somewhere. *We've been looking in the wrong place.*

"Yes," said Ember, "but we already established he isn't using the Moonbeam to get around. So he's flying out in the open?"

"I guess he thought it was what we'd least expect." I sighed. "I should have asked the ghost from my dreams, they see everything on the other side. But I didn't know she was real."

"About that," Zeph said. "How is she real? Dreams can't come to life."

"I don't know what she is," I admitted. "She's clearly a ghost, and she helped me out in there. If not for her, I might have ended up stuck on the other side with the dead."

"Come again?" said Will.

"I've been having these bizarre dreams lately," I said. "I'm standing, or floating, in fog, and there's this woman. A ghost. Like when I was in the spirit realm…"

"Maybe—" Ember faltered, looking pale. "Maybe you were."

"Maybe I what?" Then it hit me. "Wait, can necromancers go into the spirit realm when they're asleep?"

"I heard they go into a sort of coma when they leave their bodies," said Zeph, frowning. "I guess it makes sense that they can do it when unconscious. You're not actually dreaming, you just think you are."

I gaped at him. If the fiery-eyed woman wasn't a figment of my subconscious, then who *was* she?

"Did the ghost tell you her name?" Ember asked.

I shook my head. "No. But she's been there every night for at least a week. Ghosts usually disappear after a day or two and even then, they're tied to one place, aren't they? But she was in the lab, too. I saw her."

Not only that, she'd left her mark on my wrist. Now it made a little more sense that she'd been able to touch me. Ghosts were rarely able to leave a mark on the living, but she didn't strike me as a typical spirit. Not at all.

"Is she an ally, then?" asked Ember.

"I assume so." That, or Lorne had sent her to mess with my head. But he didn't have the spirit sight, and shifters and ghosts didn't typically work together.

The Moonbeam brought me back to life. What else did it do to me?

I turned to Will. "What did the mages do, ask me to check in with them?"

"Lady Clare didn't seem all that fussed, to tell you the truth," said Will. "She was more concerned with that dragonling."

"Why?" I frowned. "I thought the whole point was that we were supposed to find the cause and cure for the sickness. Which we didn't. Lord Smyth might want to hear about the fortress, but I'm not distracting them by telling them there's a shipload of dragon eggs floating around somewhere. We didn't even find any witches raising zombies using those symbols, either."

Becks padded into the shop and shifted to human form. "I heard you mention a boat. Well… I've been checking the ships that come into the river when I wander around in the early hours of the morning. Just in case someone starts up that… shifter trade again. Nothing living has been brought into London since before the Faulkners died."

Nothing living. He wouldn't have hatched the dragonlings just to have them slaughtered, right? I'd thought he wanted them as an army.

"Seriously?" said Ember. "Will—what's that on your neck?"

Everyone looked at him. His collar had slipped, showing a rash on covering one side of his neck. Will yanked his collar into place. "Ah, shit."

"When did that happen?" I asked, my heart dropping like a stone. "Did you handle anything weird, or speak to anyone who might be infected?"

"My *job* involves handling weird shit. And I've been asking all over the place about those witches. If anything, I'd have thought Cori or Ember would have picked it up first. Or Zeph. He deals with the public more than I do."

"Not so much this week," Zeph said, his face unusually grave. "How do you feel?"

Will touched his hand to his neck. "It doesn't hurt. I'm fine."

"You're not fine." Kit walked to him, his mouth trembling. "Will… let me help you." A green glow spread from his hands to Will's neck.

"Don't touch me, fool," Will berated him, stepping back. "I don't want you to catch it, too."

"There's a chance Kit might be immune to the virus," Becks said. "Faeries are immune to most human infections. Then again, you dragon shifters are, too."

The dragonling made a small, distressed noise. I looked from him to the bottle on the counter, a horrible thought crossing my mind.

Kit's glowing hands dimmed. "Did it work?"

"Your healing magic doesn't work on viruses, Kit," Will said. "Don't worry, I'll be fine. I've handled a dozen poisons today alone."

"The mages," I said hesitantly. "Uh—why exactly did they say they wanted to see the dragonling? Did they give a reason?"

"Yeah." Will pushed off the counter. "Some dickhead started a rumour there's a plague of exotic animals spreading that virus. There have been other sightings, rumours, from outside of London as well."

My stomach lurched. "Are you sure it's not—true? Just because we haven't seen the other dragonlings doesn't mean they aren't here. We found that bottle in the same room the eggs hatched in."

Silence fell, horrified expressions breaking out on the others' faces as they came to the same realisation as me. Lorne hadn't taken the dragonlings with him. He'd set them loose in London. And they were all infected with the virus.

That was why the other shifters were avoiding us, passing on rumours that we'd started it. Because I'd beaten the Faulkners in such a public setting and everyone knew they'd had dragon eggs. Hell, they'd probably seen us walking around with Thorn in public, too. It was as much their revenge as Lorne's, and they might have given him the idea for all I knew, before they'd died.

Kit moved protectively to the dragonling's side. "What is it? What's wrong with him?"

"Nothing, I hope," I said. "I *hope*. Has he bitten anyone lately?"

"Me," Kit said. "And he bit Will this morning."

Fear clawed up my throat. "I don't think he's carrying the virus, but he's not immune. We have to get him out of here before the neighbours bring out the pitchforks."

"We can't abandon him!" said Kit. "He's no safer on the other side of the mirror."

Damn, he was right. If a dragonling had got at the villagers, too... then Lorne must have released them up and down the country. Since he could fly and so could they, they'd have spread easily without the need to use the

Moonbeam as a portal. They could travel as swiftly as one of us, and given the speed at which they grew...

Jesus. Does he want *to wipe out the entire human population?*

"He did it on purpose," Zeph said grimly. "He wanted to force us to kill the dragonlings or watch the rest of London get infected. There's no winning in this situation. No matter what choice we make, he wins."

13

"There's no use panicking," Will said firmly, taking the bottle of poison in hand and marching into the back room. "Most people on our street don't believe the rumours. Otherwise they'd have been waiting for you to come back with the dragonling."

"Might change when they find out you have the sickness, though," Becks said. "It must be spread like any virus, not through biting alone. I don't see Darcy getting bitten by a dragonling and not realising."

Good point. That must be the only reason nobody had figured out the cause. Only one person would need to be bitten for everyone they knew to pick up the infection. One down-on-his-luck mercenary wandering around the darkest corners of the city, the fae-infested places nobody but the desperate set foot in. He might not even have realised it was a dragon who'd bitten him. Face it, what was one more monster in London?

"Keep the dragonling hidden," I said, following Will

into the back room. "I think Lorne is doing this on purpose, and it's a good job Thorn came with us to the fortress when Lady Clare was snooping around. I think it's safe to say we haven't seen the last of her. We should keep the shelter and hide him in there if anyone comes knocking."

"And—the virus?" Kit ran to Will's side. "What're you handling that thing for?"

"I'm already infected, Kit," he said. "Please—the last thing I want is for you to catch it, too. I'm going to use this to brew a cure."

"Once we have, we'll burn it," Ember said. "As for Thorn, keeping him in the shelter isn't a perfect solution, but taking him through the mirror when half the village is sick is irresponsible at best. I guess the first victim must have run into a dragonling while he was walking in the hills."

"And he didn't tell anyone," I added. They wouldn't have had reason to assume Lorne was involved. "The dragonling up in Scotland might be miles from the village by now. I think we'd have better luck finding the ones roaming around London."

"Slight issue," said Zeph, lowering his phone. "I just heard from my boss. The pub is shutting down, indefinitely, until the sickness is gone. We're officially a zero-income household."

———

I stared into the circle of candles, dimly lighting the gloomy living room. "I summon Jake Frey."

"He's not gonna answer," Becks said, watching with

her cat-like amber eyes from the armchair. "Sorry to be a downer, but what if that ghost of yours gets loose in the house? If we wind up homeless, we're doubly fucked."

"Gah." I scowled, waving a hand at the candles. "I summon you, wailing spirits of the dead. Becks wants to talk to you."

"No, she bloody well doesn't." Becks threw the mercenaries' logbook at me. I caught it before it could knock the candles askew.

"Hey, you're sitting in front of the circle now," I said. "That's progress."

"Only because nothing's bloody happening."

Undeterred, I walked around the circle. The fiery-eyed ghost hadn't visited my dreams in the few hours of sleep I'd snatched last night, and I wondered if I'd spoken too soon when I'd said she seemed to have stuck around an unusually long time. "I summon you, fire lady."

"Is that what you're calling your ghost?" Zeph asked from the camp bed, his voice thick with sleep. Unlike the rest of us—except Kit—he could sleep through any catastrophe. Even necromantic rituals.

"Not sure I'd call her 'my' ghost." I waved the logbook over the circle. "I should just read every name from this book one at a time until a ghost shows up." Considering the death toll among the local mercenaries, odds were, I'd get someone eventually. Not a happy thought.

"Call Darcy," said Ember, who curled up on the other armchair.

"You think he's dead?" I put down the logbook. "Can't hurt, but I doubt he got bitten himself. He just caught the virus from someone else."

I halted in front of the circle, hands inches away from

the thick grey smoke. If the candles had a battery life, I'd probably wasted half of it this morning alone.

"I summon you, Darcy Jansen."

The smoke swirled. Then Darcy appeared, very much dead.

Becks exclaimed, Ember sat bolt upright, and I stepped back, disarmed by the sight of my former boss hovering in the circle of smoke.

"What the devil is going on?" he demanded.

I stared at him. "You're dead."

"I know I'm dead, Coriander." He narrowed his eyes at me. "What do you want from me? Practising amateur necromancy, are you?"

"Something like that." My heart thumped behind my ribcage. "You know you're dead. That's better than ninety per cent of the ghosts I've summoned. Darcy, did you ever get bitten by a dragon?"

"You've lost it," he said. "Or *I've* lost it. Let me go in peace."

"I will," I said, "but we're tracking the source of the virus." *Bad move there, Cori.* If he'd been bitten by a dragonling, he'd have told the whole office from his sickbed.

"They say you're cursed, Cori," he said. "They also said you brought the virus into the city when you hatched that dragon egg."

"You must know that's bollocks." Even Darcy had heard the rumours? "Did you hear any more rumours about dragons, or—mercenaries being bitten by unusual creatures?"

"Only every bloody day," he said. "Let me go. It's bad enough they stole my body—"

"Excuse me? Who stole your body?"

Zeph, who now sat upright on the camp bed, said, "It was a witch, right?"

"Looked human from what I saw," Darcy said. "Two of them loaded my body into a truck and drove it down to the Docklands."

"To reanimate, I bet." *I think we have our witches.* "Thanks, Darcy. You've helped us a lot."

"Destroy it," he said, his voice sharp. "I'd rather my body be destroyed than turned into one of those cursed monsters."

"I will," I said, but he was already fading out, disappearing. My fists clenched. "Time to find the shitheads who are raising the dead."

———

After a lengthy argument, Zeph and I agreed to go to the Docklands with Becks. Ember tried to argue the point, but someone needed to search the dragon shifters' village in case the dragonling who'd spread the sickness was still nearby.

The smell of rot and decay was strong enough at the Docklands to mask any hiding undead. With salt canisters up both my sleeves and spares in my pocket, I was more than prepared to deal with undead, but it was the people reanimating them who concerned me the most.

Bloody mages. Lady Clare should have been handling this rather than harassing my friends and snooping around our house.

"Becks, are you sure you want to come?" I asked, noting that her pace had slowed the closer we got to the river.

"You know how I feel about keeping shifters in cages and using them to attack others against their will," she said, her hands clenching. "They're trying to turn everyone against the dragonlings on purpose."

"I doubt we'll find them here." They must have assumed someone would track the zombies eventually. The cause of death was far more lethal than the undead themselves.

"You're not even trying to be subtle, are you?" a voice said from the shadows.

I spun around, claws out, and spotted Astor crouching behind an empty-looking truck. He'd been so quiet, we'd walked straight past him without noticing he was there.

"Nice of you to join me," he said.

I shifted my claws back to hands. "You already found this place? Since when?"

"Since I followed two zombies to their source."

"And you decide not to tell us... why?" Zeph's tone carried the hint of a threat.

"You weren't around," Astor responded. "I figured they'd have a contingency plan once they realised the two noisiest dragon shifters in London were onto them—"

I shot him a warning look, but Zeph's eyes were on the warehouse. Flames flickered over its roof—and not dragonfire. A moment later, a blast engulfed the neighbouring warehouse, too.

"That," said Astor, "was their contingency plan."

"Lucky we're fireproof, then." I broke into a run towards the blaze, and a blur shaped like a person streaked past my shoulder. I skidded to a halt, but the person fleeing the warehouse had moved too quickly for me to see anything other than a narrow feminine face and a sweep of tangled hair. "I think that was our witch."

"Was she dead or alive?" Becks called.

"Ask them." Astor stepped in the way as two undead lunged at us. Only an assassin could make twin salt canisters look like machetes. The dead fell, dissolving into ashes as the salt made contact with their reanimated bodies.

A third undead approached us. Darcy's sightless eyes looked back at me, and a now-all-too-familiar symbol marked his collarbone.

"Sorry, Darcy," I said, my claws sliding out. "It's nothing personal."

I leapt, spearing him in the neck. His head fell clean off, and I gagged at the foul smell. I threw salt onto his body, dissolving it into ashes.

Zeph turned to me. "The person who fled was human. If we fly, we can catch her."

"Lead the way." I shifted into dragon form, and my tail swung around and almost hit Astor in the face. Oops.

Becks meowed a laugh and took off at a run, her cat-form appearing almost as blurred as the fleeing witch. Zeph bounded into the air, flying over the rooftops.

I followed, wings pumping, and caught sight of a human-shaped figure travelling at speed between two high-rise buildings. Becks followed at an impressive pace, gaining on her by the second.

Then Zeph landed in the street in front of the witch, fire spewing from his mouth. The witch threw herself sideways into an alley. *Gotcha.*

I landed behind her, wings touching each side of the

alley's walls. *Try running off now.* I turned human, keeping out my claws. "Don't try to run."

The witch cursed and spat. "They're already coming for you, dragon shifter." Her long grey hair hung to her waist. Her head was bowed, her hands glowing with magic. Wait—her palms were covered in those odd symbols, moving like living ink.

"Who are you?" I demanded. "Why were you raising the dead?"

The witch jumped higher than any human should be able to, latching onto the side of the building on her right and scrambling upward in a spider-like manner. I swore and jumped after her, and an undead grabbed my legs from below.

Shit. She hadn't come alone. Undead walked out into the roads, trickling out of the nearby buildings like ants.

I kicked the undead in the face, breaking its grip, and Zeph released a rumbling growl, his fire engulfing the oncoming zombies. Trusting him to handle it, I followed the witch, my claws gouging holes in the building's wall. I climbed higher, faster, catching up to her on the roof. Her hands glowed, her legs bunched, preparing to jump to the neighbouring building.

I caught her mid-jump, and we crashed into the alley, my body pinning hers down. Speed she might have, but dragon shifter strength was superior to humans'. I punched her in the ribs, hard, and she spat blood at me. "You cannot remove me from this realm, girl. Soon I will ascend."

"You'll *descend* in a minute if you don't tell me what the fuck you're playing at. Are you working for Lorne?"

"I serve nobody but the master who wields the magic of the gods." Her voice was an inhuman rasp.

"If you mean Lorne, then he's just an egotistical dragon shifter with delusions of grandeur," I said. "Whatever he promised you, he lied."

"He already gave it to me." She twitched her skinny, symbol-streaked arms. The symbols moved in dizzying patterns, as though infused with life. "This is the blood of the gods."

She's cracked. "And this is the fist of a dragon."

With a swift crunch, I punched her in the jaw. She crumpled, and I caught the scruff of her neck. "That's for unleashing an army of zombies on us. Where are the dragonlings?"

She coughed a laugh. "Right here, little dragon…"

Claws dug into my shoulders, biting through my thin jacket. I shot out an elbow, breaking the attacker's grip before its teeth sank into me.

It wasn't our dragonling. The colouring was wrong, it was smaller than Thorn, and its teeth were bared in hostility. Worse, though—symbols were carved all over its exposed flesh where the scales had come off.

One look into the dragonling's eyes told me it was too far gone to save. Its eyes were wide with madness, drool dripping from its teeth. The sting in my shoulders told me it might be too late for me as well.

I'm sorry.

I caught the dragonling and snapped its neck, dropping its limp body onto the alley floor. The witch's coughing ceased, and I blinked tears from my eyes. Damn Lorne. I wouldn't give him the satisfaction of claiming this as a victory.

I turned back to the witch. Her eyes were open, but her breaths no longer came, and when I felt for her heartbeat, it was silent. The glow from her arms already dimmed, and something rolled onto the alley floor from her pocket. A pen, like an ordinary sharpie, with a glowing point.

Is that what she tattooed herself with?

Wishing I'd got her name, I turned on my spirit sight. The witch floated before me, her eyes aglow, her hair wild. "I am ascending… master."

"Where are the other dragonlings?" I asked her. "How many did he set free?"

It wasn't a very efficient way to spread a sickness. So many monsters roamed the countryside that any dragon released outside of a city would be dead in a day and the others wouldn't last much longer. No—he'd wanted my friends and I to take the blame. To make us suffer for snatching Thorn from his grasp.

"No more," she whispered. "No more, but there's no cure. You'll die soon enough, dragon shifter."

A shadow appeared behind her, shaped like a set of gates. *The gates of the afterlife?* I watched, unable to look away, as her form drifted backwards towards the opening gates. A tugging sensation pulled at my limbs, too—

Wait. I wasn't standing but floating, among the dead. *Not again.*

Wheeling on the spot, I halted at the sight of my own body standing inert in the alleyway, visible through the grey haze. I wouldn't have seen it at all had it not been for the glowing light of the pen in my own hand.

Huh? I didn't think physical objects were visible

through the lens of the spirit realm. Just souls, living or otherwise.

A pair of fiery eyes flashed before my vision, and I jerked away.

One blink and I was in my body again, stumbling against the alley wall. Nobody was here except me, and the dead witch. Not to mention the dragonling. Sucking in a lungful of air, I tapped on my spirit sight again, and greyness rose all around me.

I guess I couldn't blame myself for thinking it was a dream world. The endless fog certainly *looked* unreal and dream-like.

"Hey," I called out, seeking the owner of the fiery eyes. "Where are you? I know you're real now. I know I'm not dreaming. Can you tell me your name?"

"Cori!" Zeph's voice shouted. I turned off my spirit sight before I floated out of my body again. "Did you kill her?"

"I did." I turned away, my gut clenching at the sight of the dragonling. "She said—he was the last one. He's—"

"Infected." Zeph swore softly, his arms wrapping around me.

I stiffened and took a step back. "His claws got me. I don't know if it can spread that way, but… don't touch me, please." My voice cracked, and I retched into the alley. *Fuck you, Lorne.*

"Cori," he said, his voice gentle. "We've all been exposed to the virus by now. I think it's random who gets it, otherwise the whole village would have been infected."

I wiped the back of my mouth with my sleeve. "Doesn't mean I want to take any chances."

And she said there was no cure. What if it was true? If so,

I was living on borrowed time.

Astor walked into the alley, eyeing the pen in my hand. "Did you get that from the witch? That's her tattoo pen."

Zeph's gaze went to the pen. "She marked herself with that?"

"Not just herself. The zombies, too." I pointed behind me, unable to make myself turn around. "And the dragonling."

Becks swore, kicking an undead's arm aside in the mouth of the alley. "You had to kill it?"

I dipped my head. "Yeah, but those symbols… I think they were like the ones on the undead. She must have used them to control the zombies. That's how they seem smart enough to avoid salt barriers and find specific locations, like our house."

Astor wiped blood off his hands. His sleeve had torn, exposing the edge of one of his own tattoos.

"What does the walking lab experiment have to say to that?" Zeph said.

"*I'm* a walking lab experiment?" He raised an eyebrow. "And just what connection do you have to the dragonlings, then? You knew they were here. Didn't you?"

"Don't be absurd," Zeph said. "I knew they must be in the city, but I didn't guess that Lorne released them up and down the country."

"Don't you two start. I'd prefer not to spend my last days listening to you argue." I touched my fingertips to my shoulders. Blood slicked the skin under my shirt. "Let's take what's left of these zombies to the necromancers. I'm more inclined to trust them than the mages." Specifically, a certain mind-reader who suspected us already. If she found out I might have contracted the virus, I'd be jailed, and Thorn would be killed or taken away from us.

"You're not going to die, Cori," Zeph said, his voice laced with certainty—and beneath that, a deeper emotion that startled me with its intensity. "Astor, if you let her die without telling us what those damned symbols mean—"

"They wouldn't mean a thing without that tattoo pen," he said. "The power is in the ink as much as the symbols. I've studied enough of them over the last week. The spells are a type of self-directed power... not regular witchcraft, but along the same lines."

"So you do admit it was magic, then," Zeph said.

"If it means that much to you, yes," said Astor. "And it could save Cori's life."

Zeph frowned. "What exactly do you mean?"

"Astor, is there a particular tattoo which makes you think you might be immune to disease?" I asked.

"There is." He rubbed his arm self-consciously. "Not a healing one, but maybe—"

"Maybe it would work on others, if a witch used the pen." I wasn't volunteering anyone to break the law, but Will had already caught the sickness, and I was more than willing to play lab rat if it meant being one step closer to a cure.

We carried the dead witch and a couple of zombies to the necromancers, after obliterating the other corpses—dragonling included. If the witch was right, there were no other infected dragonlings in the city, which left us to take the heat. No doubt that was Lorne's plan.

As usual, Owen waited outside the necromancers' place, and looked vaguely surprised to see us. Especially Astor, who he hadn't met yet. Becks, once again, lurked out of sight in cat form.

"Hey," I said to him. "I have to report a group of zombies. They were controlled by a witch."

Astor threw the bag of body parts in front of him. "We're in a rush," he said. "Tell us what you know."

The necromancer blinked, looking bewildered. "What I know? I'm no witch. And if we don't inform the families—"

"I'm taking a wild guess she doesn't have any family to contact." I indicated the witch, whose body was covered in swirling marks. "She set a pack of undead after us. I figured you had somewhere we can put her body so it won't rise and attack us, right?"

"Yes," Owen said, reluctantly picking up the bag containing the bodies. "We do. You'd better come inside."

Astor gave me a look telling me to stay put, but I ignored him, joining Zeph to help Owen carry the dead into the necromancers' place.

"So, uh, you can get into the spirit realm at any time, can you?" I asked Owen.

"Higher necromancers can," he said. "But we use candles unless we're performing a quick scan."

"Scan?"

"When we wish to know someone's identity, it's common for necromancers to use the spirit realm." He carried the body into a room on the right, which appeared to be a storeroom. "The realm of spirits never lies. We can tell if anyone is living or dead and identify them if they're an individual we've met before by using our spirit sight.

We can also see through faerie glamours in certain circumstances."

Damn. That sounded almost like shifters' abilities to sniff out other shifters, except using a sixth sense nobody other than necromancers possessed.

"Is it possible to tap into the spirit realm while you're sleeping?" I asked.

"Only for the truly advanced," he said. "Higher necromancers can also disconnect from their bodies whether they are awake or otherwise, but every time carries a risk. They use candles to ensure their body remains alive while they're on the other side."

Damn. Ember was right.

"Uh, and what if there was a specific spirit following you around the spirit realm?" I asked. "I mean, what if every time you looked into the spirit realm, you saw the same person? Is it common?"

"Following?" he echoed. "Ghosts are almost always confined to one place. The only exceptions are the strongest."

The fiery-eyed ghost *looked* powerful. She'd even managed to lay her hands on me through the spirit realm and burn me. "And if I wanted to find a particular spirit?"

"Do a summoning, of course," he said. "All one needs is the name. Like any summoning spell, but it doesn't work on the living. Only the dead."

I knew how to do a summoning—but not the fire lady's name. Nor what she was. More than a ghost, surely. She'd touched me, burned my skin through the spirit realm with fire as potent as the Moonbeam.

But was that enough to repel the poison coursing through my veins?

———

When we reached Magic Avenue, we found Kit and the dragonling watching the empty shop, Will sleeping on the sofa in the back, and no sign of Ember. She must still be searching the village for the dragonling.

"Hey." Will lifted his head. "Don't worry, I'm just resting. What's that?"

I handed him the pen. "Recognise this? It's what the witch was using to raise the zombies, by drawing symbols. Some for speed, others for—"

"Stealth." Astor pushed up his sleeve, revealing the marks on his arm. Curling lines covered the skin from his elbow to his shoulder. "And strength. This one protects me from all magical illnesses."

"You *what?*" Will said. "You mean to say you've been immune to the virus all along?"

"I don't know if I am," he said. "But I suspect so."

"Why not tell us so we can do the same to ourselves?" Zeph said, a challenge in his voice. "Didn't want to share, did you?"

"Because it wouldn't have done any good. These aren't just tattoos, and it certainly isn't regular ink," he said. "I told you—without the ink, they're not magical at all."

"You admit it's—" Will began.

"Yes, I admit it's magic," said Astor, lifting his sleeve to his elbow. "Recognise these symbols? Some of them are in your books."

"You've been reading my spell textbooks, too?" Will said. "The assassin's finally admitted we're on the winning team."

"You won't be winning anything if you don't take this

seriously, Will," Becks said. "You're not saying that those spells can be used on your *skin,* are you? Why did nobody think of it before?"

"They did, and it doesn't work." Will pushed up his sleeve and drew a line with the pen, a looping symbol. "Stealth and speed, then. I sure don't *feel* stealthy."

"Try it," Becks said. "Do that creepy thing Astor does, where he opens a door without making any sound."

"It's not creepy," Astor said. "Just because you're all content to blunder around like elephants—"

Becks exclaimed. Will was suddenly on the other side of the room, standing beside the door. "Damn, I nearly had you."

"What the hell?" I looked from him to Astor. "You're not that fast."

"The effects aren't constant," he said. "We were required to redo the tattoos every year otherwise the effects would fade—"

"So you're getting slower?" Will appeared behind him, grinning. "I could get used to this."

"You're supposed to be curing the sickness, Will," Becks admonished. "I'm not watching you drop dead because you were screwing around."

Will tossed the pen into the air and caught it. "I take it back, this is something else. Did the witch say what's in the ink?"

"The witch called it the blood of the gods," I said. "Then again, she also seemed to think *Lorne* was a god, so she probably lost her mind before he got to her."

Astor walked to Will's side, holding out his arm. "That's the symbol. I don't know if it works if you've already contracted the virus, but I assume you also have a symbol for healing?"

Will's mouth parted. "Yes… yes, we do. Rarely used, though, since healing spells are more efficient."

The pen touched his arm as he carefully drew a symbol onto the skin. The ink shimmered, like the symbols the witch had been wearing. "If this *does* work, it's a hell of an impractical way to come up with a cure, if we have to draw symbols to everyone affected in the whole country."

Ah, hell. "Yeah, and the effects might fade over time, like Astor said," I added. "Don't lose that pen."

Will twirled it in his hand. "I'll treasure it. Anyone else need marking?"

"Me," I said. "The dragonling clawed me."

"He what?" said Kit, having entered the living room with almost as much stealth as Will. The dragonling, at his side, flinched away and hid behind Kit.

Oh, damn. He probably smelled the dead dragon on me. "Not him. We were… attacked. By another of them. I'm sorry, Kit, but it was too late."

"The good news is that I'm a superhero." Will zipped to his side so fast that the dragonling panicked, breathing fire. Becks yelped and dove out the way of the flames.

Astor gave me an exasperated look. "Let him ink you, then I'll take that pen off him before he goes too far."

Will turned on him with speculative eyes. "If you have magic inside you, doesn't that make you enough of a witch to use the pen yourself?"

"Don't try it," Astor said quietly.

I stepped into Will's path. "Go on, before Ember gets back. What's taking her so long, anyway?"

"I don't know. I fell asleep." Will reached out with the pen. "All right, I won't draw a cock and balls on you."

"Will, I shudder to think what would happen if you drew erotic art on me with a magical pen. Maybe that's what Jake did to turn the gargoyles against him."

Becks made sick noises, while I held out my arm. The pen tingled, but the sensation wasn't unpleasant.

"It only works if a witch does it," Will said. "That means I have to go to the village if I want to cure them."

"I'll warn the villagers first." I wouldn't admit it, but I was starting to worry about Ember. Not to mention the implications of relying on a pen to keep the disease at bay. If it went missing or was stolen, we'd be back to square one.

"I'll go with you," Zeph said. "Will, be ready with that pen, okay? We'll just be a minute."

I hope so. I was in dire need of a shower to get the traces of the witch's blood off me and my jacket had stuck to my wounded shoulders, but that could wait. I descended the stairs into the basement, sparing a glance for the re-sealed door leading into the tunnels. The mirror's shimmering light made the ink on my arm glow brighter.

Silence waited on the other side. Aside from the dripping from the leaking basement, no sounds came from the house. My heart beat against my chest like a trapped bird, but Azalea's office light was on.

I pushed the door open. "Hey, Azalea, we have the..." I trailed off.

She wasn't alone.

Lorne sat in her office, his huge frame dwarfing the chair, a gun pressed to Ember's back.

14

Nothing had prepared me for the sight of the man himself, sitting in Azalea's house as though he belonged there. Ember's mouth was a thin line, her eyes blazing, but I could see traces of panic in her expression. *If you fire that gun, I'll rip off your head.*

"Cure?" He tilted his head. "Honourable effort, but I'm afraid you're too late."

Damn him. I'd bet he had a dozen of those pens on backup. He'd been one step ahead of us all along.

Azalea sat in the chair beside him. No gun pointed at her, but her pose was slumped as though all the life had been drained from her body.

"That's your best effort?" Zeph said. "Guns and threats, like a cowardly human. You're pathetic."

Lorne rose to his feet like a snake uncoiling, his frame seeming to fill half the room. "I'm not the one running away," he said. "Your sister seems to have run out of words, Coriander. I'd hoped you might be the one I found here, as it's you I'd prefer to speak with."

I cut my eyes to him. "Not until you get out of Azalea's house. If you want to talk to me, you shouldn't need to threaten my sister. I don't play nice with bullies."

Azalea sat frozen, looking as though her worst nightmare had come to life and walked into the room. Ember stood in front of Lorne, the gun pressed to her spine. Despite her obvious fear, she held her head high, her eyes simmering.

"Very well," said Lorne. He stepped around Ember, the gun still trained on her, never leaving his back uncovered. Armed I might be, but one bullet from that gun would kill us in a heartbeat. No cure would undo that.

The instant he stepped over the door's threshold, Azalea hurled a mug at him. The gun flew from his hands, and I snatched it up, pointing it in Lorne's face. "Go on. Get out of this village or I'll shoot you."

His eyes narrowed, and he pulled another gun from his belt. "I think not."

"There are children in this house," Azalea said shakily. "Finish your conflict outside. I want no part in it."

"I'll leave if he does." I rested my finger on the trigger, ignoring the shudder of revulsion in my bones from being so close to the bullets designed to kill dragon shifters with a single shot. Lorne shrugged and backed towards the front door, while Azalea remained still, her own fire extinguished.

I walked out behind Lorne, with Zeph and Ember at my heels.

"Help her," I said over my shoulder. "Get the kids out, if you can. I'll handle him."

Both of them made noises of dissent, but I took no notice. Lorne wouldn't walk away alive this time.

"Don't worry," he said. "I'm not going to take your cure away from them. You're free to try whatever you like, and they're desperate enough to accept anything."

"You're seriously trying to bargain with me now?" I kept my grip on the trigger, and only the identical gun pointed at my own head kept me from putting him out of his misery. "You tried to kill my friends, tried to frame us for spreading the virus—oh yeah, and tried to wipe out the country's entire shifter population. How many of those dragonlings did you set free?"

"I imagine the majority of them will have been caught and killed by now," he said calmly. "You need nothing from me, if you already have the cure."

Yes, but not if you already sowed the seeds in London to make everyone blame us. He'd lit the spark, and it had fanned into a flame without him needing to be there at all.

"Where'd you get it to begin with?" I said, unable to stop thinking of the raving witch's words. Blood of the gods, she'd said. Something so rare that even the mages had never encountered it before. They'd used it on Orion League soldiers. Astor had survived the procedure, but he was human.

"Why do you want to know that?" he asked. "Unless… perhaps, do you not trust that the cure will work as intended? Are you unsure if it will make a bad situation worse instead? If you want me to take over, I'd be more than happy to. I have no intention of overseeing the extinction of my species."

"Leave them alone, Lorne," I snarled. "If you want them to survive and thrive, stop endangering their lives."

"These people once accepted me as their leader," he said. "They will again, given enough pressure. What if I told you I have the resources to end this tragic plague before it wipes out any more of your people? To keep them safe from ever being harmed again?"

"*Our* people," I corrected. "You're a dragon shifter, too."

"I am more than you," he said. "Did you know that we are all descended from gods? The Ancients are a race that predates humanity, and all of us are descended from them."

I coughed a laugh. "Uh… right. Okay. Are you sure you didn't lose your mind in jail? Because it happens to the best of us. I know *I* don't like being caged. Maybe I'd have gone mad, too."

The wind stirred his hair, putting me in mind of the fiery-eyed lady. The ghost, who'd saved me and not him. "Where did you put the Moonbeam?" I asked. "For that matter, what in hell did you do with your cargo of dragon eggs? They didn't all hatch, right?"

"You're too nosy for your own good, Cori," he said. "That youthful righteousness of yours will vanish in time, and I have a few ideas of how I'd like you to be positioned in my new world order… but there's no place for your friends, I'm afraid. The Moonbeam helped you. I would like to know why."

"What's it to you?" I still didn't know why the Moonbeam had revived me, and I couldn't help wondering if Lorne had encountered the fire lady, too. Since he didn't have the spirit sight, I'd guess not. Either way, whatever *new world order* he was planning, I wanted no part in it.

"I don't want to fight you," he said. "Cori, I have no desire to see us driven to extinction. But I *will* find the world that once was ours, and with the gods' assistance, I will remake the Moonbeam into what it should have been."

No, you won't. Because it's mine.

Shit, where had that thought come from? I didn't want to *own* the Moonbeam, I wanted to use it to save my friends.

"Okay," I said, pretending like I was talking to a rational person. "What's wrong with the Moonbeam, and who are these, uh, gods? If you're talking immortals, like the Sidhe, I've got bad news about what they did to the world."

"Not the faeries," said Lorne. "The League's legend had it wrong. They spoke of a prophesied war, but it didn't play out in the way they expected. The gods created the Moonbeam to control all dragon shifters, but it escaped their hands. Now the gods are dead, it falls on us to repair the damage. I have the courage to make those decisions, Cori. Do you?"

I looked into those mad grey eyes. "Lorne, I know you think you're making sense, but you're giving me a headache. I thought the dragons created the Moonbeam."

"It's a lie." His jaw tightened. "The Moonbeam contains the key to unlocking the realm of the gods, where we originated. You have a bond with the Moonbeam, don't you?"

"What realm? What are you talking about?" I shook my hand holding the gun to ease the cramp in my wrist. "If you think I'm bonded with the Moonbeam, you might as well just hand it over to me."

"You didn't believe your parents came from this realm, did you?" he asked.

My grip on the gun stiffened. "What?"

"The realms on the other side of the spirit lines," he said. "They can be reached via rituals, but that type of magic seems to be limited to witches alone. All we can do is summon beings from between the realms, not travel there ourselves."

The images of the ritualistic circle came to mind. He'd been trying to open a way… *where,* exactly? God, he really had lost his mind.

"I killed your witch," I told him.

"One of them," he corrected. "And I don't need a witch to unlock the realm of our birth, not when I have the Moonbeam. All I need is for you to submit to me, Cori."

"Nah, I disagree." My finger rested on the trigger again. "What do you say we finish what we started in London? When I kill you, I'll be taking that Moonbeam back, so I'd suggest you tell me where you hid it."

"You still believe you're in control of this situation, Cori?"

He shifted, all that contained violence exploding outwards in a gust of air that sent me flying back. His own gun fell, crushed beneath his claws. I rolled over, dodging his swipe, and shifted. A roar exploded from my lungs, and I took off after him.

We grappled in mid-air, biting, tearing. A thrill chased down my spine when my teeth drew blood. Claws and teeth collided, our wings carrying us over a large expanse of water. A loch. I sliced his wings with my claws, cutting deeper, forcing him downwards. He roared in agony, dipping lower, closer to the water.

With a crash, Lorne plunged below the surface of the lake. His wings slid from my grip, and he vanished into the depths of the water.

Then his claw shot up, grabbing my foot. I struggled, but he was stronger. My body hit the water with more force than I'd expected, drowning the fire in my lungs. Spluttering, blinded, I sucked in a breath and inhaled a torrent of water.

Darkness crept in with the water, and my senses faded.

———

My sight returned, noise crashing into me from all angles. I coughed, my vision blurry from the water. Ember dragged me onto the bank by the legs. *Human* legs.

"Cori. Cori, speak to me."

"Ugh." I collapsed onto the bank, heaving up water. "Don't tell me Lorne swam off."

"Looks that way." Zeph stood beside me, his mouth tight with concern. "He must have used a spell to make himself able to breathe underwater. That, or he's holding his breath."

"What kind of dragon likes water?" I coughed again, shivering uncontrollably. "At least he broke his gun. Are the shifters okay?"

"Four more died of the sickness since our last visit." Ember crouched beside me as I coughed up more water. "Lorne just—showed up. He's been taunting me all morning, saying he was waiting for you to come. Why did he want you?"

"The Moonbeam." My teeth chattered, and Zeph drew an arm around me. "He's lost his mind. He says he wants me to fix the Moonbeam and make it work for him again."

"I don't think he's coming back," Zeph said. "We

should get you indoors before you catch your death of cold."

"And get the cure to the villagers," said Ember.

Shit. I forgot. Thanks to Lorne. "He'll be back," I said, with certainty.

———

"He was talking complete bullshit," Ember said as we passed through the mirror into the basement of our house. "He just wants to use the Moonbeam to mind-control every shifter again, and he's pissed because it helped you and not him."

"And if there was a reason for that?" I shivered. My hair, still soaking wet, clung to my face and neck. "His theory about using the Moonbeam to open the spirit lines was way too in-depth to be a lie. True or not, he believes it."

Not to mention that's what he'd tried to do with the spirit device, too. Maybe it had been his plan all along. He was certainly egotistical enough to believe he was descended from these gods, but it didn't explain why he'd worked with the Orion League.

"So he thought *you* knew how to use the Moonbeam to open this… other realm?" Zeph said. "Why?"

"Because the Moonbeam brought me back to life," I said. "Uh, he doesn't know that. He just knows that the Moonbeam defended me and acted against him, so he thinks I have mastery over it."

Which I didn't. The Moonbeam had been forged in dragonfire, created by the dragon shifters themselves. These so-called gods had nothing to do with it. Lorne was deluded, plain and simple. Maybe his captivity had stolen his ability to reason, but I couldn't afford to speculate. Curing the sickness had to come first.

"If Will's up to it, we'll distribute the cure." I climbed the stairs ahead of the others. "Take it straight to the mages, if we have enough to go around."

The hallway was quiet. I pushed open the door and found the living room trashed, a mess of ingredients littering the carpet.

"Attempted break-in," Kit said, his face white. "I used my magic to protect us and Thorn hid in the basement, but—"

He gestured at the wreckage of spells strewn around the lab.

"Bastards." My hands clenched. "What about the pen?"

"It's okay," Will said. "What the hell did you do, go for a swim?"

"Kind of." I hunted in the mess for a drying spell before I caught a cold from the lake water. "Lorne was on the other side of the mirror, trying to bait the other dragon shifters. And he's concocting a plan to break the spirit lines again. I pushed him into the lake, but he shifted and swam off."

"He'll be back," Ember said. "We need to evacuate the village. Or send one of us over there to stand guard in case he comes back."

Will swore. "Is Lorne likely to follow you through the mirror?"

"Shit. Maybe." I pushed a soaking wet wad of curls over my shoulder and activated the drying spell. "I wounded him, so he won't be able to fly until he heals. But he'll have another witch to brew him a healing spell, no doubt. There's only one way forward from here."

"What are you saying?" Ember looked at me.

"We need to come clean to the mages," I said. "Tell them everything. The instant we tell them Lorne's there on the other side of the mirror, they'll be obligated to go through and try to take him down. We'll lose the cash bonus, but the other dragon shifters will gain the mages' protection. They need it."

"You sure the mages will want to put their necks on the line?" asked Zeph sceptically.

"Better them than us," I said, looking around at the others. "Besides, it's their job, not ours. They're the ones who want the Moonbeam back and Lorne incarcerated."

"We can't let them into the house," Kit said, eyes wide. "They'll see Thorn. There's no safe place for him to hide."

"Lorne is living in Scotland—we know that now," I continued. "The League originally started up there. Maybe the mages know where his base is. Where's Astor, anyway?"

"Hunting more of those witches," said Becks. "Are you really going to the mages?"

"Either them or the necromancers." I rubbed my eyes wearily. "I still haven't told them about my spirit sight, and I don't have time to get into an argument about whether it's possible for a dragon shifter to be a necromancer. I just want the cure out there. Maybe the mages can find more of those witches and take away their tattoo pens."

"Yeah, I'm not handing this one over," said Will, turning the pen over in his hands. "They'll never give it back before I have the chance to use it on the other dragon shifters. You want to cure them before we bring it out in the open, right?"

"I'll go with you to the village, then," Ember said. "Then you can distribute the cure here and now. Before Lorne gets back. Cori…"

"I'll tell the mages we have the cure and invite them to meet us," I said. "Give it an hour or so, just to make sure you have enough time to mark all the villagers. Kit, take the dragonling into the shelter, in case Lady Clare doesn't listen to me and comes marching back here to nose around again."

There was a strong chance she wouldn't believe me, but I was all out of fucks to give. Far too many people had died already.

I hurried to my room to change out of my damp clothes and clean the blood off my shoulders. The wounds from the dragonling's claws were shallow and had already scabbed over, but the healing mark on my wrist might not last forever. I'd worry about that when Will and Ember returned—for now, it was time to find the mages.

I left my room and found Zeph waiting in the hall. "I'll go with you," he said. "For the record, I don't trust the mages, but Lorne showed his face to us. That suggests he's going to openly strike, and soon."

I was inclined to agree. "If the cure works, at least we've achieved something, but I don't think the mob will calm down that easily. They might if we ask the mages to make a public announcement that we're the ones who brought down the rogue witches and we're not the enemy, but Lady Clare would never go for it."

And even if we defeated Lorne, we might still be driven out of our home and away from London.

Everything depended on us getting the cure out there before Lorne was able to act against us again.

———

The streets lay under a blanket of silence heavier than the rainclouds, the type of silence I hadn't seen since the early days following the invasion. Minus the looting. Even the monsters seemed to be hiding away. While the witch might have claimed all the dragonlings were dead, how many people had they infected beforehand? The shifters were slowly being pushed out of their usual haunts by the threat of disease, and as I'd predicted, unfamiliar new wards adorned the gates in front of the glass-and-chrome building that housed the mages. I'd bet they prevented any outside disease from getting inside. *They don't sell those to the rest of us, do they?*

Lady Clare must have been expecting me. She appeared behind the gates less than a minute after we got there and beckoned me inside. "Come with me, Cori."

Zeph cast a concerned look in my direction, but I gave him a nod of reassurance. I avoided eye contact with the blond Mage Lord, hoping she stayed the hell out of my thoughts.

"Looks like you're having no trouble keeping the sickness away from mage territory," I said, wishing I could sense *her* thoughts.

"A necessary precaution," she said. "The last thing we need is for the supernatural community to lose their leadership at a time like this."

Uh-huh. The mages hadn't owned this part of the city for as long as they liked to pretend. I remembered as clearly as anyone the confusion following the invasion where the mages had swiftly stepped in and taken control of as much territory as they needed to house their own people and then left the rest of us to fend for ourselves.

"We're currently under quarantine," Lady Clare added. "It's looking like we're going to have to extend the spells to cover the areas of the city free from infection before it reaches everyone. I wish it didn't have to be the case, but until we find a cure, we must take action to separate the areas of the city that are affected."

But it's in our house. Lucky she hadn't seen the drag-onling—or Will. Or my injuries, come to that.

"I don't know if you heard, but my friends and I caught one of the witches who was raising the victims of the sickness as undead," I said. "I asked them to contact you."

"If they left a message, I'm afraid it's been a busy week and we haven't had the time to check," she said.

"I'd have thought you'd want to hear about them." How much did she know about the dark magic used to reani-mate the bodies? Agnes had implied even the mages didn't know it existed. Either Lady Clare didn't feel threatened by the idea of unconventional undead, or she was lying to me. "But that's not the reason I came here. I came because I saw Lorne."

That got her attention. "You saw him?"

"I almost killed him," I said. "Unfortunately, he escaped, and I have no idea where he hid the Moonbeam. But he said enough to confirm he's behind the sickness."

She halted outside a closed wooden door. Her office, I remembered from last time I'd been inside the building. "I see," she said. "He didn't have the Moonbeam with him?"

"No." Did she have to be so bloody calm? "I'd have taken it if he had."

"Then I would advise you to make it a priority," she said. "It's recently come to my attention that the Moonbeam is not what we first thought it to be. For one, it's believed to have been the catalyst for the war between the dragon clans. I imagine that is a familiar story to you?"

What the hell?

"The Moonbeam *started* the war? Who told you that?" Lorne himself sure as hell hadn't mentioned it.

"It seems Lorne came across it when he was attempting to take over leadership of the dragons," she said. "He used it to dominate them, and then when he had no further use for it, he handed it over to the Orion League."

I stared, momentarily speechless. How in hell had the mages stumbled across that information? Even the other dragon shifters hadn't told us that level of detail about the start of the war, much less that the Moonbeam had been the cause. Yet now I thought about it, I couldn't believe I hadn't guessed sooner.

"You're forgetting we have some of Lorne's former allies here in our jail," Lady Clare added. "I managed to persuade them to share some information. Lorne needs to be recaptured as soon as possible and the Moonbeam returned to our hands."

I should have remembered some of his allies were still incarcerated. I'd thought they'd all died in the battle.

"Your sister used the Moonbeam," she went on. "Used it to end the battle, they say. How was this possible?"

She's probing me for information at a time like this?

I shook my head. "I don't know. Lorne might, but he's

lost his mind. I don't know where his base is at the moment, so I couldn't follow him." I did my best to keep all thoughts of the dragonling, and the cure, out of my mind. Not that I knew nearly enough about her mind-reading power to be certain of how to resist it. My hands were slick with cold sweat. I'd escaped punishment for now, but she had the power to sentence us to death if she decided it was an adequate punishment for the information I'd withheld. Her revelations, however, had unbalanced me. The Moonbeam that had saved my life had also kick-started the war that had killed my parents?

A chirping noise came from behind the desk, and my heart sank.

"I suppose I might as well show you." Lady Clare stepped aside, indicating a cage sitting behind the desk. Inside crouched a dragonling.

"We caught three," she went on. "I assume you know how many others there are, aside from yours?"

"It's not ours," I said, keeping my voice as steady as I could make it. "Zeph was chasing the Faulkner brothers long before they started trading those eggs inside London. I don't know how many there are."

"Tread carefully, Cori," she said. "And next time you come here, I would prefer it if you brought Lorne and the Moonbeam along with you. Think on it."

The dragonling chirped, and the sound rang in my ears as I backed out of the mages' headquarters, away from Lady Clare's cutting eyes.

15

I all but flew home, my feet carrying me like wings. Zeph easily kept pace with me, but I didn't dare tell him what Lady Clare had told me until we skidded to a halt beside a gleaming ward covering the entrance of Magic Avenue.

"Quarantined," said Zeph.

"Awesome," I said. "Thanks for that one, Lady Clare."

Ducking under the shimmering semi-transparent barrier, I ran all the way home. Becks, pacing outside, shifted into her human form when she spotted us. She looked very tired. "Bad news?"

"The mages… or should I say, Lady Clare." Breathless, I opened the door into the shop. Zeph walked in behind me, Becks padding at her heels.

"What did she do?" Worry lined Zeph's voice. "Cori, you're starting to worry me. Is she coming here?"

I took in a deep breath, turned to face him. "She caught the other dragonlings and had them in cages in her office. She also spouted all this crap about the Moonbeam and how Lorne used it to win the war. She's been talking to his allies in the jail."

"I forgot any of them survived." Becks, who'd shifted to human form, leaned against the unoccupied counter. "You didn't ask her about Lorne's base up in Scotland?"

I slapped my forehead. "I forgot. Astor will know, though. Wherever he is."

"Here." Astor walked into the shop from the living room. "Ember and Will are taking a long time."

"They haven't been that long," Zeph cut in. "Stop being so twitchy. Your sister's fine, Cori. Astor, if you know where Lorne's base is, now would be a fine time to tell us."

"There's another facility," Astor said. "Somewhere in the Highlands, or so they told us. I've never been, but I suspect it's within flying distance of the village."

"You're telling us this now?" I said.

"Until recently, I thought Lorne was in London," he said evenly. "Now I know he's in Scotland, he must be at that facility. It was the League's first base before they moved to England."

"I should have flown after him," I said. "I didn't know he was that close. Now the mages know the dragonlings are spreading the sickness, we have to find him before they arrest us all. Lady Clare insinuated that unless I walk in there with Lorne and the Moonbeam, our own dragonling will be the next one to end up in a cage."

"Becks," said Zeph, his tone worried. "What's that mark on your neck?"

"Oh, shit." Becks touched her neck, opening her collar. "Dammit. Should have asked Will to mark me before he left."

"Where's Kit?" I asked, alarm flickering inside me. "And Thorn?"

"Still in the shelter," said Astor, sounding disinterested. "Kit went there as soon as you left."

"I'll go and update him, then." Entering the living room, I made for the door connecting the two houses, which we'd rarely used since the shelter had closed down. Will wouldn't manage to sell it at this rate, considering the whole street was quarantined as a high-risk zone.

I pushed the door inwards, and a quiet whining noise came from further down the hallway. Heading that way, I tapped on the wooden door which had once led to the room in which the Faulkner brothers had stayed, disguised as gargoyle shifters.

Inside the room, Kit sat hunched in the corner with the dragonling curled around him. The half-faerie lifted his head when I walked in. "Is Will okay?"

"Will? Of course. He's still helping the villagers with Ember." I closed to the door behind me. "We know where Lorne is hiding. An old League facility up in the High-lands. He must have been there the whole time, waiting for the sickness to spread."

Which begged the question of why he hadn't tried to recruit the villagers sooner. Sending in dragonlings to terrorise them from a distance ran counter to his supposed plan to reclaim his dominance. Unless he was focusing all his attention on reclaiming the Moonbeam's power and using it to open the spirit lines, that is.

Kit's head drooped. "The cure isn't permanent. What if Will dies because of me?"

"He won't—"

"Even if he doesn't, I wrecked everything." He drew his

knees up to his chest. The dragonling wrapped a wing around him, making chittering noises. "I love him, and he —I ruined everything."

"Does he know that?" I avoided the dragonling's eyes, too shaken by what I'd witnessed at the mages' place. "I mean, did you actually tell him?"

"No. We've been busy lately—"

"Tell him," I said. "Otherwise, please don't come to me for romantic advice. I'm carrying the sickness, too." *And so is Becks.* Worse, the cure wasn't permanent, which meant even if the mages agreed to distribute it, people would still die.

I made my way back into the house, but Ember and Will still hadn't returned. Zeph had gone out, while Becks was asleep. I didn't particularly want to stay indoors with a bad-tempered assassin, and besides, I had an inkling I knew where Zeph had disappeared to.

I grabbed a couple of snack bars from our depleted rations and went outside. Sure enough, I spotted Zeph sitting on the roof of the shelter. Using my claws, I climbed up to join him.

"Want to spar?" he asked.

"No." I flopped down and threw him one of the cereal bars. "Needed some air." I chewed half-heartedly on the cereal bar. It was probably out of date by now, but we had so little food left that it tasted heavenly.

"Hmm." Zeph took a bite of his own cereal bar. His face was drawn with tiredness, his usually bright eyes dark and contemplative.

How could it have only been a day or two ago that we'd flown across the Highlands, filled with hope? Now we were worn, beaten down, and the mages had us in a vice grip. The quarantine ward shimmered in the distance, and I wondered idly if it was immune to dragonfire.

I crumpled the wrapper in my hand. "You know there's no permanent cure, right? There's only one way to fix this."

Zeph looked up. "The Moonbeam?"

"Yes." I dangled my legs over the roof's edge. "I was in a coma the first time the League captured me. They used this sleeping potion that could only be reversed by touching the Moonbeam. Lorne wants to lure us in, and what better way than to make it the only permanent cure?"

He chewed on the rest of his cereal bar. "You want to walk into his trap?"

"He's injured. Now's probably our best shot." Despite my exhaustion, my mind was wide awake. "The street is quarantined. By tomorrow, word will spread. Handing Lorne in, dead or alive, is the only way to keep everyone safe."

"I wish I'd torn out his throat." He angled his legs so they were inches from mine, leaning in close enough that I could hear his steady breathing. "I thought he'd drowned you."

"What's a bit of water to a dragon shifter?" I inhaled his scent, lifting my head to meet his. Our lips intertwined, and a growl slipped between his teeth. I liked it. A lot.

He leaned over, dipping his head to my ear. "I don't want you to think I'm doing this because you're the only female dragon shifter I know."

"Apart from my sister." I shivered as his breath tickled

my cheek. "Who's dating an assassin, so I'm not the only option. If you wanted to stay friends, I'm good with that. No pressure from me."

What I felt for him was friendship, yes, but something else, too. Something other than the kinship a dragon shifter felt towards another of our own kind.

His hand cupped my chin. I breathed in the scent of him, my lips trailing over his. He made a low, pleased noise deep in his throat. "I want this, Cori. If you want it, too."

"I do want it," I breathed, running my hands over his muscled arms. Heat sparked in my middle, turning on all my instincts.

Something hit the roof a few metres away. Something that smelled of burning. Fire.

I jerked away from Zeph, in time to see a gargoyle fly past, above the flames igniting on the house's roof.

Cursing, I jumped into the air, shifting to dragon form. The gargoyle screeched and turned around, but not fast enough to avoid my claws. With one wrench, I tore off his head. His corpse thumped down onto the shelter roof—which was also ablaze. *Kit. No.*

I landed on the ground in front of the shelter door, which flew open. The dragonling ran out, carrying Kit on his back. With a relieved sigh, I turned human, opened the door to the house and ran into the shop.

"Ah, shit, the mirror." The mirror was fireproof, but Will and Ember were on the other side and wouldn't know anything was wrong.

I ran into the hall, where I found Astor halfway into the basement. "I'll warn Ember."

"Nice try," I said. "You're not fireproof, I am. Go with the others and make sure they get out."

Zeph stood close behind me. "What if Lorne's back?"

"I'll handle it, but Zeph, you're the only one who can safely stay inside the house until the smoke's cleared. Look in there and see if you can find a spell to put out the fire."

Not waiting for an answer, I ran down into the basement and through the mirror.

The problem was, the room on the other side wasn't Azalea's basement, but an unfamiliar white-walled room I'd never seen before.

Ah, hell.

Footsteps rang out, and Lorne walked in. He wore a long coat, like a lab coat. For a rare moment, I wondered if I was dreaming. Except my dreams usually involved grey smoke and Death, not white-walled labs and my mortal enemy playing Mad Scientist.

"You stole the mirror," I said.

"I did," he confirmed. "Don't worry, your friends are fine. I left them behind in the village."

"A likely story." Crap. Even if it was true, Ember and Will were stuck in the village with no way back to London.

More to the point, this must be the old Orion League facility Astor had mentioned. The narrow walls and lack of windows brought back unpleasant feelings, of closed doors and suffocating silence. Seeing Lorne in this environment was as incongruous as seeing a League member riding a dragon.

Damn. How do I warn the others not to follow me?

"Believe it or not, I don't want or need to kill your friends, Cori," Lorne said. "It's you I wanted."

I gave a disbelieving laugh. "I'm flattered. You went to all this trouble for me? Then what was the deal with the plague and the zombies? No offence, Lorne, but you could have done better. We've already found the cure—"

"You know there's no permanent cure," he interrupted. "Except for one."

The Moonbeam. Neither of us spoke the word, but I saw it in his grey eyes as surely as he would have seen it in mine. "You stole the idea from what the League did to put me in a coma. I'm guessing the virus was created the same way?"

His eyes were calm, without so much as a hint of a flame. "You're lucky that the League didn't use it on you. They only put you into a coma, not condemned you to an agonising death."

He's mad. He also wasn't carrying the Moonbeam, so it must be elsewhere in the facility, but the room had only one door. Aside from the mirror, but if I fled, Lorne would follow me in an instant. He had me cornered and he knew it.

I pretended to relax, my shoulders drooping. "Lorne, we're old friends now. Maybe we can come to an understanding."

Zeph had let himself be taken hostage when he'd gone after the dragon egg, and I should be able to do the same. Unlike him, I wasn't dealing with intelligent mobsters, but a wildly unstable dragon shifter who'd spent years languishing in jail and losing every last shred of sanity he possessed. He was proud and paranoid, a textbook definition of the type of dragon shifter who ran themselves into extinction through sheer idiocy.

Not to mention, the Moonbeam had saved me twice already. It wasn't out of the realm of possibility that it'd help me escape Lorne's clutches this time, too.

Lady Clare's words came back. Lorne himself had used the Moonbeam to start the war. No wonder he was so ticked off that it seemed to work only for me now.

"You want to talk?" he said. "I'll take you to your new home first."

He grabbed my arm, and pain spasmed through me. *Crap. That anti-dragon shifter shield again...*

I wrenched my arm free, but darkness descended and pulled me under.

16

The fiery-eyed lady watched me through the fog of the spirit realm.

"You again," I said, my voice sounding distant. "Can you please help me find the Moonbeam and defeat Lorne?"

"The Moonbeam," she said. "The fire that runs in both of our veins comes from the Moonbeam. Lorne might possess it, but the fire is ours alone."

"Please," I said. "Tell me who you are."

She spoke, but consciousness dragged me back into the waking world. I sucked in a breath, a familiar panic rising in my chest at the sight of a barred door opposite the bed I lay on.

I'm locked in an Orion League cell. Small square room. White walls, floor and ceiling. Barred door in the front. No windows. Stifling coldness pressed against me from all sides. He'd removed my clothes and dressed me in a plain grey uniform. The phantom feeling of his hands on my skin made me gag. I swallowed hard, pushed off the narrow bed and pressed my hands to the walls as though to shift my hands and break through. As tempting as the idea might be, Lorne would have dragon-proofed the room.

Besides, I'd got myself locked in here on purpose. Once I worked out where he'd put the Moonbeam, I'd be able to get my hands on it and escape.

I squinted through the bars on the door and saw an empty corridor painted in the same muted colours as the room. God, those League people were boring as shit. I was surprised Lorne could stand living in such a cramped, lightless place. Then again, he'd been busy flying around distributing those infected dragonlings. The corridors carried the silence of a place long abandoned. Except—

A faint humming sounded beneath the silence, vibrating in my bones.

The Moonbeam.

My body ached with the echo of fire, and I wanted to hold it, so badly it was a physical pain in my chest. The burn on my arm gave a sharp jolt, and I bit my lip to avoid gasping aloud.

"Hey," I whispered. "Fire lady, I could use some company in here."

No reply. The fiery-eyed ghost probably didn't like cages, either. I was so sure she must be a dragon shifter. She'd burned me, though—why? To prove she was real, maybe. I shouldn't think of her as an ally, but maybe I wasn't the only person who'd been brought back from death by the Moonbeam.

Is that my fate after I die? To turn into a ghost like her?

I paced the room, trying to shake off the unease stirred up by the thought that I'd willingly turned myself in a lab rat. I rocked back on my heels, practised a half shift, then a partway one. I gave the cage bars an experimental tap and winced at the sharp spasm of pain. Judging by my restless energy, I'd been asleep for hours. Lorne better not have lied when he said he hadn't harmed the others.

Footsteps sounded. *There he is.*

I stepped back from the bars, waiting for him to come into view. Lorne's sharp footsteps replaced the silence, echoing down the corridor until every wall seemed to ring with the noise. Then he walked up to the door, halting in front of the bars.

I gave him a little wave. "I could use another air hole or two. It's stuffy in here."

Lorne's expression betrayed no emotion aside from minor annoyance. "Do you always approach death so flippantly?"

"Nope," I said. "I just figured now's a good place to start."

"The Moonbeam likes you," he mused. "Why is that, I wonder? Your parents were nothing special. Unlike my lineage, which hails from one of the Ancients, you can barely claim a connection to the dragons at all. You lived with humans and have forgotten who you are."

My entire body went taut, claws pushing at my fingertips, but I kept my voice steady. "Look, you know how boring captivity is," I said. "I'm guessing that's why you've decided to entertain yourself by making up stories about being descended from gods. Because you have no kingdom to rule over and you're left with nothing but a shitty old bunch of labs used to torture people like you."

A spark of anger flared in his grey eyes. *Aha, I knew he*

didn't have perfect control over his emotions. "Taunting me does you no favours."

"You don't look like you're getting much enjoyment out of holding me captive, either," I said. "If I were you, I'd be dancing in the corridors. Then again, I've never had the intense desire to capture and cage my enemy either. I wouldn't have the patience for it, to be honest."

A muscle ticked in his jaw. "Perhaps I should have brought your friends with me after all."

"I've gotta say, I'm disappointed you didn't. I'd like to have someone to talk to who isn't a deluded megalomaniac."

His face twitched again. He wasn't like an Orion League soldier, trained to hide all emotion. He was a dragon shifter, and his longing to tear off my head persisted despite his attempt to school his expression into blankness. "The Moonbeam… resonates with you. Like nobody else. I want to know why, and I think you can give me the answers."

"I can't give you much from in here."

Go on. Unlock the cage door.

He held up a pair of handcuffs. "These won't hurt you. Come with me and show me how to use the Moonbeam."

The door opened. His wide shoulders filled the frame, blocking the way. He wasn't carrying the Moonbeam. I forced my body to relax. "All right."

I extended my hands to let him put the cuffs on, grimacing at the clink of metal. *It's for Ember, and for the dragon shifters. And the Moonbeam.*

"Walk behind me," he said. "There's nowhere to run. I know the only way out."

Uh-huh. I walked behind him down the blank corridor,

and I felt the pulse of the Moonbeam's presence under my skin. Anticipation hummed in my blood, the desire almost swamping the knowledge of my true purpose. The closer I got to the Moonbeam, the harder it got to recall what I was here for.

Lorne led me into another room, this one longer and filled with lab equipment. The Moonbeam sat in a glass cage, gleaming brightly. A smile tugged at my mouth. He couldn't use it to control me. He'd failed at that once already.

He unlocked the cabinet and removed the fist-sized stone. Light flickered over the surface, showing words I'd never been able to read. The symbols slid through my mind like water. "Ignessa," I muttered.

Lorne looked sharply at me. "What did you say?"

"Nothing." I twitched my cuffed hands. "Are you going to let me take these off so I can touch it?"

He gave me an appraising look, hunger stark in his expression. "I want you to understand, first, what it is that I'm asking you to do. You're going to help me unlock the way into the realm of our birth."

This again? "I thought you wanted to use it to mind-control all the shifters in London."

"I have a worthier cause in mind," he said. "If anything can help me get back to our former home, it's the Moonbeam."

Grey smoke swirled throughout the room, and I stifled a gasp. The fiery-eyed ghost floated behind him, inches from the Moonbeam. And her hungry expression matched his own.

Help me, I thought at her. *Burn him, like you did me.*

She caught my gaze. In her eyes I saw the reflection of the Moonbeam's light, brighter than anything on earth.

Is it true? I asked the fire lady silently. *Is it really not from earth at all?*

Pain seared my wrists, then a clicking sounded as the cuffs broke. At the same time, the Moonbeam's light grew piercingly bright. Lorne swore.

I launched myself at him, sending him crashing back into the glass case. A shattering noise sounded, and his grip on the Moonbeam broke. I grabbed it, tucked it under my arm, and ran like hell.

"Who are you?" I gasped at the ghost, hurtling from the room and into the corridor.

"An ally." She floated, just ahead of me, as I sprinted. "This way."

"Going to tell me your name now?" I careened around a corner after her, a stitch growing in my chest and my limbs protesting from the sudden exertion after being still for so long.

"Less talking, more running," she said.

It's all right for some. My legs burned, but I pushed harder, turning down a fork in the corridor. Ahead lay the room with the mirror. "I can't go through there. He'll just follow if I do. My friends are still stranded in the village— I need to fly there and warn them."

She made an impatient snarling noise. "Fine, grab the mirror, but make it quick."

Definitely a dragon shifter. The mirror was awkward as hell to carry as a human, given its size, but I held it in front of me like a shield, shifting my hands to claws to get a better grip. The Moonbeam, at least, was small enough to fit into my pocket. Backing out of the room holding the mirror, I followed the ghost's directions.

"That way." She pointed ahead, to another turn in the corridor, just as Lorne rounded the corner behind me.

I flat-out sprinted, hearing him gain on me with each step. As he caught up, I shifted my feet to claws, kicking him in the face. Blood spurted and I broke free of his grip, running—running—

And then I was through the doors, completing the shift and launching myself into the sky. "Bye, Lorne." I shouted over my shoulder. Grinning, I spread my wings wide, the mirror clutched tightly in my claws.

Lorne roared—not a human sound. Ah, shit. I beat my wings faster, risking a glance over my shoulder. His huge blue scaled form rose into the air, and I flew higher, into the clouds. I was smaller than he was, maybe faster, but the mirror encumbered me. If I went to the village, he'd massacre them. I needed to draw him away.

I pushed my wings to their limits, soaring over the rolling hills and dark forests until I was on a level with the highest peaks of the mountains. My breath came short. I couldn't stay this high for long. Lorne's dark shadow passed below, and I descended over a dark patch of forest.

Once I was close enough to the ground, I shifted, hiding among the thick trees. Ugly sounds of something big and snarling told me I wouldn't be able to stay hidden for long. Fae lurked in the woods, eager to feed on anyone foolish enough to trespass. As a dragon, though? Nothing would dare try to eat me.

"Stay here," said the fiery-eyed ghost. She floated behind me, a mass of thick trees visible through her transparent body.

"Who even are you?" I asked. "You're a ghost, yet you followed me across two countries and broke a pair of magical handcuffs without even touching them."

"I'm not a ghost, Coriander."

"Then what—?" I broke off, hearing Lorne lumbering through the woods behind me. Several angry roars told me that he'd run into whatever monster made its home in here.

Not a ghost indeed. What else could she possibly be?

I ran through the trees until I found a place safe to shift and then took flight once more above the mountains, heading north. At least, I thought it was north. My lungs burned with cold, and I dipped lower. If I stayed up in the air for too long, I'd either pass out in mid-air or I wouldn't have the strength to fly back to the village.

Mountains became hills, the countryside disappearing below me. A shimmering current of energy caught my eye. *The Ley Line.* Of course it must carry on through Scotland. I didn't have the faintest clue where it ended up in either direction, but perhaps it would hide me. Encouraged, I flew that way.

Without warning, the currents of energy caught my wings, carrying me along. *Whoa. What the—?*

The ground slipped past, too fast to take in. Hills became jagged coastline, and all around, white fog began to close in. Ghosts appeared on all sides, following the currents of the Ley Line.

Hands grabbed, trying to pry the mirror away from me but passing straight through it.

"Let go!" I yelled at the ghosts. "Hey, fire spirit, help me!"

Death whispered over my skin, calling to my spirit. The ghost wasn't going to save me this time.

I did the only thing I could think of—I shifted.

The instant my wings vanished, I free-fell. An instant later, I turned into a dragon again, but a hill loomed out of nowhere, coming towards me with blinding speed.

This is gonna hurt.

I slammed down onto the hillside, and my tail swung and knocked three people over. The mirror hit the earth, and I shifted to human form, struggling to catch my breath.

The Ley Line's vibrant currents ran through the air above my head, but the ghosts had vanished, to be replaced with several bewildered-looking faeries standing on the hill's peak. It looked like I'd crash-landed into the middle of a faerie gathering.

"Sorry for crashing the party." I gasped, sucking in air. "As you can see, my costume is malfunctioning."

The faeries stared at me. They'd seen me turn from a dragon into a human in the most public manner possible. At least the mirror was still in one piece. That was dragonfire-created glass for you.

"I'm very sorry," I said to the faeries. "A giant dragon is chasing me, so I had to make an emergency landing."

The faeries continued to stare, apparently lost for words. A couple of them were armed, but dragons falling out of the sky were probably a rarity even for the half-Sidhe to witness.

Picking up the mirror, I crossed my fingers and toes that it'd stop glowing so damn bright so Lorne wouldn't see it from above. The faeries wouldn't know what it was for, but I wouldn't be able to leave it unattended without someone trying to steal it—or worse, walking through it into our house in London.

Holding the mirror, I walked down the hill, frowning at the city below. That definitely wasn't the Highlands. *Where am I?*

"Cori!" yelled a voice. "Get down here and stop being so conspicuous."

What in the world was Agnes doing here?

17

"You don't do things by halves, Cori, do you?" Agnes shook her head at me. "You flew all the way here with that thing?"

'All the way here' meant Edinburgh. The Ley Line had carried me along to the nearest key point—on top of Arthur's Seat. Hence the faerie party. If I hadn't flown halfway across the country on the orders of a ghost carrying two rare artefacts, I'd swear she was taking the piss out of me.

I walked down the path alongside Agnes, awkwardly carrying the mirror. "I didn't have much choice. How'd you know it was me?"

"I looked up at the hills and saw a dragon," said Agnes. "Since there are only two red dragons I've met, I knew it was either you or Ember. Why in the name of the gods did you decide to fly through the Ley Line?"

"Got lost," I said. "Long story. How'd you get here, anyway? I thought you lived up in the Highlands."

"I frequently travel here for business," she said. "And it

looks like I picked the right time. I guess you're in trouble."

"You're telling me," I said. "So I let Lorne kidnap me—"

She gave me a sharp look. "That's why he's flying around looking for you. I spotted him in the air first, and I came here to warn my allies."

"He doesn't know I'm here." Mostly because I hadn't intended to. What was the Ley Line playing at? Unless—it wasn't the Ley Line. The Moonbeam glowed inside my pocket, and when I put my hand on it, Agnes's eyes widened.

Then she muttered a curse. "You'd better come with me. And for god's sake don't get that thing out in public."

Walking around Edinburgh's streets with the mirror made me feel exposed, but there was no sign of Lorne in the sky. As we walked, I did my best to explain the situation to Agnes. I'd have tried to take in the winding cobbled streets and ancient stone buildings and memorise the way back, but it was a little difficult to ignore the semi-visible currents of the Ley Line going right through the city, and I was too busy focusing on not dropping the mirror on my toes. The damned thing almost blocked my view, meaning I had to carry it sideways.

Agnes reached a narrow stone house and opened the gate. "This place is a safe house. You can stay here until Lorne is gone."

"I have to kill him." I dropped my voice, following her into the hall. "I should have killed him there and then, but I need to get the Moonbeam to my friends first—and he's left two of them stranded in the village, including my sister."

Agnes gave another curse, pushing open a door into a

small living room. It contained little in the way of furniture, just a couple of musty armchairs. I sank into one with relief, still trembling from my impromptu landing.

"Why do your friends need the Moonbeam?" she asked.

"Because it's the only cure for the sickness." I let out a ragged breath. "Believe me, I'd rather not bring it out into the open, but I've already been exposed to the sickness and so have two of my friends. Our entire street is quarantined, and we're set to take the blame. I have to kill Lorne and drag his corpse back to London if I want to clear our names with the Mage Lords."

Agnes tossed her long braid of silvery hair over her shoulder, looking wearier than the last time I'd seen her. "You're been exposed to the virus?"

"I have. We tried a temporary cure, but I'm told this is the only true cure." I took the Moonbeam out of my pocket, admiring the gleam on its shimmering white surface. The glow enveloped me, and I held it still to avoid being sucked into the portal.

"Is that the virus?" Agnes indicated my neck. With difficulty, I twisted my head to look down. Sure enough, a smattering of rash-like marks disappeared under my shirt.

"I guess it is." My grip on the Moonbeam tightened. "Come on—cure me."

The glow brightened. Agnes sucked in a sharp breath. "The marks are vanishing."

So they were. The light shone over me, and a rush of invigorating energy poured through my veins.

Agnes frowned. "I should have guessed that Lorne would have ensured the Moonbeam was the only cure for the virus, but why did he let you get your hands on it to begin with? Did he think you could force it to serve him?"

"You've got it," I said. "He tried to use it to control me and it backfired and helped me instead. He's driving himself Out of his mind trying to figure out why."

"There are a few things you should know about Lorne," she said. "And the Moonbeam, come to that."

"Was Lady Clare right?" I asked, unable to keep the question in. "She... she seemed to think he used it to kill the other dragon shifters in the war. Including my parents."

Agnes looked at the Moonbeam's glowing light, a meditative expression on her face. "I'm sorry, Cori, but it's true. The Moonbeam came into existence... or at least, it was first heard of at the time of the dragon shifters' war. Lorne did indeed use it to ensure his victory."

My heart sank. "So it really was used to control the dragons against their will? I thought... I thought we created it. I thought it was on our side."

Ember would be devastated. She'd always thought the Moonbeam was forged by and for the dragons. I'd believed it, too. After all, she'd begged it for a miracle, to return me to life, and it had done exactly that.

"It was," she said. "I don't know how this Lady Clare found out, but it's true."

"She asked Lorne's former allies." I dropped my gaze. "You're... you're part mage, aren't you? How did you and your sister come to be involved with the dragon shifters?"

"I am," she confirmed. "I'm related to the mages who currently run Aberdeen's mage guild, but I fell out with them a long time ago. I'm closer to my witch side. There's a reason I stopped using my power... Lorne asked me to wipe the memories of a rival. He became quite... fixated on it. And then he asked me to erase his *own* memories."

"He—what?" I blinked, dumbfounded. "Why would he do that?"

"To forget the past," she said. "Lorne wanted to create his own history, a past of glory and descent from the noblest of dragon shifter clans. It's been sixteen years since that war, Cori. I'm assuming you have little memory of it. Lorne... he wanted to forge his own history, become someone else. I refused. My mind-erasing powers brought me nothing but grief and trouble. Magic can be a wonderful gift, but everything has its price." Her gaze flicked to the Moonbeam. "My family has always been involved in supernatural matters, and Lorne's conquest wasn't as long ago as he'd like to pretend. The dragon shifters didn't always live—"

"In this realm," I said. "Right? He... he said he wanted to unlock the way to another realm."

"He did?" She shook her head. "The arrogant fool. There *are* other realms on the other side of the spirit lines, like the one ruined by the war that devastated the dragon clans. If Lorne expects to find a kingdom to rule over, he'll be sorely disappointed. The dragons left that world for a reason."

Lorne was telling the truth? "They left that world and came here..."

"From what I gather, they once travelled from one world to the other at will, using those mirrors," she said. "Lorne is right in that his clan dates back to a time before humans, but he didn't create the mirrors or the Moonbeam. That stone... it contains magic I've never seen before. Magic that is known to have belonged only to the Sidhe and their gods."

The armchair tilted beneath me. "The... gods? Lorne wasn't lying about that either? He said we—all of us dragon shifters—were descended from gods. And that he's superior for that reason. I thought he was talking complete bullshit."

"If he claimed himself a god? He's wrong," she said. "That said... there *was* a race of beings who called themselves gods and were worshipped as such. Many could change forms into animals, like dragons. They had weapons with astonishing powers, and... and it is my belief that the Moonbeam is one of those weapons."

Her words punctured me in the chest. "It can't be. The Moonbeam is the dragon shifters'. We created it."

Agnes leaned forwards, her eye on the glowing stone in my hands. "What language is that? On the edge?"

I turned the Moonbeam over, so it caught the light, and text flickered across the surface. "I don't know, but I can read it."

The light reflected in her eyes. "You can? Have you always been able to?"

"Yes—and Ember, too." I frowned in confusion. "I know it's not English. I thought it was some kind of dragon shifter language—"

"It isn't," Agnes said. "It's a text used by the fae—and by their gods. By the Ancients, beings that lived long before humans *or* dragon shifters walked the earth."

The gods.

The Ancients.

Lorne was telling the truth?

The Moonbeam had saved my life, had restored breath

to my lungs. Maybe it had been created as a weapon once, but then again, so had we. I couldn't let the truth distract me from my mission. And yet… did the lady with the fiery eyes know? Why was she fixated on the Moonbeam—and on me?

"Don't dwell on it, Cori," Agnes said. "The Moonbeam has spawned countless stories among shifters, rumours and myths. Lorne used to claim a prophecy told him to claim it and use it to control all other dragon shifters."

"That's bullshit, too."

"I agree," she said. "However, the idea of controlling the future is an appealing one to humans as well as dragon shifters. Look at the League. Their whole operation was based on the assumption that there would be a war between supernaturals and humans. In the end, there was, and it didn't turn out the way they expected."

No kidding. But I could hardly believe Lorne's deluded ravings were rooted in truth.

And where did that leave *my* connection with the Moonbeam?

"I'd suggest you leave the Moonbeam with me," she said. "And use the portal to get back to the mirror, to your friends."

I shook my head. "I have to use it to cure the other shifters. And I need to take the mirror back to the village, otherwise Will and Ember will be stuck there. I'm not sure the portal still works, besides." There'd be time enough to test it later, but I'd been unconscious for hours in the lab. Ember would be worried sick.

"In that case, be very careful with it," she said. "If you let that out of your hands, Cori… one way or another, I fear for what Lorne will do to this world."

The genuine worry in her voice chilled me to the bone. I wished I could leave it somewhere until Lorne was dead, but I needed to save the others first, and deal with Lorne only when the virus was banished from London.

I put the Moonbeam into my pocket, but the light never left my hands, and its heat vibrated through me like wildfire.

———

The flight back took longer, or maybe it was that I wasn't fleeing for my life this time. I flew away from the Ley Line to avoid being caught in its currents again, but the journey dragged, and so did my flight pattern. My entire body ached, my head pounded, and Agnes's words mingled with Lorne's in my mind until I no longer knew what to think about the Moonbeam.

By the time I found my way back to the dragon shifters' village, night was falling, and my legs were trembling with exhaustion. My wings folded as I laid the mirror carefully onto the ground, praying that Lorne hadn't returned to look for me here.

My heart dropped as a dragon approached. Another *red* dragon. Ember shifted to human and ran to my side.

I staggered along the path. "Hey, Ember."

Ember hugged me tightly. "Cori."

"I'm okay." I hugged her back, wrapping my arms around her and squeezing hard. "I'm so glad you're okay."

"I thought you were dead." Her hands felt the round shape in my pocket. "You got the Moonbeam?"

"Yeah, I got it," I whispered. "Is Azalea here?"

"She is, but—dammit, Cori, where *were* you?" She

rested her head against my shoulder, and I felt dampness soak my shoulder.

Tears burned my own eyes. "I'm sorry, Ember. I came to get you through the mirror and found myself in Lorne's hideout. So I stole the Moonbeam and ran away, but I had to fly around for ages to get him off my trail. Good news, though—the Moonbeam does work as a cure. It worked on me."

Ember let out a stifled sob. "You're brilliant."

I had to break it to her, and to Zeph, that the Moonbeam should be returned to Agnes once we were done curing the others, but that could wait. "We'll help the villagers first. I don't know if I can use it on more than one person at once, but I think they all have to touch it for the cure to have any effect."

I made for Azalea's house first. Ember walked beside me. "Will's back there. Azalea isn't happy, but nobody stepped in to fight off Lorne when he marched in there and took the mirror. He threatened to take her son instead, and well—"

The door flew open and Azalea appeared. "You brought it back, Cori. Thank you."

"More than that." I held up the Moonbeam. "I can help your son. Is he—"

"He's dying," she murmured. "Please—save him."

She didn't need to tell me twice. I ran for the stairs, pulling the Moonbeam out of my pocket. The smell of sickness choked me, but the Moonbeam's light shone over the room and the limp figure in the bed. *Come on... heal him.*

The boy twitched. Then the rash began to disappear from his face, so fast that I nearly dropped the Moonbeam in shock. His harsh breathing steadied, his hands twitching in sleep.

Azalea put her hand on my shoulder, making me jump. "Is it working?"

"It is." I swallowed the lump in my throat. "He'll be fine, but I have to go and cure the others."

Azalea ran to her son's side, allowing me to retreat downstairs. There, I found Will sitting in the hallway. "Go to the others first," he said. "I'm fine. I mean, I've had angry dragons yelling at me all day, but considering—"

"I'll be back in a bit." I was still worn out, but the Moonbeam's resonant humming bolstered me, filling me with renewed hope.

One by one, I moved between the houses, curing anyone still suffering, offering condolences for those who hadn't made it. Every smiling face, every recovering dragon shifter renewed that hope, even alongside the grief of those whose loved ones couldn't be saved. By the time I got back to Azalea's, my legs trembling and my heart full, I was on the brink of tears.

"Will already went through the mirror," Ember said, waiting for me in the hall. "We should leave—"

"Stop." Azalea walked down the stairs to stand across from us. "We need the Moonbeam."

"We have to take it to London," I said. "To save the others."

She didn't move. "It belongs to the dragon shifters. The mages will take it from you."

"I know," I said, "but the sickness has spread throughout London, and it's the only cure."

Sparks flared in her eyes. "You lied. You want it for yourself."

"I used it to cure your son." I stepped back as she reached out for it. "Let me go."

The Moonbeam glowed, once, and a spasm of disconnected rage went through me. What was the matter with me? I'd heard every word Agnes said against it, and I believed her. Azalea was worn down by grief and suffering and didn't know the Moonbeam's unhappy history. I wasn't about to enlighten her during what was supposed to be a time of celebration.

"I'm sorry, but dozens of people are dying," Ember said. "We'll discuss what to do with the Moonbeam when we've cured all the victims."

A growl rose in her throat. "Give it to me."

A shadow fell, then a flash indicated a witch spell. Azalea crumpled, unconscious, and Zeph walked up the stairs from the basement. "Don't worry, it was only a knockout spell."

My gut tightened. "I'm sorry. Gods, what am I going to tell the children?"

"She'll wake up in a bit. She'll be fine." His gaze softened as he looked at me. "Come on, we should go."

"Nice to see you, too." I pushed the Moonbeam back into my pocket and climbed over Azalea's inert body, wrapping him in a hug.

"It *is* good to see you, but—" He released me, and backed down the stairs to the basement. "We need you on the other side."

"Things are that bad?" I followed him through the mirror, Ember on my heels—

And found a knife pressed to my throat.

"Astor!" Ember protested. "That's Cori. What in hell have you been doing?"

Astor lowered the knife. "I assumed Lorne had the mirror."

"He did, but I stole it back." I sagged against a wall, dizzy with tiredness. "And can someone please find me a change of clothes?"

Several confusing minutes later, I found myself in the living room. Will lay on the sofa, and Becks curled up on the rug, still unconscious.

I took the Moonbeam and held it out over Becks. "Work," I muttered to it. "Cure her."

The glow spread over her, and she stirred in her sleep, opening her eyes. Her body shuddered. Then she shifted back to human so abruptly that she kicked me in the face.

I yelped and held my chin. "Becks, you okay?"

She groaned. "Damn, that glow is bright."

"She's fine," Will mumbled. "I, however, feel like death."

"Calm down, I'm getting to you." He did look pretty rough, but being yelled at by dragons for the last day and a half probably hadn't helped. I held the Moonbeam out, and its glow spread over him. Immediately, the tiredness disappeared from his face.

Kit burst into tears on the spot, while the dragonling made a faint trilling noise, wrapping his wings over both of them.

Ember appeared behind me with a change of clothes. I took them from her, giving her another hug. "Thanks. Prison wear isn't flattering."

"Prison." Her body stilled. "Lorne locked you in the League's place?"

"He tried." I attempted a shrug, but the memory of the barred room wouldn't leave me for a long time. "He got it into his head that I could help him unlock the Moonbeam, but I stole it instead. Then I flew to Edinburgh by accident. It's been what, a day and a half?"

"Nearly two days by now," said Kit, his lip trembling. "I thought—Ember and Will were stuck on the other side, and we didn't dare follow you in case Lorne killed us. Becks helped put the fire out, but she's in a bad way."

"I'm fine now, just tired," she mumbled.

"So am I." I'd intended to change clothes, but they made a comfortable pillow. I leaned back and found Zeph's head inches from mine. "Glad you're okay."

"So am I," he said. "I can't believe you flew all the way to Edinburgh."

"Believe me, I'm glad you pushed me so hard in our lessons together."

"You're amazing."

I smiled despite myself. "Hey, don't stroke a dragon shifter's ego. Simple lesson there."

"I take it you stroked Lorne's?"

"That sounds so wrong."

He laughed. The sound was like music to my ears.

I should have told them Agnes's warnings, that the Moonbeam couldn't be trusted, but my eyes were closing, and my body cried out for rest. Their voices blurred together until oblivion claimed me.

18

A humming noise pursued me into endless fog. Once again, the fiery-eyed ghost floated before me, outlined against the grey.

"I know I'm not dreaming," I said. "I'm just not in my body. Like a necromancer."

"No," said the woman. "You're so much more than that, Cori, my dear."

"Who are you, if not a ghost?"

"A friend."

Hmm. I looked at my burned arm. Even transparent, I could see the shape of her handprint against the skin.

"I had to prove to you that I was real, since you refused to believe what you saw," she said.

"I never thought I could disconnect with my body while still alive, let alone asleep," I said. "Wait, does that mean *your* body is still alive somewhere? You're doing the same thing?"

"Yes." She was suddenly closer to me, her breath like

ice on my cheek. "And you can help me find my body, Cori, if you use the Moonbeam."

I jerked my eyes open. My hands were pressed to the mirror, the Moonbeam tucked under my arm.

Zeph looked blearily down the stairs to the basement. "Cori, what are you doing?"

"Sleepwalking." Damn. Was the ghost influencing me while I slept now? I'd wandered all the way down to the basement without even waking. Sleepwalking wasn't something I'd ever done before.

Zeph blinked a couple of times. "Is that the Moonbeam? It was glowing while you were sleeping. I saw it."

I shook my head, more irritated than I had the right to be that I hadn't got to carry on my conversation with the spirit and find out what in hell she was on about. *You can help me find my body,* she'd said. Did that mean she'd been separated from her body somehow? Like me—when I'd died?

A dozen questions bloomed in my mind. She still hadn't even told me her name. But she'd helped me escape Lorne and retrieve the Moonbeam. That seemed to suggest she was another dragon shifter like me, right? Did she think I owed her? Was it even possible to owe a favour to a ghost?

I followed Zeph up the stairs and back to the living room. "Did I fall asleep on the floor?"

"Yes, you did," he said. "You passed out with that Moonbeam clutched in your hands like the One Ring."

"Ha." Agnes's words came back to mind. the Moonbeam did engender some rather... out of character possessiveness. I mean, look at how Azalea had tried to stop me bringing it back here. It had an effect on us, and I'd be a fool not to acknowledge it.

But my reasons for hanging onto the Moonbeam weren't selfish. We needed to use it to cure the other shifters. After that... I'd see about taking Agnes's advice.

No matter what a certain ghost said.

I went to shower and change out of my muddy prison clothes, which had seen better days. So had my hair. No wonder those half-faeries had all been dumbstruck when I'd crash-landed among them on the hill. The claw marks on my shoulders had vanished. The Moonbeam had done more than heal the symptoms of the sickness: it had removed all my injuries, too.

Invigorated, I went to join the others in the living room again. Nobody looked like they'd slept much, but there was a renewed aura of hope among our group. Especially Ember, who sat in an armchair turning the Moonbeam over in her hands. My gut tightened, and a startling twinge of jealousy hit me. *Hey, that's my sister. She brought me back from the dead with the Moonbeam and used it to stop a war. She's entitled to hold it.*

Ember smiled up at me. "We're all virus-free. Once we've visited everyone on the street, the mages will have to remove the quarantine spell."

"They will." I looked around at the others. "We need to take it directly to every person with the virus. Or hand it over to the mages, but do you trust them to make sure everyone gets cured before they lock it up?"

"She has a point," said Zeph, glancing at the Moonbeam. "Given what I've seen of them, I think it's safe to say they're more concerned with their own safety than ours. We should distribute the cure before handing it over to them."

"Do you expect the gargoyles to let us walk around without throwing fire bombs at us again?" asked Ember. "I don't agree with handing it over to the mages right away, but if we ask the shifters to come to us, we'll get trampled."

"You think I'm scared of a little fire?" I reached and took the Moonbeam from her. The text appeared on the surface again, words which by rights I shouldn't be able to read, and yet…

Zeph leaned over my shoulder. "Can you read that?"

"Yep," I said. "I don't know what language it is, only that it must be coded into our DNA or something. Nobody aside from dragon shifters can read it. Agnes was surprised I could…"

"Huh," he said. "It says… it says the Moonbeam is forged in dragonfire."

"I know." I turned the Moonbeam around to show him the other side. "I didn't know this, but Agnes said the language isn't from this world."

Zeph's jaw dropped. "What?"

I drew in a breath. "So, it turns out Lorne was right."

His eyes grew round, disbelieving. "Not from this world? From where, then?"

The others stared at me with rapt attention while I explained everything Agnes had told me, about the dragon shifters' realm, the war, and the Moonbeam's involvement.

"Lady Clare was right, then," Ember said. "Lorne did use the Moonbeam against the other dragon shifters to ensure he won the war. Then he handed it over to the Orion League so *they'd* be able to use it against us."

She was taking this more calmly than I'd expected. "Sorry. I know you used it to save my life—"

"I always knew it wasn't inherently good," she said. "I also knew it was dangerous, come to that."

"Because it can be used to control shifters against their will," I agreed. "And, if we believe Lorne, open the spirit lines and possibly kick off a second faerie invasion. So, when we've cured the shifters, Agnes asked me to bring it back to her. She said she had somewhere safe to store it."

"You trust her?" Zeph asked.

"More than Lorne."

More than the fire spirit, though? Well—yes. Except Agnes couldn't reach me in my dreams. I had no way to alert her of any potential danger. And I'd have to tread carefully if I wanted to cure all the affected shifters without alerting the mages.

Zeph paused. "Maybe, but she's not a dragon shifter. What if Agnes ends up giving it to the villagers and they draw Lorne's attention again?"

"Lorne's already watching them," I said. "I just—don't trust the mages at the moment. Lady Clare seemed way too interested in it, and it can be used against us by anyone." Even our allies.

An image of Ember wielding the Moonbeam filled my head, holding every shifter in London under her thrall. I remembered watching her, awash in grey light, her eyes blazing with inner fire as she pleaded with the Moonbeam to return me to life.

"Ember," I said. "Did the Moonbeam ever… communicate with you?"

Her brow wrinkled. "No. I mean, I can read the text on it, and I can sense its power when I touch it. When I brought you back to life, I went by instinct. But in terms of actually speaking to it, no. Why, has it spoken to you?"

I shook my head, but the sense of unease didn't go away. "Not exactly." If it was a tool created by the gods, as Agnes had said, why would dragon shifters believe we'd created it?

Maybe she was wrong, but she had better judgement than the majority of people I knew. Her sister Madison had been our parents' friend, too. That was reason enough to trust her word.

"Let's get this done," Zeph said. "I don't think we should all go out. There's a chance the gargoyles might attack the house again while we're gone."

"Let them try," Will said, and the dragonling let out a growl.

"I'll go," I said. "Ember…"

She rose to her feet. "One of us should watch the mirror. I don't like the idea of letting you go out alone—"

"I'll go with Cori," Zeph said. "I'll take good care of your sister, Ember, don't worry."

I hugged Ember. "Take care of the others."

She squeezed me back. "Good luck, Cori."

Nodding to Zeph, I made my way through the living room and into the hall, retrieving my coat and shoes and a new stash of weapons. Lorne had taken everything I'd been carrying, not to mention my favourite unicorn socks, but it couldn't be helped.

"Okay," I muttered to the Moonbeam. "Work your magic. How do we find whoever's affected?"

"Look for which areas the mages quarantined," Zeph

said, taking my arm. It was an unexpected gesture, but I let him, his smile bolstering my courage.

The Moonbeam glowed in my pocket. I zipped it closed, but the glow spread as we left the house, bright enough that its reflection ignited in the nearby windows like white flames.

"Stop that," I muttered to it. "What the hell are you playing at?"

Zeph stopped walking. "Cori, what's going on?"

"I don't know."

Was the portal linking to the mirrors turning on again? Or was the Moonbeam somehow reaching out to the other shifters? The light refused to die down, and before I could retreat, several doors opened all along the street. Shifters, witches and other people stared at the glowing light as though hypnotised.

Shit. Had its hypnotising power kicked in without my permission?

"Are you using its power?" asked Zeph.

I shook my head. "Of course not. Hey, Moonbeam, dim the lights. I need to cure the shifters, not put a giant beacon on my head."

The Moonbeam's glow spread, bathing the street, and spreading beyond. I spotted a row of figures beyond the barrier at the street's end, and my heart sank.

Shifters gathered, a crowd of them stretching into the distance, and every single one of them was looking at the Moonbeam.

Okay... that's kinda creepy.

"Coriander." Lady Clare's voice rang over the ward on the street's end. "Hand that over."

I tensed, holding still, but the shifters moved in closer,

forcing Zeph and me to advance towards the barrier. "Hang on. I can't get it to stop glowing."

"I hoped you'd see sense," Lady Clare said, holding out a hand. "Go on, Cori."

I shook my head. "I need to use it to cure everyone affected by the shifters. I don't know why it's... hypnotising them."

Had Lorne done something before I'd taken it? Or did the Moonbeam have a mind of its own after all? Either way, I didn't want to give it to the mages. Especially someone who looked at it with such stark avarice in her eyes.

"Give it here," she said. "This is your last warning."

Pain stabbed behind my eyes. I pressed my free hand to my forehead, gripping the skin as though to hold myself together, and a second stab almost drove me to my knees. I looked up, eyes watering, stunned. She'd attacked me using her mind power.

Beside me, Zeph was doubled over in pain, his hands pressed to his forehead.

I gritted my teeth, my vision wavering as another stab of pain hit me. "You could be jailed for using your power on a civilian, Lady Clare," I gasped out. "Where in hell are the other mages?"

"Gone," she said. "On my orders. Now, do as I say, Cori."

Despite my swimming head and blurred vision, I wasn't imagining the wanting in her voice. Or the hunger in her eyes when she eyed the Moonbeam. Yet she was human, and she shouldn't be affected by its power.

I'd already suspected the Orion League had had insiders among the mages... to say nothing of the

Faulkner brothers. They'd been confident enough to attack us in broad daylight without fear of repercussions, and the mages had hidden behind a barrier and let them run amok. I'd always known the mages didn't have our best interests at heart. Even when they'd rewarded us for helping them, they'd always been looking for an angle. But this—no.

"No… chance," Zeph snarled. "Stop probing my mind. You won't find anything you like in there."

"I don't care for your memories, dragon shifter, I want that Moonbeam. Give it here, Coriander, or—"

"Don't bother with the theatrics. She's as stubborn as any of us."

Someone else had stepped up beside her. Someone who shouldn't be here in London.

Lorne.

19

Lorne reached his hand out across the spell-barrier for the Moonbeam. "Thank you for charging this for me, Cori."

Charging? The Moonbeam glowed, the brightness spreading towards Lorne. I jerked my hand out of reach, my heart thumping. At least the pain in my forehead had gone.

Lady Clare's mouth fell open. "What the devil—"

Lorne barely glanced at her. "Do keep quiet. This doesn't concern you."

"You're a wanted criminal."

I gave her a glare. "And you enabled this. I won't hand the Moonbeam to either of you. Whatever bullshit reason you think you deserve it for, Lorne, it's not yours."

It's mine. The words resonated through my head, whispered in my ears. It scared me, the way the Moonbeam's presence affected my mind. It was like trying to reason with a drunk person. Except it wasn't alcohol that intoxicated me. It was the thrum of power vibrating within my bones and blood, filling me with a reckless wanting that felt utterly foreign to me.

The fiery-eyed ghost appeared, her gaze fixed on Lorne. From his calm expression, he couldn't see her. Nor could Lady Clare, who continued to stare at Lorne in open horror. Serve her right for assuming she had control over the situation. I should have guessed Lorne would fly here instead of the village. He needed both the Moonbeam and me, after all.

"The Moonbeam is merely a tool," he said. "But it feeds on the life force of shifters, and now it should be more than ready to unlock my way to the realm of my birth."

"What the *hell* did you do?" I whispered.

"I didn't do a thing, Cori," he said. "It was you who made me see the light. You and the Moonbeam have a connection. And when you laid your hands on it, you enabled it to reach its full potential."

"Whatever you're planning will end in disaster, Lorne." I gripped the Moonbeam, its vibration making my teeth rattle. "It's not yours to take."

"Don't you feel it?" The Moonbeam hummed alongside his words. "You're merely an ignorant child. You haven't seen its true potential in action."

"Potential?" I spat. "When you used it to start a war, or handed it over to the Orion League so they'd let you claim the village? I'd cut off my hand before giving it to you again."

"Yet you're outnumbered."

"He's wrong," the fire lady murmured from my side. "The shifters are in the Moonbeam's thrall. Turn them on him, Cori. Go on."

I can't. If I set the other shifters on Lorne, they'd die unnecessarily. I needed to kill Lorne myself.

More to the point—if I wasn't controlling the Moonbeam, was the *ghost* doing it?

"Do it," she hissed.

"Use your army on me, Cori," he said. "I will take every one of them to pieces."

"They're not my—"

The ghost was the person controlling the Moonbeam. She was much, much more than a simple spirit.

"Be careful," murmured the fiery-eyed spirit. "As long as you hold that Moonbeam, Cori, supernaturals dead or alive will be drawn to its lure. The instant you turn your back, those shifters will all turn on you. So I suggest you use it as intended."

The truth sliced through me like a knife blade—she *wanted* me to start a war. She had something to gain from the chaos, and she'd sacrifice the other shifters in order to do it.

I wouldn't let her have her way.

Lorne's gaze showed puzzlement, shock—and then his eyes found the ghostly figure floating beside me, bathed in the Moonbeam's light. "So it's true that the dead are on your side, Coriander?"

"I am no lost spirit," said the fire lady. "Perhaps you will be a worthier host after all."

Host? Worse, Lorne could clearly hear her. And so, judging by her ashy white face, could Lady Clare.

"What madness is this?" she cried, her voice high, reedy. "I demand you leave, spirit—"

Flames engulfed Lady Clare. Her voice rose in a high scream, quickly cut off. I gaped, the Moonbeam tight in my hand, as the fire lady's magic consumed the Mage Lord until nothing remained.

Ashes scattered to the road in the place Lady Clare had stood. Zeph remained still, as did I. Lorne looked startled, but not shocked.

"Tell me," Lorne said to the ghost. "Why do you favour Coriander? Why is she able to use the Moonbeam and not I?"

What the fuck?

Zeph swore loudly at my side, but a flash of fire pushed him back, and from its heat, I knew it could hurt a dragon shifter as easily as anyone else. Just like the fiery-eyed ghost's touch.

The ghost turned to Lorne. "Because the Moonbeam brought her back from death."

"No," I whispered.

Lorne turned to me. "Now I see it. The Moonbeam brought you back to life, and its magic runs inside your veins."

"Yes," whispered the fire lady. "It does."

Traitor.

Lorne cast his gaze around at the immobile shifters. Then he turned into his dragon form, breathing a stream of fire over the rooftops. Houses ignited, shifters snapped out of the Moonbeam's spell and fled through the streets.

I turned to Zeph. "Can you hold the Moonbeam? I'm going to kill him."

"Cori—that thing is lethal." His voice was quietly stunned, and while the fiery-eyed ghost had gone, the pile of ashes in place of Lady Clare was a reminder that she could burn any of us the same way. Dragon or not.

She was more than a ghost, more than human. But *what* was she?

"All the more reason not to take it anywhere near him." I handed the Moonbeam over to Zeph, even as my instincts screamed at me to stop. "Please—if that ghost appears, don't listen to her. She's not on our side."

"Trust me," he said. "I'll take care of it."

I trust you. I leapt into the air, shifting in an instant. My wings spread wide, beating fast, gaining ground.

Once more, Lorne and I collided, biting, tearing. My claws raked across his chest, drawing blood, but his thick scales prevented me from reaching any vital organs.

The Moonbeam's glow bathed me from below. Beyond control, beyond reason, crashing through my veins like a waterfall. Maybe it did contain strength enough to break the wall between the worlds, but I wouldn't be the person who gave Lorne what he wanted.

My claws scraped at his scales, tearing them loose. Glad of all the lessons I'd spent practising with Zeph, I slashed deep, opening a wound on his neck. He was stronger, but I was much faster, and the Moonbeam still hummed along with my heartbeat, lending me its strength.

Then Lorne grabbed me by the wing, and I screamed as the membrane tore.

My one remaining wing beat twice as hard, but as I fell, so did he. Currents of magic rose to surround us. The Ley Line—near Hyde Park. The place I'd died, torn out of my body...

No. I won't die here. This time I would spill his blood in the same place the Moonbeam and I had first bonded.

My blood dripped onto the trees as we descended in a

spiral, but Lorne was bleeding, too, from deep scratches in his chest and arms. A tremendous roar came from above, and then Zeph pelted towards us, the Moonbeam in his hands, his wings beating.

"Get that away!" I screamed, but all that came out was a roar of agony as Lorne tore at my injured wing.

The air shimmered, the currents of magic growing stronger. Ghostly figures appeared all around us. *No...*

"Almost there," the fiery-eyed ghost murmured.

The lines flickered. Then a hazy green blur appeared on the other side of the grey, like looking through a foggy window.

The Moonbeam fell from Zeph's hands, drawn towards mine, fitting into my palms. Lorne didn't appear to notice. He stared rapturously at the fog, at the green blur.

Then he gave a final lunge at me, grabbing the Moonbeam. I pulled back, but my uninjured wing gave out, sending both of us spiralling into the fog.

20

Softness lay beneath my back. Grass, maybe. Fog swirled above, masking everything else. I sat up, the Moonbeam still clutched in my hands. Beside me, Lorne sat looking slowly around. His face showed a mixture of awe and fear.

"We made it," he said. "Cori… we're in the other realm, the place of our birth."

What the hell? Wherever we were, it wasn't London. No city was this quiet and empty. From the fog, I might have mistaken this place for the realm of Death, except the ground was solid, as was the Moonbeam in my hands.

"How do you know that?" I climbed to my feet. "There's no landmarks. We might be anywhere."

Lorne stood, scanning our surroundings. "This is a place between the spirit lines. A liminal space."

"Great," I said. "How do we get out of here, then?"

Lorne turned on the spot, not looking at me. "We don't. The spirit lines sealed, and the Moonbeam is spent."

"Are you saying you got us stranded over here?" I

threw the Moonbeam at his head, where it bounced off and rolled back to my feet. Then I grabbed it again before he could snatch it up. "Congratulations. You've reached the home of your ancestors: the village of Fuck All. I need to get back home."

My friends would have watched me vanish from the sky. The other shifters might not remember Lady Clare's death, but if they did, they might even think Zeph had killed her, given the absence of anyone else to blame. That aside, I didn't want to spend the rest of my life stuck in the middle of nowhere with only my mortal enemy for company. No thanks.

My wing's injury had gone away when I'd shifted to human, but I'd lost a lot of blood. Lorne was also bleeding from his arms and chest where I'd clawed him. At least the Moonbeam had stopped glowing like a disco ball.

I looked down at the fist-sized stone. "Okay, Moonbeam, take me back to London. Not him, he can stay if he wants to. I don't know what you're playing at, but seriously—"

Lorne marched over to me, his eyes narrowing. "You're talking to it," he said. "You and the Moonbeam are communicating."

"Does it look like we are?" My head throbbed, and my whole body felt bruised. Like the Moonbeam had taken something out of me to cross us over. And I was no longer sure if I had anything left to give. "I've no clue where we are, how we got here or how to get out. This was your goddamned idea, Lorne. Tell me how to get home."

"This is our home. Give that to me, or I will make you regret crossing me."

"If you kill me now, you'll regret it later when you

have nothing to eat. I'll let you know if you start to smell appealing."

Lorne merely blinked in evident confusion. He really did have no sense of humour to speak of.

I tapped on my spirit sight, unnerved when the fog thickened without any ghosts appearing. "Hey, fire lady. You here?"

Lorne's eyes narrowed. "Who are you talking to?"

"My imaginary friend." The fiery-eyed ghost was the one who'd really been controlling the Moonbeam, even when I'd thought it answered to me. *She'd* wanted to open this realm and send the shifters to war against one another. "Never mind. It's just you and me now, shithead."

Lorne hissed out a breath, staring into the fog. "There it is."

I opened my mouth to tell him to shove it—then stared. The outline of several buildings became visible through the fog, like a mirage of a distant city.

The mist cleared a little more, revealing twin statues on either side of a platform. Carved dragons lined the path, etched in stone. My heart seized, and every scrap of doubt, every piece of certainty that he was lying—it all disappeared the moment I set eyes on the city.

Huge stone houses lined wide paths, with larger buildings in between. The shadow of a mountain appeared at the back, while the ground sloped uphill.

Is this where my parents grew up? Where Ember and I were born?

I shoved the thought away. Maybe someone lived in the city who'd be able to help me get home.

"The two realms used to be closely linked," murmured

Lorne. "My father told me before he died that the mirrors connected this realm with ours. Before the war."

"The war *you* started," I said. "With this."

The Moonbeam's glow reflected in his eyes. "Who told you that?"

"Agnes," I said. "You probably haven't a clue who she is. Nobody who isn't one of your allies matters to you."

"I know who Agnes is," he said, in somewhat absent tones. "She thwarted me once. I punished her sister as a consequence."

Anger clenched around my heart. "You're not getting out of here alive, Lorne."

Is *anyone alive in here?* I peered through doorways, windows, yet I saw no signs of life. Or wherever the fire lady had disappeared to. If she'd found her body, I'd punch her in the face for getting us stuck over here.

"This," he said, "is my goal. Not London. No simple human home will do after this. I knew this city was waiting for me, and I came to reclaim it."

"You're assuming nobody else already lives here, yes?"

I wasn't about to let him declare war on whoever might live in the city, even if he deserved to get his arse kicked. But the houses appeared to be deserted, abandoned.

"They left," he said. "*We* left. You might not remember—"

"I was five years old when I went to London, Lorne. I wouldn't remember even if I'd stayed in Scotland. And I'm glad my parents got me away from you before you could terrorise Ember and me like you did to everyone else."

"You think I'd have tortured you?" He shook his head. "I only punish those who disobey. I have no interest in slaughtering infants. Yes, I know I have a son, too… and he is under the watch of my allies, until he's old enough to be of use."

A soft gasp escaped. "You—?"

"I'm aware that one of my consorts was carrying my child when I was jailed, and I assume you had a hand in helping her escape."

"Ember did," I said. "But you won't live to see your son."

My hands shifted to claws, cupping the Moonbeam. It had stopped glowing by now, but a thin trickle of light led from the stone up to a statue in the middle of a square ahead of us. A large dragon, fearsome and majestic, real scales glittering all over her body.

"Who is that?"

"The ancestor of the dragon shifters." He spoke in a tone of reverence. "She is a goddess, the fire goddess. The city is hers."

Uh-huh. "Who exactly told you all this?"

"My father." His words were quiet yet precise, his eyes darting around. "His position was taken from him unfairly. To avenge him, I took the Moonbeam. I gave it my life. But I don't understand why it chose to revive you instead."

"Because I died, and my sister didn't want to watch me disappear. You wouldn't understand, Lorne. You don't care about any other people, so nobody gives a shit about you, either."

His eyes widened a fraction. "You were protecting her when the Moonbeam caused you to shift. Can it be that the Moonbeam is actually connected to your sister and not you?"

"Would it matter if it was?" I shook my head. "You need a serious wakeup call, Lorne. I don't care whose it is. Once I get out of this hole, it's going back into hiding."

"No," he said. "Now the stone has awakened, even if I died, it would keep searching for someone to revive its power. It must be close now."

I took a step backwards. The light grew brighter. "I thought you wanted to come here. What the hell are you talking about?"

His eyes were intense. "There's nowhere to run here, Cori."

"Then there's nowhere for you to go, either." My heart beat faster. "What in hell is happening to the Moonbeam?"

"It doesn't matter."

"Like hell. This is the crux of it all. The reason you killed innocent children with that virus and set those dragonlings loose in the city—too bad both of those things backfired."

"On the contrary," he said, "they didn't. The remaining dragonlings have yet to hatch, but when they do, they will destroy the rest of that world and remake it anew."

"You have got to be kidding me."

He stepped onto the path behind me. "I'm willing to make a deal, Cori. Give me the Moonbeam and I'll use it to save your friends before the dragonlings hatch. When they reach my people, they will infect every single dragonling with the virus, enough to spread to every shifter in the country. By the them they're done, there will be none remaining, and few humans, too. The remainder can easily be tamed to serve me."

He's cracked.

I had to get out. If it was true—if some of the eggs had

yet to hatch—then they'd be on a boat somewhere, with nobody having a clue they were rigged to destroy the human race. And I was stuck here in the place the dragons' wars had started, with a maniac who'd tear two worlds down to get what he wanted.

The Moonbeam glowed, brighter. *Like the portal.* Encouraged, I leaned into its light, drawing on the fire inside me.

Please. Take me home.

Light swallowed me up, and I stumbled out into an unfamiliar room.

Not the lab. Not the village, either. The room appeared to be a library, containing tall shelves lined with ancient-looking leather-bound volumes, plush rugs, ornately carved wooden furniture.

First the dragons' home world, now a room that looked like it had been preserved from before the faerie invasion. Someone very rich lived here.

I turned on my spirit sight, looking for any ghosts who might give me a clue, and a pair of sharp eyes stared back.

Someone else was here. Someone who definitely wasn't one of my friends. A woman with a long black coat adorned with what looked like medals, looking me up and down through the open door.

"Hey," I said. "Sorry, is Agnes here?"

"She went back home," she said. "Months ago. Who are you?"

"I'm Cori. I was here... did you say months ago?"

"The name's Lady Montgomery," she said. "Leader of Edinburgh's necromancer guild. What exactly were you doing in the spirit realm?"

21

Oh, bugger. The woman standing before me was a necromancer, and I'd looked into her eyes using my spirit sight. No explaining that away.

Lady Montgomery was stern-looking, with grey in her dark hair. How in the world had she got hold of the mirror? Given her collection of badges, she'd proved herself in battle more than once. She could yank my soul out of my body without a thought.

"My name's Coriander," I said. "I'm not here to attack you. I'm just here to meet a friend. Agnes... uh..."

"I assume you mean Agnes Briar," she said. "How did you find this mirror?"

"It belongs to some friends of mine," I said. "If I'm in Edinburgh... how did it get here? Where am I?"

"This is the headquarters of Edinburgh's mage guild, and the mirror is currently in their possession."

"How?" No way could the mirror have migrated all the way here and fallen into the mages' hands in the space of an hour or two. It shouldn't be possible. "I mean, I've never met the mages of this city before. I didn't know my friends were acquainted with them, either. We're from London."

Lady Montgomery gave me an appraising look. "The mirror is stored here for safekeeping while its owners assist me. I'm in the middle of hunting for a gang of witches who are practising an illegal form of magic on the dead and the living alike."

"A gang of witches." Crap. It couldn't be— "Are they by any chance raising the dead using symbols?"

Her eyes narrowed. "Yes, they are. Do you know of them?"

Holy shit. The zombies, and the virus, were here. Lorne must have started the whole scheme in Edinburgh, before bringing it with him to London. But if his people were here... did that mean this was where he was planning to unleash his booby-trapped dragonling eggs?

"Ah—damn," I said. "I mean, I think I know who they are, or at least who sent them."

Problem: Lorne was on the mirror's other side. I wasn't sure he'd be able to follow me—or even if he'd want to, given that he'd have to leave the Moonbeam behind to do it—but if the dragonlings hadn't hatched yet, Lorne's witches must be waiting to receive them. I couldn't let that happen.

"Then perhaps we can be of use to one another," said Lady Montgomery. "If not, then I'm afraid I'll have to take you into custody. How did you access the spirit realm? You're no necromancer."

While Lady Montgomery shouldn't be able to read my

thoughts like Lady Clare, she had a similar cutting stare which suggested she could see through any lie.

"No, but I have the spirit sight. Uh, do you know Lord Glover?" I asked. "From London?"

"Oh, yes," she said.

"He can vouch for me." *I think.* If you dismissed the fact that I'd disappeared in suspicious circumstances right after Lady Clare's death. Had the mages arrested my friends, and was that how they'd got hold of the mirror? If that was the case, then it would make more sense for it to be with London's mages, not all the way up here.

"What do you know about those witches?" asked Lady Montgomery.

"I know that the enemy is using tools manufactured in a lab that belonged to the Orion League," I said. "I was trying to track him in London, but he must have been operating here, too. The zombies all have symbols drawn on them, right?"

"Yes," she said. "The same happened during the aftermath of the invasion, but they died out. I assumed the art was forgotten."

"It's the same source," I said. "The Orion League stole the technique from the witches. Now Lorne's doing the same. He might—he might come through this mirror. Do you know where it links to?"

"As I said, the mirror isn't mine," she said, her sharp gaze skimming the glass. "I'm told it links to another mirror in the Highlands, or so Agnes told me. She warned me you might be coming, but I expected you sooner."

Damn. So my friends had brought the mirror from London, which meant the other one was still in the shifters' village. But what had caused them to travel this far north?

"Sooner?" A horrible possibility seized me. "How long have they been here?"

"At least two weeks."

My jaw dropped. "What? It's only been a few hours."

No wonder she'd said Agnes had left months ago. *Oh, god, Ember.* She'd think I was dead. So would the others.

I moved to leave the room, but the leading necromancer barred my way. "I've met your sister. She doesn't have the gift. How long have you been able to see the dead, exactly?"

I didn't have time to dawdle and I expected she knew it, but what was a few more minutes when I'd already lost weeks? Besides, Lorne would make sure the whole world knew before long.

"It's complicated, but it involves the Moonbeam," I relented. "It's a magical creation that functions as a portal linking to this mirror. That's why I wanted to warn you Lorne might follow me here. He has the Moonbeam now. He used to be in the custody of London's mages, but he escaped."

"I've heard the name," she said. "I will inform the Mage Lords and tell them to prepare."

With a snap of her fingers, she summoned someone to her side. "River, take Cori to the others."

A boy of maybe twelve or thirteen, with curly blond hair, appeared behind her in the doorway and nodded to me. "Come this way."

His ears were pointed, indicating he was a half-faerie, but he wore the black cloak of a necromancer. He gave me a curt nod, opened a door and revealed Agnes waiting behind it.

My jaw unhinged. "What the hell are you doing here?"

"Is that any way to greet an old friend?" Agnes said. "You left a tremendous mess behind you in London, Coriander."

"Uh. Yeah. That's one way of putting it." I rubbed my forehead, wondering how many more surprises this endless day would bring. "I disappeared. I'm here to help deal with the witches. Also, Lorne sent his last shipment of dragonling eggs here and he's planning to infect them all with the sickness, so I really need your help."

"I suppose we could give you a hand," said Will, from behind her.

Smiling at my shock, Agnes stepped aside. All my friends were inside the room: Will, Kit, Becks, Ember, Astor, even the dragonling.

And Zeph, who embraced me with such force that my arms were pinned to my sides. "I knew you were still alive."

"Mmph," I said, my voice muffled.

"Don't keep her all to yourself, Zeph," said Will, grabbing my hand. The others swarmed me—except for Astor, that is, but he never voluntarily touched anyone except Ember. My sister caught me in her arms, stroking my hair like we were little kids again.

Ember finally let me go. "I can't believe it. Cori, you've been gone... a month? Five weeks? I lost track."

"It hasn't been that long for me," I said. "An hour at most. How is that even possible? I was in London just then, and now... you're here." I sank into a vacant chair, overwhelmed.

"The other realm operates rather like Faerie," said Agnes. "You've all heard the stories of a human who wanders into the woods and returns to find a decade has passed? You're incredibly lucky you only lost a few weeks."

"With any luck, that means Lorne won't be back for a decade." I leaned forward. "He's lost over there. Maybe he'll follow me, but that would mean giving up the Moonbeam."

"He survived?" asked Ember.

"Last I saw," I said. "This has been the longest day of my life."

A door rattled somewhere behind me. "I ordered takeout," Will said. "I think the delivery guy was kinda freaked out when I asked for it to be delivered to the mages' headquarters."

"I can't believe we're in Edinburgh's mage guild." I looked around at the others. "I don't get it. I thought the mages in London would want our heads on a platter, considering what happened to Lady Clare."

"We'll tell you if you explain where you've been for the last month," Zeph said, patting the seat next to him. I moved over, sinking into the warm sofa. He smelled of dragon, and home.

The others listened to my account of our visit to the dragons' city while we ate. Like me, the others hadn't truly believed it was a real place, rather than a figment of Lorne's delusions. Agnes disappeared halfway through to speak to the mages, so I made a mental note to update her later.

Eagerly shoving fries into my mouth, I looked at the others. "Okay, your turn. How did you get here? I'm guessing it involved flying?"

"When you vanished, I was alone in front of a crowd beside the ashes of a dead mage," said Zeph. "I had to run. Obviously, the shifters were totally out of it, but if the other mages had found me there, they'd have blamed her death on me."

"He showed up on the doorstep bleeding and babbling about you vanishing into thin air," Ember went on. "We'd already packed up ready to run, so we followed your idea to come here to Agnes. With the mirror, since leaving it behind wasn't a great move. Zeph's an effective pack horse when he wants to be."

Zeph reached for a few fries. "Had to do something useful."

"Damn," I said. "You flew all the way here... with the mirror. And you handed it over to the mages?"

"Didn't really have a choice," Becks said. "They were expecting us."

"But..." I looked at them—Ember, eyes aglow with happiness, Becks, lounging on the rug, Will and Kit, sitting with the dragonling between them. The only person who didn't look delighted to see me was Astor, and he never looked happy anyway. "I thought they blamed us for the sickness."

"Luckily, the news hadn't spread this far north," Will said. "Agnes argued for us, including Thorn... and they agreed to let us stay. On condition that we find and exterminate Lorne's allies. The sickness hasn't been as bad here, but the zombies are worse, much worse. The necro-mancer guild has their work cut out."

"I met their leader when I came out of the mirror. She said she was going to tell the mages…"

"Ah," said Ember. "That means they'll come back and interrogate us again, in all likelihood. I know for a fact they've been having behind-the-scenes meetings about the mirror, and they've been on the phone to Lord Smyth in London."

I groaned. "It's the bloody Moonbeam all over again. I mentioned Lorne might follow us, assuming he can bear to let the Moonbeam go."

"So you left it behind," Zeph said. "I'm sorry I let go of it. I don't know what the hell happened."

The image of the Moonbeam flying towards me as though propelled by an invisible force filled my mind. "I don't, but I can guess. That thing has a mind of its own, and it *wanted* me to rip open a way into the other realm."

Ember's mouth dropped open. "So… it was on Lorne's side?"

"No clue." I pushed away the takeout box, frustration rising at the memory. "Lorne didn't seem to care about it so much in the end, not when he set eyes on the city. He acted like he'd stumbled upon a gold mine and spouted all this nonsense about the ancestors of all the dragon shifters living there—his ancestors, that is. I doubt he cares that I vanished."

"So you're saying he *won't* follow you?" Becks said. "I suppose there's nothing to stop us from going back and snagging the Moonbeam, if he has no allies to defend him."

"Except the fire lady—the ghost." I slumped back against the sofa. "She's the one who killed Lady Clare."

"Who—" Zeph broke off. "That ghost from your dreams? *She* turned the Mage Lord to ashes?"

"She did," I said. "I know she helped me at first, but she sided with Lorne when I refused to use the Moonbeam's power on the other shifters."

"That's fucked up," said Ember. "How could a ghost burn someone alive?"

"She said she was more than a spirit," I said. "I think she must be related to the dragon shifters, but hell if I know how."

"Glad you left her behind, then," Becks said. Kit nodded in agreement.

"Never mind her," I said. "Turns out Lorne didn't set all the dragonlings loose. There's a bunch of eggs still out there, and they're set to bring the virus into the country any day now. Given that the witches are here, I'm assuming they're coming to Edinburgh. If they hatch…"

Ember paled. "It'll come here. The virus. And the Moonbeam is stuck in the other realm, with no other cure."

"Exactly." Lorne could wait. We'd only get one shot to save the other dragonlings and stop the virus. "Does Agnes know who the witches are? Where they're hiding?"

"We've brought down a dozen of their hideouts," said Zeph. "But no dragon eggs. If it's been over a month… maybe they're already loose."

"You'd know if they were," I said, though my heart sank at his words. "We still have a shot to find them and end this. Maybe they're still on the boat. If you keep killing Lorne's people and the man himself is missing, maybe they didn't see them as a priority."

The door opened and Agnes came in. "The mages are on their way," she said. "In the meantime, we're operating under the assumption that the mirror should be kept under 24/7 guard. They know the village is on the other side, but they refuse to believe my claims about the other realm."

"Do they expect me to take them there as a tour guide?" I shook my head. "The other dragon shifters don't need the mages hassling them either. We have to get that mirror away from the village. Take it somewhere else."

A rapping on the door made me jump. Two more cloaked individuals entered the room. Their styled hair and polished attire marked them as mages. The first was a tall, broad man of between fifty and sixty, his black hair streaked with grey, while the woman was younger, thin and blond.

"I am Lord Sutherland of Edinburgh's mage council," the man said, in a distinct Scottish accent. "And this is Lady Anders."

The blond mage nodded in greeting. "And you are…?"

"Ember," said my sister. "This is Coriander, my sister. That's Zephyr, Will, Becks, Kit, and Astor."

The mages hardly looked at each of us. Their attention was trained on the dragonling. "And what exactly is that? When Agnes mentioned another dragon, I assumed it was a shifter."

"This is Thorn," Will said. "Our ally."

"We don't allow pets in our headquarters," said the mages.

Kit looked alarmed. "But—"

"The enemy is attempting to infect the remaining dragonlings with a virus," I interjected. "If we set him free, the same will happen to him. He's well-trained."

The dragonling spat a mouthful of carpet out. Agnes walked to the mages, talking in a low voice. While they still didn't look happy, Lord Sutherland gave a short nod.

"Do as you will. But we have one request," he said. "Along with Lorne, I would like you to hand over the Moonbeam. I believe that is what the late Lady Clare would have wanted."

"It's… gone," I said. "We were forced to leave it on the other side of the mirror. I don't know how to retrieve it, and that place isn't safe to go into."

Agnes whispered to him again. I strained to catch the words, which sounded like, "You can keep the mirror for now, but for god's sake don't go blabbing about it."

Despite his nod of assent, I recognised the avarice in Lord Sutherland's eyes. It mirrored Lady Clare's, which would have bothered me if I didn't have bigger problems to worry about than the mages.

Like the dragons' city. I'd barely caught a glimpse, and part of me wanted to go there myself and tread the paths my ancestors walked. Maybe even my parents, if it had been abandoned as recently as Lorne claimed.

If I killed Lorne, I could give the other dragons a chance to see it. But first, I'd save the dragonlings and obliterate the last of Lorne's witches, before he came back into this world.

No pressure.

22

The door closed behind the mages, and Agnes scowled. "That one's trouble."

"Who, Lord Sutherland?" I asked. "Why bring the mirror here when you knew he'd want to claim it?"

"This is the safest place in the city aside from the necromancer guild, and that place is covered with wards which might make using your… talents difficult."

"You mean my ability to see ghosts," I said. "What use is it now? Lorne's allies are either alive or zombies—and not the type of zombies necromancers can banish, either."

Agnes shook her head. "I'm not an expert, but the necromancers have more sense than the mages do. They wouldn't allow me to bring the mirror into their domain. You're very lucky Lady Montgomery didn't take you with her for an appraisal—she'll want a word with you later, Cori."

"I'm still not sure I should have told her," I said. "I didn't expect her to see me using my spirit sight. And I doubt the mages will drop the whole Moonbeam issue, even though…"

Agnes tilted her head. "Even though what?"

My head drooped. "You… you were right. The Moonbeam *wanted* Lorne to open the way into the dragons' city. I had no control over it in the end. The fire lady, the ghost, *she* did."

Something she wanted was over in that realm, which meant I couldn't count on her coming to help us now. We were on our own.

Agnes wore an expression I couldn't read. "I'm glad you came to your senses. That Moonbeam… it's said to have corrupted other dragon shifters in the past. You wouldn't be the first. Just be glad it left your hands before it could do any more damage."

"Corrupted… how?" I frowned. "Where did it really come from? Agnes—"

"Now isn't the time for that conversation," she said. "The mages expect you to make progress tracking the witches by this evening. If you don't want to be waylaid by Lady Montgomery, I'd suggest you start with that."

"But I have no idea where the witches might be hiding," I protested. "I couldn't even find them in London. Unless Will has a tracking spell and a zombie I can use?"

"That's how we caught the others," Will said. "But they've been sending the zombies out in packs. The witches are too bloody good at hiding themselves. They're inked with their own stealth and speed spells, so they always leave their location before we reach them."

"And—the dragon eggs?" I asked. "Lorne implied that they're infected with the virus, but they haven't even hatched yet. That I know of. If they're still on the boat, that implies the witches must be waiting somewhere near the coast."

"The beach," Agnes said. "Edinburgh lies on the centre of a number of major spirit lines, including the Ley Line, and was also where the League initially captured witches from. Cori, you have the ability to search the spirit realm, don't you? I might have many strengths, but that isn't one of them. I'm not a necromancer. I think your ability will enable you to find them."

Oh. That's what she wants me to do with it. "I can try."

Turning on my spirit sight was second nature now. Between one blink and the next, grey filtered in. No wonder Lady Montgomery had spotted me right away. The world appeared wreathed in grey, and the others shone within like spotlights. Spirits. There must be a way to distinguish between those who were alive and those who weren't, but there didn't appear to be any nearby ghosts to question.

I turned off my spirit sight. "No ghosts in here. Guess the mages won't let the dead wander into their headquarters. I think I'd need to go outside to have a proper look around."

"At least they got *that* right," Agnes said. "Lady Montgomery has been unable to track the witches, and since they aren't necromancers, they've managed to hide themselves. Did Lorne give you any other hints?"

"No..." I thought back to my unceremonious arrival in the city the first time around. "Might they be hiding on the Ley Line? Or any spirit line? A key point would hide their magic."

Agnes nodded slowly. "The thought did cross my mind. We'll start with the Ley Line and go from there. It does pass through the beach, but if the boat hasn't reached the shore yet, it's possible that the witches are avoiding the area. There's definitely a key point on Arthur's Seat somewhere. Be careful, though—that line also leads into the faerie realms."

"Hope I don't crash any faerie parties this time around, then."

———

We set out as a group, on foot. Flying was only an advantage when you wanted to make an impression, so that had to wait until we found somewhere less public. Besides, it was best that the witches didn't know we were coming.

Agnes walked in the lead. Ember and Astor followed close behind. Then Zeph and me, and then Kit, Will and Becks brought up the rear with Thorn trailing along. We were bound, all of us, and would do anything to protect one another. Just like my friends had all waited for me. Bonds stronger than blood united us.

Whatever Lorne said, my fate wasn't tied to the dragon shifters' past. And I'd forge a future that would allow everyone to exist without fear and persecution.

Zeph's hand brushed mine. "Worried?"

"A little." I let him take my hand, squeezing it. "Lorne implied the eggs were on their way to the coast, but that was weeks ago. I didn't expect to lose so much time."

"Don't forget that he hasn't been around to give orders, either," Zeph said. "Without him, the witches might have left the eggs in a safe house. Or even on the boat, if they were concerned about the eggs hatching with him not there."

"He did imply he gave them orders." But I'd bet he hadn't accounted for all my friends flying to Edinburgh to help out. "Then again, he wasn't exactly... with it. But I can't deny the possibility that he might try to follow us."

"Assuming he's willing to leave the Moonbeam behind." He walked down the cobbled street at my side. "I can't believe the mages want it back after Lady Clare's death."

"You believe me, then?" I asked. "I mean, about it having a mind of its own? Because we're still... bonded, in some way. I had no control."

His eyes darkened with embers. "I saw your face when Lady Clare died. You looked terrified. But Cori, you're not responsible for what Lorne did. Don't ever think that. The Moonbeam is gone, now, right?"

"For now, but it's still the only source of the cure," I said. "The whole time we thought it was on our side, and..."

"It's not on Lorne's side either," he said. "Doesn't mean he can't use it against us, but it's as likely to backfire on him as anyone else. Now he's stuck in another realm with no allies, fawning over dead gods. I'd say we have a good chance of thwarting his plan long before he ever figures out how to get back."

I dipped my head. "I *want* the Moonbeam to stay over there with him, but part of me doesn't want it to, either. Its magic is in me, because my sister used it to bring me back from the dead. It *took* something from me, and the other shifters, when it opened the rift. Our energy."

Zeph grimaced. "When the League were developing

those spirit devices… that's what they were trying to mimic. He and the Faulkner brothers must have been trying to recreate the same power."

"Except the Faulkners had nothing to gain from opening the other realm," I said. "It's not their realm. But you're right—Lorne has no idea what he's messing with."

As we neared the foot of the hills, the shadow of a dragon passed overhead, wings splayed over the peak.

"Shit," said Ember.

No. It can't be.

Zeph tilted his head back to look up at the sky. "Lorne…?"

It wasn't Lorne. A grey-scaled dragon shifter landed in front of us, blocking the road. He shifted to human form, becoming a tall man with grey hair to match his scales.

"If I were you, I'd turn back," he growled.

"Lorne did leave some allies behind, then." My hands shifted to claws. "Let me guess—he asked you to stop us from reaching the witches' hiding place. What did you have to gain, or did you not bother to ask questions?"

The dragon shifter's mouth tightened. "The witches will cleanse this city, and the world. When they're done, we'll be free to fly again without opposition."

"Whatever he told you is a lie." But I could see the white light reflected in his eyes. He'd put his hands on the Moonbeam. He was from the village.

The Moonbeam had corrupted them.

I lifted my clawed hands. "This is your last warning. Get out of my way."

"So be it." He shifted into dragon form, flying directly at our group.

Ember got there first, her claws digging into his throat. She growled a warning.

The dragon shifted to human, spitting out blood. "I would rather die than submit to you."

"What in hell is wrong with him?" Will whispered behind me.

"The fool," Astor said. "He's marked."

"He—" *Oh, bugger.* As he writhed beneath Ember, his coat tore, exposing marks etched onto his arms. *The witches marked him.* "Ember, he's not in control. Don't—"

The dragon roared, shifting once more and throwing my sister at the rest of us. Our group scattered, and Zeph and I both turned into dragon form, too.

"Stop!" The word came out as a roar. "I can help you."

Zeph flew, his claw latching onto his fellow dragon's wing and bringing him crashing to earth. Below, the misty hill merged with the sky, rippling currents of energy marking the Ley Line as it travelled further north, towards the sea—

Sparks flew from the hill. *There are our witches.*

Zeph snarled, indicating north. My heart free-fell at the sight of a large ship approaching the beach. The dragonling eggs were almost here.

We had to stop the witches before they could reach them.

With a roar, Zeph tackled the dragon shifter again. The two collided on the road, further scattering our group. I shifted to human form as I landed beside them.

"Why not kill him?" Astor demanded, holding onto Ember, whose arm was bleeding.

"He's marked," I said, breathless. "He's not in control of his own actions. Lorne's witches marked him with those symbols, the same ones he used to get the dead to obey him. Guess they work on the living, too."

Astor stiffened. "So that's why the upper soldiers of the League were always so… cold."

"So were you," Will put in.

He gave a humourless smile. "I guess it's a good thing for all of you that the League fell before I ever got to that stage. Are you going to leave him, then?"

"I'll watch him," Agnes said, to my surprise. "I'll see what I can do to those symbols. I'm no fighter, but you…"

"Need to find the witches," I said. "The ship's almost at the beach, which means the witches will be leaving their hideout soon. And we'll be waiting for them."

And with that, we moved towards the hill. The rippling currents of the spirit line made it hard to see where I was going. Flickers infiltrated my vision, grey paths lined with grey trees. *Creepy.* I faltered, and Agnes glanced at me. "You can see through the Ley Line?"

I squinted. "I can see… grey. What is that?"

"That," she said, "is the realm the Sidhe of Faerie threw their gods out of. I'd advise you to tread very carefully, Cori. Paths to Faerie are usually one-way."

"Wow, I feel so much better." I stepped forward, regardless. The others were counting on me.

"Stay close to me, Cori." Ember took my arm. "I won't let you wander off."

"Nor me," Zeph said. "We'll take out those witches no matter what tricks they pull."

Gratitude welled inside me. I kept one eye firmly on the hillside as we climbed, concentrating on the solidity of the ground beneath my feet. The pulsing currents of energy became more distinct, and the see-through path revealed a stone construction of some type.

I stopped walking. "Please tell me you guys can see what I can."

"A building?" Ember said from my right. "Yeah, I see it."

"Good. Because it looks exactly like something from the other world—"

Kit shouted behind us. I whirled on the spot, seeing the others had pulled out weapons. Three huge winged monstrosities lurked overhead, just like the monster from the lab.

Looked like the witches knew we were coming.

Zeph, Ember and I all shifted at once, launching ourselves at the winged beasts. My claws dug into foul flesh and tore one of their throats open. Ember wrestled with the other, while Will threw witch spells and Kit hurled handfuls of faerie magic. Astor, meanwhile, crept towards the rippling, semi-transparent stone construction. I prepared to shout a warning, but Astor caught the blurred figure that appeared from the fog, tackling her onto the hillside. The dragonling breathed a stream of fire, piercing the mist and hitting another fleeing figure. A witch.

I let go of the limp body of the monster, spitting out a mouthful of its foul-tasting blood, and landed beside Astor on the hillside. My claw caught another witch, piercing her in the chest. Behind me, the monsters' screeches and cries rang through the fog. I beat my wings, searching for my friends, but the fog of the liminal space coupled with the roaring currents of the Ley Line made it impossible to see my surroundings.

Then a roar cut to my ears—*Zeph.*

I took flight, in the direction of the sound. More witches were leaving the construction, moving down the hillside at the rapid pace gifted to them by the marks they wore. I breathed fire as I flew, hitting each witch until they turned to ash. And further up the Ley Line—

The ocean, vast and blue, curling around the coastline, and the shape of a large ship disappearing beneath the water.

Zeph.

His head broke the surface of the water, his distress clear. The dragonling eggs… they were sinking.

No.

With a roar of fury, I dove down, digging my claws into the ship to stop it from being submerged. Zeph growled, kicking out of the water and tearing into the ship's innards. He reappeared a moment later with a crate grasped firmly in his claws. The ship continued to sink, disappearing below the water's surface.

We landed together on the beach, wet and shivering.

"We need to put them somewhere safe," Zeph said, once we'd shifted to human form on the sand. "They must be close to hatching by now, and we can't set them loose here."

"But where?" If we released them into the wild, they'd either fall victim to wild fae or start attacking human settlements. That left one option.

"We'll take them through the mirror."

———

"You're absolutely sure Lorne is dead?" Ember asked, as our group reassembled in the library of the mages' guild. The mirror remained at the back, glittering against the bookshelves. Agnes had let us bypass the wards by talking to the guards, leaving us to carry the crate of dragon eggs inside.

I shook my head. "No, but where else are we supposed to leave them?"

"The village?" suggested Becks. "I guess Azalea wouldn't be keen on that idea either."

Agnes swore. "Work it out. The mages are coming. I'll divert their attention, but if they see that crate, you'll have one hell of a lot of questions to answer."

"Damn," I muttered. "All right, we'll do it. If Lorne's there, he'll be weakened. I can kill him."

I hope.

I took the lead, making my way through the mirror—

And found myself faced with the furious stares of a dozen dragon shifters.

23

The dragons from the village crowded around us, wearing expressions of hostility. Most were in dragon form, but others were in their human guise. Including—Azalea. The other dragons filled the stone steps of the dragons' city, for all the world like they'd flown here.

"How did you all get here?"

I already knew the answer: Lorne had used the Moonbeam to get through their mirror and dragged every one of them here into his deranged kingdom to declare himself leader over them.

I should have made sure he stayed dead.

The others stood behind me, equally stunned. Including Zeph, laden with the crate of dragonling eggs.

"It looks like we have our first intruders to fight off," said an echoing voice. Lorne came into view, his eyes aglow, and he held the Moonbeam in his hands.

"Last I saw you were bleeding to death." I kept one eye on the other dragons. They couldn't all be on his side, right? They'd be able to overpower him—unless he used the Moonbeam.

The Moonbeam, which served him once again.

"The goddess herself healed me," he said. "Give me those dragonling eggs."

"You think I'm letting them anywhere near you? You planned to infect them with a poison to wipe out all life on earth." I scanned the other dragon shifters for any hint of recognition in their eyes, but there came none. The Moonbeam held them all in its thrall.

You were supposed to be on our side.

He held up the Moonbeam, which flickered with fiery light. "I have been chosen by her, the goddess of fire herself."

Dread curled in my chest, and I knew before she appeared that the fire lady was watching me. From Lorne's side.

Or rather… the fire goddess.

"I can speak to the fire inside the stone." He held the stone before him. "The stone is asking me to join forces."

"Yes," purred the fire goddess. "You and I will be one, and I will take everything you craved."

Lorne didn't seem to hear her voice. A jolt of under-standing hit me—nobody except me *could* hear her, because for all her power, she was a ghost. Not only that, she was tied to the Moonbeam, and my ability linked me to her as well. She'd still chosen to take Lorne's side, but maybe I could use our link to my advantage.

"Lorne," I said. "You have no idea what you're messing with. Do you honestly think any goddess of dragons would side with you after what you did? You slaughtered your fellow dragons. You murdered my parents. You drove the dragon clans into a war that nearly destroyed us all."

"Don't you understand?" he said. "The goddess of fire is bound to the Moonbeam. The Moonbeam enabled my victory. Our goals are in alignment, and the goddess and I are on the same side."

Everyone was silent. Under the Moonbeam's thrall. Only Kit and Astor would be unaffected, and they couldn't fight off an army. Even the dragonling's attention was fixed on the gleaming stone.

"Don't do this." I met the spirit's eyes. I should have known she was much more than a ghost. After all, she'd managed to burn me. The only thing that could burn a dragon was the fire of a goddess… our own ancestor.

Wait—hadn't she said she was looking for her own body?

"Lorne!" I shouted. "The goddess doesn't want to be on your side. She wants to destroy you and take your place. Don't let her!"

"The Moonbeam and I are one." He held it up and the glow brightened, covering him, covering all of us. His voice deepened, merging with the spirit's. "We are one again. I am the fire who burns in your veins…"

Lorne broke off with a scream, his skin igniting. The Moonbeam glowed, a white spot amid the whirling flames. Lorne, burning alive. In seconds, his body turned to fire and ashes.

The Moonbeam clattered to the ground. For a long moment, nobody spoke. Tension hummed in the air. Then, I turned to look at my friends. As I suspected, the spell had broken.

Where in hell did she disappear to? I thought she planned to take Lorne's place.

"What just happened?" asked Becks. Like the others, her attention was trained on the Moonbeam. "Did Lorne just burn from the inside out?"

"She killed him. The fire lady… or rather, the fire goddess." I looked at my sister. "Did you see her?"

"I saw," she confirmed, her eyes wide with shock.

"As did I." Zeph's attention was on the Moonbeam. "She burned him—but where did she go?"

One of the other dragon shifters moved to pick up the Moonbeam. I stepped forwards, my heart thumping against my ribcage, my spirit sight scanning for any trace of the ghost.

"Nobody else touch that," I warned. "It's cursed."

"Says who?" responded the other dragon.

"You saw what it did to Lorne." I looked at the others, whose expressions had melted from anger to bafflement. "It burned him alive. Or rather, *she* burned him. She's not on our side."

She never had been. The fire goddess had helped us for her own gain—though that didn't explain why she'd brought me back to life and tired my life force to the Moonbeam as a consequence. Maybe the Moonbeam could be used independently of her after all. Not that it mattered. She was gone, and—

Wait.

I looked more closely at the ring of glowing light surrounding the Moonbeam. "She travelled via portal."

Which brought her to—

"The mages," Ember said, aghast. "She's in Edinburgh."

I broke into a sprint towards the Moonbeam's portal

of billowing light. The other dragon shifters shouted admonishments, but the light sent it spinning into my hand—

And then I was gone, into the room with the mirror once more.

The fire goddess hovered in mid-air, draped in shimmering white light, above several terrified-looking mages. And Agnes, who glared up at the spirit, holding a pendant in her hand.

"You cannot destroy us," she said. "Ignessa. Your body is not in this world. You're wasting your time."

Ignessa. I'd said that name, involuntarily, without knowing what it meant. I'd read it from the Moonbeam's text… and Lorne must have worked out who she was.

"That trinket will not protect your people from destruction," Ignessa said, flames shimmering around her transparent form. "I will become your queen."

Great. She's just as power-mad as Lorne. No wonder she took his side. At least until she burned him to ashes.

"No chance," I said. "You're a ghost, which means any necromancer with a smidge of talent can set up a candle circle to trap you. The leader of Edinburgh's necromancer guild is right here in this building. I guarantee she can banish you in the state you're in now. This is your last warning."

A snarl escaped, remarkably dragon-shifter-like. "I will not be banished. You *will* bow to me, when I find my body."

She whirled around, avoiding the item that Agnes held in her hand, and dove through the mirror's glass.

"What *is* that?" Ember asked, staring at the pendant.

"A gift, given to me by your people," said Agnes. "It

makes me immune to dragonfire, including hers. Don't let her escape."

"What the blazes is going on?" bellowed Lord Sutherland.

Agnes snapped her fingers, and the mages fell unconscious. "I'll have to erase their memories of this," she muttered. "That goddess isn't alive, but if you don't stop her, she soon will be."

"You knew she was coming?" I stepped back towards the mirror.

"I suspected," Agnes said. "Madison told me enough of the Moonbeam's legends before she died. Including that the Moonbeam is a talisman. It contains a fragment of the goddess's magic."

"And thanks to me, she has it back," I said. "Or thanks to Lorne, at any rate. Which means—what?"

"Nothing, since she's without a body," Agnes said. "I suspect she thought she could take Lorne's, but his mortal body was too fragile to hold her."

Her words collided in my skull. "What—where in hell did she even come from? Why did she focus her attention on me?"

"Sorry, Cori," said Agnes. "I'm afraid it was you who woke her. Her spirit came back when you returned from death. Ember brought her back."

Ember's jaw dropped. "No."

"Life comes with a price," Agnes said, a shadow crossing her face. "I'm sorry."

"Then..." I paused. "Is she back for good now? I take it her body isn't dead?"

"I'm afraid I don't know," she said. "But she manages to find one, this world and all others will burn. Unless you destroy the Moonbeam. That will take away her power and confine her to the form of a regular spirit until she expires."

My heart contracted. She was tied to the Moonbeam. If we destroyed it, she'd be killed... and the other dragon shifters would probably take us to pieces.

Speaking of whom...

I sucked in a breath. "Agnes, whether we make it back or not, I need that mirror in the dragon shifters' village to be taken into safe hands. If you can. We'll try to come back, but if the Moonbeam is destroyed..."

We might be stuck on the other side. Forever.

Agnes nodded, while Ember moved to my side. "We can do this, Cori," she whispered.

Then once more, we leapt through the mirror.

Fog surrounded us, blurring our surroundings. The outline of a building appeared, a stone construction on a grassy hillside.

"Where are we?" I whispered to Ember. "This isn't the city."

I searched for the Moonbeam's light, but it seemed to have dumped us into this realm at random. We weren't in the city, and the other dragon shifters were nowhere to be seen.

"Cori," hissed Zeph's voice. "Over here."

I peered into the gloom, the outline of a building becoming more distinct. A stone temple-like construction beckoned us inside, and there, between mossy, half destroyed pillars, sat my friends. All but the back two pillars were broken and worn down with age. The crate containing the dragonling eggs lay open in the centre, along with the Moonbeam.

"You got it away from the others?" I asked.

"I took it," Zeph said, his jaw set. "It was affecting the other shifters, and when they started brawling, I managed to fly off with it. If they'd got through the mirror, the mages would have arrested them. Where is that ghost?"

"She's here. Somewhere."

And considering she'd left a minute before us, she must be close.

"I thought she was dead," Will said. "Right? Since when could ghosts burn people alive?"

"She's a *goddess*, Will," Kit said tremulously. "Like the gods the Sidhe used to worship."

"Now isn't the time for a history lesson." Astor was on his feet, his eyes on the sky. "Cori, you're the one with the spirit sight. Where is she?"

"I don't—" I broke off. The crate trembled, the outline of a white figure appearing above our heads. "Get away from there!"

Kit lunged. Fire exploded, white flames licking at us, only to collide with a solid green shield. The shield folded around our group, including the dragonling eggs, protecting us from the flames.

"I can't hold it for long!" Kit gasped. "Get the Moonbeam out."

Zeph had already grabbed it, but the fire goddess turned away from the others, eagerly reaching for the Moonbeam in Zeph's hands. Her palms passed right through it, but more flames licked out, and Zeph yelled aloud, his arms burning.

"Stop that!" I ran to his side, grabbing the Moonbeam from him. The flames licked at my arms, and I gritted my teeth against the pain. *We're bound, you and I. I don't know if you did it on purpose, but I won't let you burn my friends. I won't.*

"Cori!" Zeph shouted, as I reeled on the spot, white flames surrounding me. She wanted to burn me like she'd done to Lorne.

No...

I gripped the Moonbeam, looking at the text rippling across the surface. Words filtered their way into my brain. It was living dragonfire, but in the end, the Moonbeam was just a repository of energy, like any spirit device. It could only hold so much before it exploded.

The fire goddess smiled. "Give me your life, Coriander."

My life. Before, when the Moonbeam had ripped open the spirit lines, it had taken the life force from the other shifters in order to do it. It was still alive, trembling with energy, and that same fire burned in my own veins. It was *giving* me energy.

So I could give it back.

Power pulsed from my hands, straight into the Moonbeam. Its glow brightened as I fed more of my life force into it, feeling my body grow cold, the trembling growing worse. Zeph tried to grab it, only to be repelled by the force of the burning energy.

I dropped to my knees. *No... I can't have given it all already.*

And then Ember was there, at my side. I screamed a warning, but she took the Moonbeam from my hands, the glow transferring to her.

The goddess screamed in rage.

No. My sister... no.

With a wrenching crack, the Moonbeam shattered, a

hundred pieces of shimmering white scattering over the grassy hillside.

The fire goddess vanished in an instant, and Ember collapsed. My vision wavered, my knees hitting the ground, reaching for her hand, but she wasn't breathing, and her spirit—

Her spirit hovered over her body, a ghost.

My heart cracked in two. Tears burned my eyes, spilling over.

Ember was gone.

24

Fire woke me. Fire, and tears so sharp they burned. Softness blanketed my head. The grass. I lay inside the temple, the others' whispers like sandpaper against my ears.

Zeph's form wavered above me. "You're awake. Cori—I thought—"

I coughed, my eyes stinging. "Ember..."

Zeph spoke. "She's alive."

Alive.

I lifted my head. "What? She..."

"She's alive." Zeph's voice broke. "Cori, she wants to see you, if you can walk."

"If I—" I was already on my feet, my body trembling, my heart beating too fast. The others watched, but didn't speak, as I stumbled towards the dragon-shaped figure outside the temple. I'd come close to giving up my life to the Moonbeam, and there wasn't much of me left. But Ember—

A familiar growl sounded. And then I was running

287

down the misty hillside, towards the ruby red dragon stretched outside the temple.

"You shifted," I whispered. "You lived."

"I did," said a voice from my shoulder.

I jumped. Ember floated there, ghostlike, before her own dragon form.

"What the—?"

"It's what the Moonbeam does," said Ember's spirit. "It suppresses the human side until the shifter is all that's left. As long as I'm here, she's trapped with me."

"But she's not dead?"

Ember shook her head. "She can't get out."

"And neither…" My throat was dry. "Neither can you."

"Not as long as the Moonbeam is broken."

I dropped to my knees again, the fight going out of me at the sight of my sister—in Death. While I'd heard her accounts of the battle in Hyde Park, I'd never taken in how it must have felt for her to see me floating there, unable to return to life. No wonder she'd been desperate enough to bargain with the Moonbeam to bring me back.

The Moonbeam, which lay in white shards over the hillside, no longer gleaming. Its power was gone.

"You saved everyone, Cori," Ember's spirit said. "The fire goddess and Lorne are gone."

"But you—" I broke off, looking to Zeph in desperation. He stood behind me, giving me space to talk to my sister. "There must be another way."

I held my breath as dragon-Ember padded to my side. Her tail curled around me and a growl rumbled in her chest.

My sister was still alive in there somewhere. And as long as she existed, I refused to give up on her.

"She won't attack me," I said to Zeph, who had gone tense. "She knows me."

But she'd given up her fire. Her *life.*

"Your friends," said Ember's ghost. "Go to the others. They're worried about you."

I wrenched my gaze away from her, away from the Moonbeam. Pieces of shattered white stone littered the ground, all that remained of the fire. I trailed after Zeph back into the temple, wiping my eyes.

Within, Will and Kit sat with the dragonling. Becks stretched out, sleeping, but looked up when I walked in. Astor—I almost felt sorry for him, sitting alone, no longer able to communicate with Ember.

"The Moonbeam's broken," I said. "Isn't it? We can't get home."

Zeph dipped his head. Will nodded. Kit clung to the dragonling, while Becks made a noise of assent.

"I'm sorry," I said. "You're stuck here with me. All of you."

"Are you kidding?" said Becks. "We already lost everything. We're more fortunate than those poor souls left behind."

"And we saved the dragonlings," added Kit.

"Not to mention ourselves," Will said. "The virus is gone. And now, so are all of Lorne's allies."

True. But we had no supplies. We'd lost everything. I had nothing but the clothes on my back. We'd lost our home. I'd lost the life my parents had wanted to give me. Ember had lost her freedom. Astor had lost her, and everyone else.

"The spirit lines opened once," said Zeph. "Maybe they can open again."

"Not without a huge surge of energy," I said. "Unless you have another of those spirit device things sitting around somewhere—and even then, I think they only work on key points. I don't know if there even *are* key points here. Or if there's a spirit realm, come to that. This isn't Earth."

"The mirrors and the Moonbeam were created here," he said. "Right? That means the other dragon shifters created a means of travelling between realms. They must have left others behind."

"Maybe," I said, rubbing my eyes. "But every minute we spend here is a lot longer back home."

"Maybe it'll be a world that's friendlier to dragon shifters when we get back, then," Zeph said.

"That's a bit too optimistic. London was a hot mess when we left."

"All the more reason to keep the Moonbeam the hell away from them."

I looked back at the shattered pieces outside the temple's entrance. I could no longer sense its fire in my veins. "It's tied to Ember and the goddess. She said—the only way to free her is to repair it."

"What?" Zeph looked alarmed. "I mean, I want to free Ember, too, but that fire goddess was a power-hungry maniac."

"I know." I bit my lip. "Ember doesn't deserve to pay the price for our mistakes. The goddess is still alive, in ghost form, like Ember, but she can't hurt us."

"That's not a good thing," said Becks. "Cori, you aren't seriously thinking of—"

"I summon you," I said. "Ignessa, the fire goddess."

I had no candles, no props, but my voice rang out into

the foggy temple. And then she appeared, her eyes like flames, flickering in the fog. "You dare to summon me, like some common spirit?"

"I'm not afraid of you," I said. "Tell me how to free my sister."

Her eyes lit up as she grinned. "You will envy her fate in the end."

"Shut up," I said. "It's not like I actually know *how* to remake the Moonbeam, besides. Is it really the only way to set her free?"

"Yes," she said. "It is. If you re-forge the Moonbeam and unite the dragon shifters under my rule, then your sister will be released along with me."

I looked around at my allies, and then past her, towards the city where the other dragons had found themselves stranded. They'd survived in ways I'd never imagined, despite the unspeakable horrors they'd suffered.

Fire burned in my veins, and my hands curled into fists. The Moonbeam's power ran in my blood and in my sister's. The fire goddess was reduced to almost nothing. We were stronger than she was. And we'd find a way to beat her.

I promise that.

The dragonling growled from behind the fire goddess, promising vengeance of his own design.

I could get on board with that plan.

"We will get her back," I vowed. "You haven't won this, Ignessa."

ABOUT THE AUTHOR

Emma is the New York Times and USA Today Bestselling author of the Changeling Chronicles urban fantasy series.

Emma spent her childhood creating imaginary worlds to compensate for a disappointingly average reality, so it was probably inevitable that she ended up writing fantasy novels. When she's not immersed in her own fictional universes, Emma can be found with her head in a book or wandering around the world in search of adventure.

Find out more about Emma's books at www.emmaladams.com.